He shook his head and said, "No."

Charlotte cleared her throat. "So it's just a coincidence that we're at the same place at the same time—again."

The grin on his lips was no more than a shadow. "Not exactly."

The man was too charming for his own good. And cute, handsome, sexy—

Charlotte took hold of herself. "Look, I'm sure you're used to sweeping women off their feet. But it's not going to happen here."

"I was merely returning your sunglasses."

How on earth could she have thought that this gorgeous man had followed her for any other reason? She took a deep breath. "Thank you," she mumbled. "And it was wrong of me to assume—"

"That's not the only reason I'm here."

"It's not?"

"Nope." One corner of his mouth lifted in a sexy grin. "I'm here because I want to be with you."

Dear Reader,

Every one of us knows that there's a special guy out there meant just for us. The kind of guy who's every woman's fantasy—but only one woman's dream come true. That's the kind of men you'll meet in "The Ultimate..." miniseries.

Whether he's the man that'll follow you to the ends of the earth or the type to stay right in your backyard and promise you a passel of babies or the guy who'll pull out all of the stops in his seduction, the men you're about to meet are truly special.

Nikki Rivers continues the miniseries. Nikki loves writing stories where the ordinary heroine gets "the fabulous man, the best job, the greatest kids and the coolest house. That's what Harlequin is all about," she says. "Women who win."

We hope you enjoy all the wonderful stories and fabulous men coming to you in "The Ultimate..." series.

Regards,

Debra Matteucci
Senior Editor & Editorial Coordinator
Harlequin
300 E. 42nd St.
New York, NY 10017

Her Prince Charming

NIKKI RIVERS

Harlequin Books

TORONTO • NEW YORK • LONDON
AMSTERDAM • PARIS • SYDNEY • HAMBURG
STOCKHOLM • ATHENS • TOKYO • MILAN
MADRID • WARSAW • BUDAPEST • AUCKLAND

To Deb Kratz—for yesterdays shared, todays enjoyed and tomorrows dreamed of—and for bugging the staff at San Francisco International Airport for me.
A special thanks to some of the good people of Madison, Wisconsin: John Peterson and Ann Voss Peterson, who answered all my questions cheerfully, and Nick and Katherine Galanos of Badger Candy Kitchen. Their wonderful shop provided inspiration—and some really good hand-dipped chocolates! And a thank you to my friend, Tom Bruce, New York actor, writer and director, who came to my rescue more than once, and to my daughter Jenna who helped me hatch the idea while we ogled waiters at a sidewalk café.

RECYCLED PAPER · RECYCLED PAPER

ISBN 0-373-16723-7

HER PRINCE CHARMING

Copyright © 1998 by Sharon Edwin

Printed in U.S.A.

Chapter One

"Uh, excuse me," Charlotte Riesling said, quickening her step to catch up to the bellboy. "Uh, I'm not sure I'm in the right hotel."

The young man didn't stop, just turned around and walked backward, placing his other hand on the luggage cart to keep it rolling along smoothly. "Excuse me?" he asked, lowering his brows.

The carpet at her feet, though plush and obviously expensive, was rather...well, she'd expected a floral pattern of muted pastels, not geometric shapes of neon-bright color against black. Her grandfather had assured her that this was one of the oldest, most staid hotels in San Francisco. So far, nothing she had seen looked particularly staid.

"What I mean to ask is," she amended soberly, "this is the Cameron House, isn't it?"

"Well, ma'am, sort of."

She gave him a level look. "Sort of?"

He shrugged. "Well, the old man died and left the place to his son. He renovated."

"So I see," she commented dryly.

"Yeah. So now it's mostly called Cameron's."

The bellboy turned to face forward again as he walked. Charlotte followed until he stopped at room 1822. While she waited for him to unlock the door, she thought how

appropriate the shortened name seemed. The heir to the
throne had taken the *house,* or home, out of the place, and
had obviously been very eager to make changes. *Change.*
Charlotte thrived on routine. Hated the unexpected. How
ironic that she should come to stay in such a place at such
a time.

She followed the bellboy and the luggage cart into the
room, barely listening while he did the usual rundown on
how to control the air conditioner, then gave him a tip and
shut the door behind him.

Like the corridor, the room was a kaleidoscope of color,
with a platform bed and ultra-sleek furniture. Charlotte was
more the overstuffed-chintz sort. Well, she would only be
in residence until Monday. She supposed she could endure
the abstract lithographs and the lamps that looked like ref-
ugees from a fifties junk shop until then.

Still, the whole thing was too much like a sad joke. Charlotte had come to the venerable hotel to try to ward off the
effects of just such a "renovation" at WEND, her grandfather's radio station in Madison, Wisconsin.

Not *ward off,* exactly. It was too late for that. Her grandfather, Barnabas, had stood firm on his decision to change
the format at WEND from classical music and intelligent
conversation to classic rock and happy talk. Charlotte
nearly shuddered at the thought. She'd practically gown up
at WEND. The fondest memories of her somewhat-
unorthodox childhood were of sitting in Barnabas's leather
desk chair, worn soft and dull from years of use, her feet
barely touching the floor as she entered numbers into a
ledger her grandfather kept just for her visits. And all the
while the classical music that had soothed the worries of
her young life magically swelled from the very walls of the
one place in her small, disheveled world where she felt safe.

She moved to her suitcase on the chrome stand where
the bellboy had left it. She could no longer avoid a con-

frontation with J.J. Tanner, the man who was going to change her life. But first, she would take a nice hot shower and trade her bulky sweater for something a little cooler, then set out to storm the enemy unannounced.

She fished the tiny key out of her skirt pocket and unlocked her luggage.

"What?" she said aloud to the empty room wondering if she'd ended up in the wrong place after all. Was this really her hotel room? Because these certainly weren't her clothes.

Gone were her long, flowing skirts in dark colors. Absent were her long tunic tops, baggy sweaters and oversize shirts. Missing was her favorite pair of cotton tailored pajamas.

For long moments she stared down at the colorful mass of silks, satins and slinky-looking knits, muttering, "This is crazy, absolutely crazy."

Well, no, she thought again. It wasn't crazy. She'd probably picked up the wrong suitcase at the airport, that was all. Except why did her key work in this lock and the luggage tags match her baggage-claim check?

"This is my suitcase. But no way are those my clothes."

Charlotte eyed the colorful fabrics spilling from the suitcase, trying to imagine what kind of person would steal her old denim skirt and well-worn pajamas and replace them with a wardrobe that was up-to-the-minute chic. She also tried to imagine explaining the situation over the phone to someone from the airline.

She looked at her watch. Time was passing. She wanted that shower and change of clothes. She wanted to head over to WEXL and face the enemy. There had to be something in that suitcase that would tide her over until she straightened out this mess.

HALF AN HOUR LATER Charlotte was staring at herself in the mirror.

"Oh, Lord, this will never do," she murmured.

The least revealing things she could find in the suitcase were a pair of jeans and a black, scoop-necked bodysuit. Or at least they seemed the most modest until she tried them on.

Standing in front of the full-length mirror, she twisted this way and that, wondering how the jeans could feel so comfortable when they looked so tight. The denim revealed the hips and rear end she had been hiding most of her life. And the bodysuit accentuated breasts that she'd always thought were much too full.

She couldn't confront the enemy looking like this!

"There has to be something else in here—"

She rummaged in the suitcase again. But everything was too short, too low-cut, too bright, too totally un-Charlotte-like.

She thought about putting on her traveling clothes again—her standard Friday ensemble: long brown challis skirt and bulky-knit sweater, rounded off with brown leather hiking boots. But San Francisco in October was a lot milder than the Madison, Wisconsin, autumn. She would swelter in the heavy sweater and long skirt. She couldn't afford to face J.J. Tanner sweating and disheveled.

The man already had the term "rat" penciled in after his name as far as she was concerned. He had refused to speak to her on the phone, and all because she'd lost her temper that first time. From that point on he'd insisted on speaking only to Barnabas. Which was ridiculous since Charlotte was, after all, going to be his boss. But Barnabas had put up with it simply because J.J. Tanner was supposed to be some sort of wizard program director, adept at transfusing radio stations in need of new blood. Well, maybe Barnabas owned WEND, but Charlotte, as general manager, ran it.

And she wasn't about to let an employee cut her out this way.

J.J. Tanner was just going to have to accept that even though she'd lost the war to keep WEND classical, she was still the "general" in charge and he would have to learn to deal with her.

"WHAT DO YOU MEAN he's gone?"

The receptionist cracked her gum again before answering. "J.J. doesn't work here anymore, that's what I mean."

"Well, I know he's leaving," Charlotte acknowledged, "but not until next week."

"Wrong. J.J. checked out on Monday."

"You're sure?"

The girl gave Charlotte a disbelieving look. "Honey, if J.J. was still around, I'd know about it. He's not the kind of man you can exactly ignore, you know. I mean, the man is a hunk. If I'd had a chance, believe me, I would have—"

Charlotte decided to interrupt before the girl could go into detail. "Could I at least get his home phone number?"

"Doesn't have one."

"He doesn't have a phone?"

"Naw, I mean he doesn't have a home. At least, not in San Francisco anymore. He's gone, lady. Someplace in the Midwest. Some little burg where I can't imagine what he's gonna do with his nights. If you ask me, a man like that will just be wasted on all those farm broads and—"

"Well, I didn't ask you, did I?" Charlotte interrupted testily.

The girl looked Charlotte up and down and she tried not to squirm in her bodysuit. "You one of his women?" the receptionist finally asked.

Inexplicably, Charlotte could feel hot color creeping up her neck and flooding her cheeks. "Of course not!"

The girl gave her a hostile stare. "Right. Look, lady, I got work to do."

With that, she cracked her gum again and buried her face in the pages of the latest issue of *Cosmopolitan* magazine, leaving Charlotte to wonder if something in the water at WEXL was causing all this rudeness. Because she would certainly have to say that in her one brief phone encounter with J.J. Tanner, he'd been just as rude as the receptionist.

But Charlotte wasn't giving up that easily.

"I want to see your station manager," she demanded.

From behind the picture of the supermodel on the cover of the magazine came a heavy sigh. An aggressively manicured hand thrust out and pressed a button on the phone.

"Someone here to see you, Heather," the receptionist said without putting down her magazine. "I think it's one of J.J.'s girls."

Charlotte grimaced at the description and wished she'd worn her challis skirt and bulky sweater after all.

TEN MINUTES LATER she was back out on the street with absolutely no idea of where to find J.J. Tanner. After displaying her identification, Charlotte had finally convinced Heather that she wasn't a J.J. groupie. But she still couldn't get any information out of her. What on earth did the man do to women to engender such fierce loyalty and protectiveness?

Well, Charlotte knew what he probably did. And what really irritated her was that Heather and the receptionist obviously thought he'd once done it to Charlotte, too. And the thought of that made her want to eat chocolate. Or pasta. Yes, that was it. As if on cue her stomach growled, reminding her that she hadn't eaten since the bagel she was served on the plane.

She would go back to her hotel, have a nice meal in the restaurant, and then she would call the airline and book herself on the next flight out. Because if J.J. Tanner was no longer in San Francisco, he must already be on his way to Madison. And, one way or another, Charlotte was determined to confront him before he showed up for work a week from Monday.

CHARLOTTE LOOKED UP from her shrimp fettucine. There was some sort of commotion at the entrance to the restaurant.

"The seafood is already dead—I don't think it'll care if I'm wearing a jacket and a tie," a man was saying.

Charlotte couldn't quite see him clearly since the maître d' was doing his best to block the man from entering.

"But *we* care, sir. And so do our patrons. Perhaps if the gentleman weren't in jeans…"

Charlotte winced at the word, looking down at her denim-clad legs, then back up toward the entrance just in time to see the man peer around the shoulder of the maître d' and look straight at her.

"There seems to be some sexual discrimination going on here."

"I beg your pardon?"

"The lady with the shrimp on her fork—"

Charlotte looked down at the fork halfway to her mouth. Sure enough, a shrimp dripping in olive oil was perched there. The man was referring to her.

"She seems to be wearing jeans."

By now a few diners were looking her way and Charlotte resisted the urge to stand and recite the reason she was wearing what she was wearing and simply prayed for the dessert cart to come rumbling by to get those eyes off her and onto a chocolate éclair.

"That is true, sir, but the lady in question is a guest of the hotel. We make exceptions in such cases," he added a little disdainfully—disdainfully enough for Charlotte to not be so sure she liked being one of the exceptions.

"So, you're saying if I go out to the lobby and register for a room, you'll seat me?"

"Well, sir, I would hate to put it that way…"

"What about guests of guests?"

"I beg your pardon?"

"If I were the lunch guest of someone staying at the hotel could I eat my lobster wearing jeans?"

"Well, yes, I suppose—"

Before the maître d' could finish, the man had brushed past him and headed right for Charlotte.

"Sorry, I'm late, love, but you know those cable-car lines," he said as he took the seat opposite her.

The maître d' bustled over. "Sir, please—"

The man across from her gave a theatrical sigh. "Now what?"

"I'm sure this lady doesn't want to be bothered."

"Is that true?" he asked, stabbing her point-blank with a pair of dark eyes that danced with such mischief she could scarcely look away.

"Uh, well…" she stammered.

"Madam, shall I call security?"

A sudden hush settled over the room and Charlotte didn't have to worry about breaking the hold that dark gaze had on her to know what was happening. The scene had "spectacle" written all over it. And she was at the center. Only one thing to do as far as she was concerned.

She forced herself to look away from the man's eyes. "Of course not," she told the maître d' with several ounces of her father's haughtiness borrowed for the occasion. "Please bring my *guest* a menu."

The maître d' paused for only a moment longer, then, with an elegant shrug, and an apologetic glance at the rest of the room, he signaled a waiter.

Charlotte became aware of the shrimp still dangling from her fork. All at once it seemed imperative to get it into her mouth. Her lips closed around it as she looked back at the man across from her. The mischief in his eyes was waiting.

JACOB LOOKED FROM THE woman's confused eyes to her wide mouth—the lips naked of artificial color and glistening slightly with the oil dripping from her shrimp. He watched as her tongue came out to lick those lips and thought about what they might taste like.

Beside him the waiter coughed discreetly. "Does the gentleman wish to order?"

At the moment, the "gentleman" didn't feel like taking his eyes off the strong-jawed, unpainted face of the woman across from him.

"'The gentleman' wishes a lot of things," he said, trying to hold back a grin when her brown eyes flared and sparked. "But, he will be happy to start with lunch."

"Of course, sir," the waiter murmured.

"You think I'd like the shrimp?" he asked her.

She hesitated for only a moment. "I'm sure I have absolutely no idea what you might like."

Her tone was so haughty that he couldn't help himself. He just had to push her a little further.

"Oh, I think you might," he drawled, deliberately letting his gaze slide to her mouth. "I think you might have a very good idea of what I might like."

Then he put his hand over hers, guided her fork to her plate, speared a shrimp, and brought it up to his own mouth, biting the end of it off with a snap of his teeth.

"But I'll start with the shrimp," he said while he chewed.

"Sir?" the confused waiter asked.

The woman jerked her hand out of his and let her fork clatter to her plate. "Bring my *guest*," she said, hesitating just briefly on the word, "the fettucine. And bring me my check."

"Yes, ma'am," the waiter hastened to assure her, then hurried off.

Jacob laughed softly. "That tone gets results."

"I beg your pardon?"

"Miss Nob Hill."

"I have no idea what you're talking about," she said, refusing to look at him as she gathered her purse. "Now, if you'll excuse me—"

He laid his hand on her wrist. "But I don't."

Startled, she looked from his hand to his face. "What?"

"I don't excuse you. Stay and eat with me."

She looked down her rather long, narrow nose at him. "You've got to be kidding."

"No," Jacob answered, suddenly realizing that he hadn't been quite so serious about anything to do with a woman in a very long time.

He'd spent the morning haunting places that were already haunted. Places he'd frequented with his wife, Michelle. She'd been gone nearly five years, now. Her passing had left a hollow place in his heart along with a motherless child who had been scarcely a year old. But five years was long enough to mourn, by anyone's standards. So Jacob had checked into a hotel—one he never could have afforded back when they had spent their honeymoon in San Francisco—planning to spend the next five days saying goodbye.

But he was on sentimental overload. He needed a break. He figured the restaurant of a luxury hotel on the edge of Union Square had definite possibilities for diversion. Especially since he was wearing his scruffiest jeans and most washed-out T-shirt. He'd expected trouble, and he'd gotten it. But he hadn't expected to find a woman who totally captured his senses.

"Stay," he repeated, not at all sure he liked the softening of his tone.

She stared at him for a moment and when she finally spoke, the haughtiness in her voice was gone, replaced by what he could have sworn was regret.

"No," she said. "I can't."

Then she pulled her hand out from under his and stared at him for a moment longer before saying, "I have to—uh—go," and took off as though she was afraid he was going to follow her.

Jacob sat at the table for a few minutes before it occurred to him to wonder why he wasn't—following her, that is.

By the time he reached the lobby, she was nowhere in sight.

Ten minutes later he was still trying to convince the desk clerk to give him her name.

"Sir, surely you must understand—"

"No, surely *you* must understand—this is the only woman who...who..."

"Who what, sir?" the clerk asked blandly.

"Well, who..."

What could he say? This was the only woman since his wife had died five years ago who had more than mildly interested him. How could he explain that he was practically pleading with this guy in a suit to give him her room number on the strength of the way she chewed on a shrimp? On the delicious contradiction between the haughtiness in her voice and manner and the softness of her abundant body in clothes that made her look like she belonged a few blocks over, in North Beach, instead of ensconced in a luxury hotel on Union Square?

"Who what, sir?" the clerk prodded.

"Forget it," Jacob mumbled gruffly as he headed for the door that led to the street. He had only a few days in San

Francisco. Only a few days to do so much. The last thing he needed was the complication of a woman.

"WHY DON'T YOU STAY OUT there for a few days, Charlotte? Have a real vacation."

"Barnabas," Charlotte said into the telephone, "you know that's impossible. There's so much to do."

"No, but there *will* be a lot to do once Tanner is here. You won't have another chance for a little vacation in many months, my dear."

She knew her grandfather was probably right, but somehow she felt she had to be on the job more than ever, now that Tanner was coming. She felt like she was going to have to prove herself all over again. She felt like she needed to be there just in case—just in case... Charlotte frowned at herself in the mirror over the desk. Just in case of what?

Well, she didn't know what. All she knew was that a man who was going to change her life was on his way to WEND and she had to be there to strengthen her position.

Didn't she?

"All right," she said, sighing. "The airline can't book me until an eleven o'clock flight tonight. I might as well spend the night here and take an early flight tomorrow."

"Charlotte," her grandfather said to her in the same voice he'd used so many years ago when she'd insisted on studying yet another musical instrument instead of going to the movies or a dance or just hanging out with kids her age, "that isn't exactly what I had in mind."

"I know, Barnabas," Charlotte replied. "But I need to be there right now. I'll see you tomorrow—"

"Charlotte," Barnabas interrupted. "There is absolutely no point in your cutting your trip short. Tomorrow is Saturday. The day after is Sunday. Your days off, remember?"

Charlotte sighed. "You know I haven't taken an entire weekend off since all this started."

"My point exactly, Charlotte," he said, the aloofness in his tone making her wince—not to mention shrink backward to the age of eleven. Barnabas had a way of separating from a situation he didn't know how to deal with, and dealing with a preteen girl wasn't something he'd always known how to do. At such times, he merely stated his opinion with the air of one who expected that opinion to translate into an order by the time it hit the recipient's ear. "I'll expect you back on Monday. That still gives you another week before the transformation is complete."

Barnabas may have sounded like he had twenty-five years ago, but Charlotte was long past reacting the way she had at age eleven.

"Listen, Barnabas, I—"

Her grandfather's deep sigh stopped her. "Charlotte, give me this one, please. Don't make me pull rank."

Charlotte grinned. *Don't make me pull rank*—that was what he'd always said just before he pulled it.

What the hell, she thought. Three days in San Francisco was hardly a punishment. "All right, Barnabas," she said. "I'll give you this one."

There were several heartbeats of silence at the other end of the line. Then, "Charlotte, this is you, isn't it?"

Charlotte laughed. "You win, Barnabas—this time."

She could still hear his deep chuckle as she hung up the phone.

Leave it to Barnabas to tackle what she saw as a monumental problem with the unemotional approach he used for all life's big decisions. It was the little things—like the time she'd saved her allowance for a box of linen handkerchiefs with "Grandfather" embroidered on them. Or the Christmas decoration she'd made him when she was five and still hung on the tree every Christmas. Those were the

things that could turn the man into emotional mush. But
something like changing his beloved radio station into
something for people to listen to while stuck in traffic jams
instead of enriching their lives with the classics and he
acted like life was merely taking another turn and he was
equipped to handle it.

No wonder he'd never been able to understand her need
to cling to some sort of permanency, some semblance of
tradition. He went his own way—always had—so it was
hard for him to imagine the fierceness of the longing she'd
always had to be accepted by her parents.

Her father was a brilliant concert pianist and could make
any instrument he touched sing with emotion. Charlotte had
barely conquered chopsticks. She'd gone from piano to violin to cello, never succeeding in coaxing even a slightly
musical sound from any of them.

Her mother, who had a brilliant mind for business and a
fantastic ear for talent, had been her father's manager. As
a young child Charlotte had traveled with them, a silent
witness to their tempestuous relationship.

She had neither her mother's beauty nor her brains and
none of her father's grace and talent. Even as a very young
child, she'd known she was more of a disappointment to
them than anything else and often thought that the reason
they took her with them was to keep up the myth of the
brilliant young family for the music press.

By the time she was five years old her parents were leaving her in the care of Barnabas more and more. It had been
almost a relief to her when they'd divorced and stopped
traveling together. Her father went on to another manager,
her mother went on to other clients and Charlotte was to
remain entirely in Barnabas's care until things were
"calmer." Somehow they never were and with the excep-
tion of one or two excruciating weekends in New York
every year with both of her glamorous parents, they mostly

forgot that she existed. She became Barnabas's alone. Not long after that, she'd learned to love the radio station only slightly less than she loved her grandfather. It had been her life for years.

And now some West Coast hotshot was going to take it away from her.

"Oh, hell," she muttered as she jerked the barrette from her hair. A weekend in San Francisco wasn't going to make matters any worse. She picked up her brush and punished her hair for a few minutes until she became aware that she'd been staring at the movement of her breasts against the tight spandex of the bodysuit. She stared for a moment more, before blushing and turning away.

She was really going to have to do something about these clothes. Go shopping for a blazer to wear over the bodysuit and jeans, and maybe a shirt for tomorrow—something long and tailored. Something that would cover her behind and blur her bustline. Because she was convinced that the clothes must have something to do with what had happened at lunch. The man, the one with the closely cropped dark hair and the dark eyes full of mischief, would never have insisted on sitting at her table, would never have flirted, sort of, with her if she'd been dressed in her "real" clothes.

Things like that just never happened to Charlotte.

SHE WAS STANDING BEFORE the window of a boutique, staring at a blazer in a shade she would never wear, when she saw *him*. Or more precisely, saw his reflection in the glass. He was crossing the street behind her. Charlotte pulled her sunglasses slightly down her nose for a better look. Yes, it was him. Unmistakable. No one else could possibly have that determined-yet-arrogant stride. Charlotte stared at the reflection for a moment longer before she realized that he was coming straight for her.

She pushed her sunglasses back into place, ducked her head and started walking.

She was just relaxing her shoulders, thinking she'd made a clean getaway when a voice behind her, the same voice she'd heard the day before, ordering shrimp, spoke.

"A shame. That color would have looked great on you."

Chapter Two

"I never wear that color," she told him over her shoulder and Jacob grinned, lengthening his stride to try to keep no more than two paces behind her.

"Well, you should. It would bring out those amber flecks in your eyes."

Her step faltered at his words and Jacob chuckled to himself. But then she seemed to want to punish herself—or perhaps him—because as soon as she recovered she started walking even more quickly.

In no time at all, she'd lengthened the two paces to four, but if she thought that might deter him, she was dead wrong. He let his gaze move up and down her tall frame. The view was good enough that he was beginning to wonder if he cared whether he caught up with her or not. Her long stride was doing very nice things for her curvy backside. Her brown hair was confined at the nape of her neck and he wondered what it would look like, free and blowing in the wind. With her wide shoulders and soft womanly figure, he could easily imagine her in a miniskirt and a tie-dyed T-shirt—the ghost of a flower child.

He jogged a couple of paces and pulled up alongside her.

"You know if you're really looking for clothes, the best place to go is The Haight."

Her eyes flickered toward him and away again, just perceptibly enough to let him know that he'd gotten her interest.

"Yep. Got the coolest stuff there. Resale shops run by old hippies. Lots of atmosphere. Vintage clothing."

She looked at him again. "Vintage clothing?"

"Yep," he assured her, certain there were visions of tie-dyed gauze dancing in her head.

She looked away again and they walked in silence for a moment more before she stopped so abruptly that he'd walked on a few paces before he realized she was no longer beside him. He stopped and turned around.

"How do I get there?" she asked him.

He did his best to keep the grin off his face. "Well, you see, that could be a problem."

"Why is that?"

"It's a little complicated." He shrugged and looked at his watch for effect. "But, what the heck, I'm not doing anything right now. I'll take you there."

Her brow rose, her jaw tightened. "Are you crazy?" she asked.

It wasn't the first time in his life someone had asked him that.

He gave her his best maniacal grin and wiggled his brows. "Certifiable."

She shook her head, but he knew she was having a hard time keeping a straight face. Her eyes had given up the pretense already. She bit her lip and looked away from him, staring down the street as though there was suddenly something important to see. "Look," she finally said, "I'm sorry, but I don't know you, and—"

"We can remedy that," he interrupted. "I'm very knowable. By the time I've escorted you to the intersection of Haight-Ashbury, we'll be old friends."

"That won't be necessary. I'm sure I can find it if you'll just give me directions."

He shook his head. "Nope. Can't. It's a secret only us

crazy people are in on." He thumped a finger on his chest. "You need one of us to get there."

She stared at him.

He grinned. "You could do worse, you know."

Her brow rose again: "Excuse me?"

"I'm one of the least of the crazies."

For a moment her wide mouth twisted and he thought she might smile, but she reined it in, leaving just the trace of it to dance in her eyes.

"That I find hard to believe."

"Naw—it's true. I'm certified as a level-one crazy. Just crazy enough to know how to get to The Haight."

"Well, unfortunately, I'm not crazy enough to pick up a complete stranger on the street and let him take me shopping," she said as she started walking again.

Jacob watched that long stride for a moment, then hurried to catch up. "But you aren't picking me up. *I'm* picking *you* up. Makes a world of difference."

"Does it?" she asked dryly.

"Absolutely. This way, nothing that happens is your fault. From the moment you put yourself in my hands, it's out of your control."

She gave him a long, sideways look. "That's exactly what I'm afraid of."

He laughed at the wry sarcasm in her tone. "Come on—I'm the perfect gentleman."

That brought her to a stop again.

"Really?" she asked, deliberately looking him over.

Jacob made a show of smoothing his battered T-shirt. "Well, don't I look like one?"

Her mouth twisted. "No, you don't. And you don't act like one, either," she added as she started walking again.

He scurried to catch up. "You're going to wear me out, love."

"I can only hope," she muttered.

He laughed. "There are better ways to do it, you know."

"I'm sure there are. Why don't you go and do them?"

"Why don't you come with me?"

She wanted to laugh off this comment the way she'd laughed off most of his other outrageous remarks. But this particular comment was made in a deeper, more intimate voice than he'd used before. A voice that made her step falter enough that she might as well have stopped. So she did. But her gaze didn't. She looked him over more thoroughly than she had before. He had a clean-cut jawline and a gently squared chin. His brows were thick and arched low over those darkly alive eyes. He was only a few inches taller than her five feet nine inches, but his golden-tanned flesh was definitely all in the right places. The word *certifiable*—his word—came to mind. The man was certifiable, all right. But what he was certifiable *as* was what Carrie, WEND's receptionist, would call a "babe." A *male* babe. A male babe who was asking her if she would like to come with him and do something that might wear him out.

And the little grin on his face let her know exactly what kind of activity he had in mind.

For just one moment, for no longer than it took for her to blink, she wondered what it would be like if she said yes. Wondered what it would be like to see those dark eyes glittering with passion instead of mischief. Wondered what it would be like to have that quick, clever mouth on hers. Wondered what that crisp dark hair would feel like under her fingers.

Then she blinked again and wondered what she was thinking of.

Charlotte was a woman who lived by rules. If the sign said Don't Walk, she didn't walk. If a library book was due on the third, she returned it on the second. A woman wasn't supposed to talk to strangers. So Charlotte didn't talk to strangers.

Yet here she was, not only talking to one but contemplating what it would be like to—what it would be like to—

She started walking again, closing her eyes in a brief but fervent wish that he wouldn't follow her.

No such luck.

"Come on," he said, bobbing along beside her like an irritating adolescent. "You know you want to."

She felt like giving a shout of laughter at his audacity. But she couldn't. Because he was right. She did want to.

"I know a pub where you can tip a pint, shoot a few darts and nosh on some incredible shepherd's pie."

"I thought I was going shopping."

"Afterward, love. After I help you find a white gauze shirt and a tie-dyed T-shirt. After I—"

Charlotte suddenly knew she didn't want to know what else the man had in mind to help her do. She swerved toward the entrance to a building and pushed at the door with her shoulder, thankful, indeed, when the door swung open.

The place was hushed. The cool air was filled with the soothing notes of a Brahms concerto while figures dressed in black walked without sound to and fro. For one dizzying minute she wondered if she'd barged into a funeral home.

"Does madam have an appointment?"

"Wha-what?" Charlotte managed to stammer. Was it some New Age Californian thing to make an appointment at a funeral home well in advance of dying?

"An appointment?" the man repeated. "Because, if madam is simply a walk-in she is fortunate, indeed. One of our clients just canceled and—"

"Canceled? Can you, uh, do that?" Charlotte asked, picturing a Nob Hill matron telling the Angel of Death, "Not today." He would have to come back at a more convenient time. It was the servants' day off.

"Well, it's frowned upon, of course," the man answered.

"But in this case, an old and loyal customer, one makes exceptions."

The man peered at her and Charlotte wondered if she looked anything like she was about to die.

"You won't want the dye job she had scheduled but I should think it would take most of the extra time to give your hair a complete treatment."

"My hair?"

"Yes. A deep-conditioning treatment, a superb new cut." His hand fluttered near her chin while he studied her. "Something chic yet easily maintained."

Charlotte raised her brows. "Uh, maintained?"

"Yes. I'm sure madam has a busy life."

Life. Charlotte suddenly liked the sound of that word. But was it an appropriate subject for a funeral parlor? She looked around, seeing for the first time the clues she'd missed when she'd rushed in off the street. The black clothes were smocks. The marble tables were heaped with upscale magazines. The glass case held designer hair care products.

She'd wandered not into a funeral parlor, but a hair salon. A very posh one, at that.

"Well, I didn't really want the full treatment, you see. I was just—"

She gestured toward the door she'd entered and did a double take. *He* was still out there, lounging against a lamppost like an illegally sexy vagrant. He gave her a grin and a wave but didn't attempt to come inside. Apparently, even though he didn't draw the line at causing scenes in restaurants, he did draw it at entering a beauty salon.

"How long did you say all this would take?" she asked, her eyes still on the man outside.

"Oh, two hours, I should think." He studied her hair again, frowning as he added, "At least."

Two hours. Even a certifiably crazy man wouldn't stand

out on a street and wait for two hours.

"Okay," she said, with an emphatic nod, "let's do it."

JACOB LOOKED AT HIS watch. Half an hour. He'd been leaning on the lamppost for the past thirty minutes while she was having whatever done to her hair inside Antonio's Parlor. He couldn't wait out on the street for her much longer. Next thing he knew, she would be having him arrested as a stalker.

"What a world," he muttered to himself as he looked at his watch again. It had gotten so a man couldn't even follow a beautiful woman around, making a nuisance of himself until she accepted a date with him. Not that Jacob had ever done such a thing. And not that this woman was all that beautiful. No, she wasn't beautiful, but somehow she was stunning with her innocent pink-tinged complexion, wide naked mouth, and body of a Hollywood starlet, circa 1955.

Ah, well, he thought, glancing again at the door to Antonio's. He'd promised himself a sunset over the bay and the afternoon was rapidly closing. He would chalk this one up to a fleeting bit of insanity. Maybe he would think about her a little as he tried to sleep tonight. By tomorrow, she would be forgotten.

HE'D BEEN DISAPPOINTED in the sunset. This morning in The Haight was an improvement. Maybe because Michelle had never liked The Haight. She hadn't seen the romance of the age of "flower power." She had never wished that she could have been a teenager during the "summer of love" as Jacob had. She'd preferred the view of the Golden Gate Bridge—or watching the sunset from Ocean Park. He hadn't seen a sunset from the park in years. Last night he'd stood at the edge of the ocean and waited to feel what he'd felt that night after their wedding when he'd held her in his arms and watched the fire that joined the sky and the sea.

He hadn't felt it. But he'd felt something else. He'd felt,

finally, that he could say goodbye. By the time the sun had slid into the ocean he'd known he was right: It was time to move on with his life.

Much later, as he'd lain in bed at his hotel, he'd scarcely taken the time to be surprised that the woman on his mind was the woman from the restaurant.

When he'd woken from a very restful sleep, he'd decided to give himself a morning in The Haight. He was in the mood to walk Haight Street all the way down to Golden Gate Park and back again.

By the time he'd reached Cole Street, he was whistling a rock song from the "summer of love" and enjoying the passing parade of local eccentrics, tourists and yuppie interlopers. The breeze was in his hair, there was music coming from somewhere—there always was in The Haight— and he was feeling mellow enough to consider buying a tie-dyed T-shirt. So mellow, in fact, that when he first spotted her, the thought went through his mind that he was hallucinating.

But there she was, her back to him again, standing in front of a shop window, gazing in. Just as she had been the day before when he'd found her. Was he destined to live out that scene forever in some weird hope that he would get it right the next time and she would come with him?

But, no, he thought as he watched her. Something was different.

And then she turned.

My God, he thought, *it's like the sun coming out.*

Her hair had been cut to just below her jawline and it hung straight and shiny, like skeins of fine silk thread. Something in her face had changed, too. Something had coaxed the beauty that had been waiting just under her skin to the surface. She looked—there was no other word for it—*radiant.*

She started to move away from the shop, then paused,

turned toward it again, and went inside. It took him about two seconds to decide to follow her in.

A bell jangled over the shop door when he entered. She was tall enough for him to spot her right away near the back of the store. He strolled over to a rack of men's ties, fingering a few, his gaze returning to her again and again. He cleared his throat, hoping she would investigate where the sound was coming from. He imagined her looking up, her face lighting with pleasure when she saw him. But, she didn't even glance. She seemed too engrossed in something else.

He let go of the wide paisley tie he'd been pretending to consider and began to slowly work his way to the back of the shop.

"YOU MUST BE CRAZY."

Charlotte spun around, almost dropping the dress she'd been holding. Her heart—already in overdrive from being startled out of her contemplation of the dress—leaped another notch when she saw who'd spoken to her. He was leaning against a support column, the same scruffy jeans molded to his hips and thighs, a black T-shirt with the sleeves rolled up and with an oblong hole big enough to answer the question about chest hair. He didn't seem to have any. Just smooth, golden flesh. Charlotte got her mind off that hole, and what lay beneath the rest of the shirt, and looked into his face.

"'Crazy?'" she repeated, borrowing her tone from her father again. "You must be thinking of someone else. Such as yourself? Because I'm not the one following anybody around San Francisco—"

He grinned and she suddenly felt foolish. Why would this man be following her? He could probably interest any number of nubile young women. Charlotte had never been "nubile" and, at thirty-six, she was getting further away from "young" with every passing moment.

"Maybe not. But you were crazy enough to make it to The Haight on your own."

"Ah, yes. The neighborhood you have to be crazy to find. Well, I did find it," she replied, searching for the price tag on the black dress she was holding.

"You must be really certifiable if you're thinking of buying that thing."

Charlotte looked at the dress in her hand. "What's wrong with it?"

"It's black, for one thing."

She eyed him. "Like your T-shirt, so I have to assume you have nothing against the color."

"No, I don't. Black is a noble color. Just not for you."

"Really?" she asked dryly.

He grinned again. "Truly."

Before she could stop him he'd taken the dress from her hands, placed it back on the rack and started pawing through the rest of the clothes hanging there.

"Of course," he said, "the color isn't the only thing wrong about it."

"No?"

"No. It's too long."

"Too long?"

"Right. You need something to show off those legs."

"Now, wait just a minute! You know nothing about my legs and I prefer to keep it that way, if you don't mind."

"Ah, but I do mind. And I know enough about those legs to know they should never be in anything but tight denim or short skirts."

Charlotte's mouth fell open. "Of all the—" she started to say.

"Here," he interrupted her, pulling a dress from the rack. "This is the one for you."

The dress was burgundy velvet with a wide, scoop neckline and long flowing sleeves. It was gorgeous. But Charlotte knew it wasn't for her. For one thing, the skirt was barely longer than the sleeves. For another, that low scoop neck would leave very little to the imagination about the breasts she'd tried to hide most of her life. The things had sprouted up practically overnight when she was twelve. While all the other girls had those cute lacy bras, Charlotte's mother had bought her something that looked like a harness and felt much worse, Charlotte was sure, than anything a horse had ever had to wear.

"You must keep them contained, my dear," her mother had warned her. "After all, you don't want to come across as blowzy or cheap, do you, darling?"

Her mother would never approve of that dress.

"I would never wear anything in that color," she declared haughtily as she headed for the door.

"Well, you should," he replied, coming right after her. "It would bring out the red in your hair."

"I don't have any red in my hair," she stated firmly as she pushed the door open and went out into the street.

"Oh, yes, you do. And whatever Antonio did to your hair yesterday brought it out even more. The sun is setting your hair on fire, love."

Charlotte stopped and turned. "It—uh—is?"

He took a step closer to her. "It is," he said, his voice deepening a little, his dark eyes dancing dangerously, alluringly.

Alluringly? Charlotte blinked, then shook her head. She was getting downright corny. You would think she was in the middle of a romance novel or something.

She started walking again.

He was right behind her. "You were pretty before. But now you're really a knockout."

Charlotte almost tripped over her own feet. A knockout? Her?

"Oh, please—" she managed to say over her shoulder.

"You don't have to beg, love, you can have anything you want."

Now she did stumble. My goodness, was there really a gorgeous man following her around San Francisco saying things like that to her?

And was she really going to fall for it?

No, of course she wasn't. She wasn't born yesterday.

"Good. Then what I want is to get on with my morning in The Haight—" she shot him a look over her shoulder "—alone."

She expected at least a token argument. It didn't come.

"Then you've got it, love," he said.

Startled, she turned around. He was already cutting across to the other side of the street.

Well, good, she thought.

HE'D ALMOST REACHED Golden Gate Park when something caused him to turn the corner and wander down streets he wasn't familiar with. He was just enjoying the sunshine and the day, feeling the freedom of having no particular place to go.

Of course, as he wandered the streets, she wandered in and out of his mind with a freedom over which he seemed to have no control.

The sudden bewilderment in her dark eyes before she would catch herself, rein herself in—in that one flash of pure emotion, he saw something in her that needed coaxing out. It was impossible not to wonder what it would be like to be the man who accomplished that.

He did his best not to. It was something of a losing battle.

His mind on the woman and the sunshine, he suddenly realized that he'd been skirting Buena Vista Park. He left the sidewalk of Buena Vista Avenue and started up the paved path. In seconds the city was forgotten. The thick forest of twisted pines, redwoods and cypress entwined above him like a natural canopy as he wove upward toward the summit of the park. He nodded at a few people who were walking their dogs, but the place was virtually empty, the air taken over by birdsong and brush rustling in the breeze, dimming the sounds of the city below. He liked the feeling of being all alone in the world that this pocket of wilderness evoked in him.

Or, at least he thought he did. Until he came out of a stand of pine and there she was again.

Somehow he wasn't that surprised. It only seemed right that this woman who seemed to be invading his life would choose to explore this unlikely place at the same time he had.

He would have liked to stand and watch her for a while, but he was mindful that if she turned and saw him she might become even more skittish. And in today's climate, who could blame her? So he carefully started toward her, waiting for her to notice him.

He was only a few yards from her when she turned her head and looked right at him. Her hair blew across her face and she pulled it back with the tips of her fingers. He saw something flare in her eyes for just a second before she put her sunglasses on.

"I should have known," she mumbled when he reached her.

"What should you have known?" he asked gently.

"That you wouldn't be doing the usual tourist things."

"Ah, such as the Golden Gate Bridge?"

"Yes. Or Fisherman's Wharf."

"I've always liked the view from here."

"You've been here before?"

He nodded, looking out past the pitched roofs of Ashbury Heights and farther north where the spires of the Golden Gate were visible against the vibrant blue of the bay. This was one of the few places in San Francisco that held no part of the past for him. It had always provided a solitary space in time for him. A place where he'd made no memories with another human being. From now on, it would make him think of her.

He turned back to her. She was looking out on the same vista as he had been. Her strong jawline provided a contrast to the soft sensuality of her wide mouth. He looked at that mouth and saw candlelight in a dark room, rumpled sheets and tender caresses. He looked at the determined jawline and saw a woman stubborn enough to resist.

She turned to look at him so suddenly that her sunglasses slid down her nose and he saw her eyes again. Dark, confused, innocent. The word *seduction* swept into his crowded thoughts, the ones so full of this woman. She would take some seducing, he knew, before he could have her.

That he wanted her, there was no longer any question.

"Hard to believe," she murmured, pushing her sunglasses back into place, "that this is right in the middle of the city. It's so wild. So untouched."

"Wild and untouched," he repeated. "Very seductive."

He'd meant the words to disarm her. And they did. She looked at him and he didn't need to see her eyes behind her sunglasses to know he'd gotten to her. Her lips had parted. Color had flared in her cheeks.

He wanted to push her a little further. Some devil in him had to do it. He took a step toward her.

"And secluded. A lonely spot where one doesn't really want to be alone."

"Wh-what?" she stammered, her sunglasses slipping down her nose again.

"Have you ever made love in the woods? On a bed of leaves. Under a canopy of tree limbs. The wild wind brushing your flesh. The sun dappling your skin."

He reached out a finger and pulled her glasses farther down on her nose so he could see into her dark eyes. "After all," he whispered, "making love is a natural act. It should be enjoyed in the midst of nature."

She bit her lip to hold back a gasp. Her skin felt suddenly hot—and all she could think of was how the wind would feel against it. For one dizzying moment, she wanted the picture he'd painted with his words. And she wanted it with him.

Sex with a stranger?

No, that wasn't her.

Was it?

She looked into his dark eyes and forced her mind to answer: *Absolutely not.* And on the heels of the words her mind had sent to her heart came a shaft of regret from the longing that seemed to be flooding her body.

Vaguely she heard the rustle of leaves under his feet as he moved closer to her, felt his fingers brush her face as he removed her sunglasses. She looked at his mouth and wondered what it would feel like against hers. She looked at his hair and wondered what it would feel like under her fingers. She looked at his eyes and wondered what they would look like if he—if he—

His eyes had darkened with something new and the thought flew into her mind that she didn't have to wonder what his eyes would look like full of need and want and intent. Because that was what she swore she saw in them now.

His gracefully formed mouth came closer. And the whole universe seemed to shrink and center on his lips. All at once she knew with clarity that he wouldn't be a gentle kisser. His mouth would take. And demand. It would *own*.

And suddenly, Charlotte wanted to be owned.

She had a moment to wonder if that low, needy moan had come from her before the pocket of the world she was lost in exploded with the sound of branches snapping, dried leaves being kicked up and a deep growl that Charlotte was pretty sure wasn't coming from her.

A huge dog bounded from the underbrush with such force that it hit her in the backs of the knees. She went down like a ton of bricks.

A young girl, all arms and legs, broke through the thicket. "Oh, gosh," she said, "I'm sorry! You okay?"

Charlotte took a deep, slightly shaky breath. "I'm fine. Just fine."

"Let me help you—"

A cacophony of barking rose from somewhere in the trees and the girl gave her a harried look, again said, "Sorry," and ran on.

He squatted down next to her and brushed the hair from her eyes. She thrust her head back, trying to dodge the touch, but it was too late. She would have thought that getting knocked on her butt was enough to knock any lingering lust out of her head, but the feel of his fingers in her hair was telling her body something else entirely. She scooted backward on her rear, away from him, and scrambled to her feet.

"You sure you're okay?" he asked, standing again and making a move to touch her.

She stepped back. "I'm fine," she answered, refusing to look at him. Nothing like displaying a little clumsiness to dampen the ardor. Not, of course, that she was sorry to see it dampened. Kissing a stranger in an enchanted forest high above one of the most romantic cities in the world would hardly be playing by the rules. And Charlotte always played by the rules.

True, thumping to the ground like a ton of bricks wasn't exactly the device she would have chosen to make herself stick to the rules. But one couldn't look gift pratfalls in the mouth.

And one certainly didn't want to look this strange, irreverent man in the mouth, either.

Not again. She simply didn't trust herself.

She started for the paved path that led down to safety.

"Where are you going?" he called.

"I've got sights to see," she called back, her eyes on the ground before her. Tripping on a tree root would strip her of the last ounce of dignity she was clinging to.

"I'll come with you," he said as he started to scramble after her.

"No, you won't."

"Oh, come on. Four eyes are better than two. Besides, I know my way around. I'll be your official tour guide."

He would be her official downfall, she said to herself. Out loud, she said, "I have a guide book, thank you," as she held it up so he could see it over her shoulder.

"Oh, but I'm so much better than a guidebook."

His voice had slipped into that low tone of intimacy he'd used on her before.

"I can show you things Michelin never even thought of."

A jolt of longing pierced her lower belly again at the low, lazy hum of his words and she had absolutely no doubt that he could show her things *no one* had ever thought of before. Not that she was going to let him.

"I'm apparently more conventional than you think. Right now I'm headed for Golden Gate Park, which I'm sure is much too…normal for a nonconformist like you."

"Oh, I can flaunt convention wherever I am."

"I'm sure you can. And I'm sure there is plenty of convention all over San Francisco just waiting for you to flaunt it. So don't let me keep you."

His rich, seductive laugh rolled over her and up into the trees, growing fainter and fainter as she started to trot down the rest of the incline to the street.

When she reached the bottom, she was, once again, alone.

Chapter Three

Shakespeare's Garden.

Charlotte was enchanted as she wandered the tiny place, examining plants and trying to remember the relevant lines from Shakespeare's plays. Such a romantic place. She should be wearing a lacy, tea-length dress and a graceful hat with a large brim shading her eyes.

Or *something* shading her eyes, she thought as she squinted at the quotations on the plaques set in the garden wall. Where on earth had she left her sunglasses? She started rummaging again in the soft leather shoulder bag she carried, but at the sound of a voice behind her, her fingers became paralyzed suddenly around a nearly toothless comb.

"The reddest rose," the voice behind her said, "would pale in company of the flame the sun ignites in your hair."

Charlotte resisted turning around. After all, she didn't really have to. Once again she recognized the voice. "Nice try," she said as blandly as she could manage, "but I don't believe that's Shakespeare."

"Nope. It's not."

She still wouldn't turn around. "Then who is it?"

He moved up next to her and leaned a shoulder against the wall. "Just me, love."

She gave him a look designed to quell, but his dark

eyes—showing just a shadow of amusement as he watched her—definitely put her in second place when it came to being disarming. Those eyes managed to steal away every once of her concentration for just a moment or two until she remembered that irritation was the proper response.

"Are you following me?" she asked, trying for the haughty tone she'd used on him earlier. But first she'd had to cough out the frog in her throat. Something was lost in the process.

He shook his head and murmured, "No."

And there went her concentration again. She cleared her throat for the second time. "Right. And it's just a coincidence that you wound up in Golden Gate Park."

The grin on his lips was no more than a shadow. "Not exactly."

The man was too charming for his own good. Of course, he was a lot more than charming. Other adjectives came to mind. Cute, handsome, sexy—

Before her mind turned completely to mush, she took hold of herself. "Look, I'm sure you're used to sweeping women off their feet. But it's not going to happen here. So I suggest that you just—"

"You left these at Buena Vista," he interrupted. "I thought you might need them."

Slowly, she looked from his face to his outstretched hand. Her sunglasses were dangling from one crooked finger.

Much as she'd hated ending up on her backside in front of this man, at the moment she was fervently hoping for another Doberman to come running out of the heather. Or better yet, an elephant. Something that would plow her down for good.

How on earth could she have thought that this man had followed her for any other reason? He was a babe. A certifiable babe. And if Charlotte was sure of anything, she was sure that she wasn't the kind of woman who attracted a male babe.

She snatched the sunglasses from his finger and thrust them onto her nose, ducking her head to hide the flush she felt creeping up her face.

She took a deep breath. "Thank you," she mumbled gracelessly, hoping it would be enough.

But she should have known he wouldn't let her off the hook that easily.

"And?" he asked.

She took another deep breath, still keeping her head down. "And it was wrong of me to assume..." She couldn't seem to get the rest of the sentence out. How on earth could she admit to this man, this certifiable babe, that she had been about to accuse him of following her around San Francisco to—to—*to put the make on her?*

She stole a look at him. The amusement on his face had come out of the shadows and she knew he was going to take great delight in making her say it.

Well, she wasn't going to.

"Quit gloating and leave me alone."

She started to move away but he was quicker. He stepped in front of her, bracing his hands against the garden wall behind her on either side of her head. She should have felt threatened, but she knew the thudding of her heart had nothing to do with fear.

He shifted his body, bringing himself almost imperceptibly closer to her, his dark gaze moving to her mouth, then back up to her eyes again. "I'm not here to gloat," he said.

"I know—you're just here to return my sunglasses."

His smile grew slighter, sweeter, and she wondered briefly if he practiced ways of being charming in the bathroom mirror when he shaved that dangerously handsome face every morning.

"Well, that's not entirely true."

His words came out as gently as his smile and she had to swallow hard before she could speak. "It's not?"

He shook his head. "Nope."

"Then, uh, what are you here to do?"

He hesitated and made a small noise in his throat, his gaze skittering away for only a moment before he looked into her face again. On any other man she would have interpreted it as a moment of insecurity. But that wasn't possible with this man, was it?

One corner of his mouth lifted. "I'm here," he said, "because I want to be with you."

She sucked in a shaky breath. "Wh-what?"

"I want to spend time with you. Show you *my* San Francisco."

"But...but, why?"

Her heart pounded in her ears while she watched him watching her, his brow furrowed, his mouth tilted, his eyes lost some of their amusement.

"Maybe because every time I've run into you you vacillate between being a woman who knows how to take care of herself, knows how to put a man in his place, and a girl who..."

He hesitated, removing one of his hands from the wall behind her. And for a moment she thought he was going to touch her. But his fingers stopped just short of her throat. Thank God, she thought, because her pulse there was jumping like it was trying for an Olympic record.

If he didn't finish his sentence soon, she was going to explode. "A girl who what?" she whispered.

"A girl who trembles like a virgin."

Hell, she thought. Bloody hell. She forced herself to say, "That's ridiculous. I don't tremble."

"Yes, you do. You're trembling right now."

She lifted her chin. "I am not!"

He did touch her then. Gently, he took her hand and lifted it. "I can feel your pulse beating in your palm."

His fingers played over her palm and something inside her leaped. She gritted her teeth and snatched her hand away.

"I'm thirty-six years old and I don't tremble like a...like a..." She almost choked but finally managed to get the words out: "Like a virgin."

His grin was as gentle as his touch had been. "There's something else I want, besides the chance to spend the day with you."

"What's that?" she asked warily.

"I want to kiss you."

"What?" she gasped.

"I want to kiss you. May I?"

She opened her mouth but nothing came out. She shut it, then tried again. "No! No, of course you can't!" And finally she stopped trembling enough to push herself away from the wall. She brushed past him and started walking. Fast.

He, of course, came after her.

"Why not?"

"You're being absurd."

"I'm a good kisser."

She almost laughed. No kidding, she thought. He was probably an expert by the time he turned twelve.

"I'll take your word for it," she said over her shoulder.

"But I'm a stranger. How do you know you can trust my word?"

"Exactly!" she shouted triumphantly. He laughed and she already knew how it would look on his face.

She headed for the California Academy of Sciences building, planning to take a look at some of the artwork in the museum. He followed right behind.

"You know, if you'd tell me where you're going I could arrange to meet you there. Or better yet, we could walk together."

"I don't think so," she said, thinking that maybe she

would have to adjust her plans and spend some time staring at the dioramas. That should make him lose interest. He didn't look like the kind of man who would be content spending such a glorious day inside staring at the life-size exhibit of an African watering hole.

"Don't tell me you're going into the museum?" he asked from behind her.

"That's where I'm headed," she confirmed. "I'm sure it's not your cup of tea, so I'll just say goodbye and thanks for returning my sunglasses."

He took her hand. "Let me show you something more interesting."

"If you don't mind," she said, trying to tug her hand out of his, "I'd like to see—"

"Dead things," he interrupted. "The place is full of dead things. Let me show you a place that is intensely alive."

He started pulling her along and it took her a few paces before she could dig in her heels and halt his progress. He turned around to face her, but held fast to her hand.

"Come on," he said in that disarming way he had. "Let me show you one of my favorite places in the park."

She sighed, feeling a little like she was dealing with a willful child. "Then will you leave me in peace?"

"I'll tell you what," he replied. "If you don't like this place as much as I do, I'll go away and leave you alone."

She raised a brow. "Really?"

"Absolutely. I'll abandon you forever. I'll even cross the street if I see you coming."

He grinned at her and she could feel the pad of his thumb brushing the edge of her palm. A spear of sensation shot down through her lower belly. The man knew how to work with what he had, that was for sure.

"Please?" he cajoled.

She grinned and shook her head. "Does anyone ever say no to you?"

"Only you."

That made her laugh out loud. "Well, we can't break your record now can we?"

"Then you'll come?"

She nodded. "I'll come."

He tried to pull her along again but she stood firm.

"Remember what you promised."

"What's that?"

She rolled her eyes. "That if I don't like what you show me as much as you do—"

"I'll forget I know you," he finished.

"But you don't know me," she said.

"Not yet," he answered in that soft, steady voice that was even more disarming than his grin. "But I will."

Her mouth dropped open, but then he was pulling her along again and she had to close it quickly or she would gulp enough air to give her hiccups.

"Will you slow down?" she asked petulantly as he started up the steps of the Academy of Sciences building.

"No."

"No?" she asked between pants as she struggled to keep up with him.

"No—being breathless will help heighten the experience."

That didn't sound good. Not good at all.

They entered the academy and she got a brief flash of something that looked like an African safari to her right. And then they were in a courtyard, winding their way through groups of people clustered here and there around a fountain.

"Penguins," she said, but he just kept going.

"Oh, dolphins. I love—"

"You'll love where I'm taking you even better," he insisted and the dolphins were nothing but a blur as they scuttled past.

Suddenly, he stopped. She bumped up against him, almost losing her balance when she ricocheted off him.

"Close your eyes," he said.

"What?"

"Just close your eyes."

"Look, this has gone far enough. I'm—" She had absolutely no idea what she'd been about to say. Every shred of coherence fled. All she was aware of was the sudden gentle brush of his finger on her cheek and the soft light in his dark eyes.

"Trust me," he said.

How could she trust anything with the way her mind had flown? With the way her breath was so still in her lungs? With the way her skin seemed about to melt?

"You can, you know," he murmured as his gaze traveled her face.

She closed her eyes. He didn't move at first. The sounds of children laughing and parents calling receded and dimmed. There was only the feel of his finger moving on her cheek and the warmth of his hand engulfing hers. And then he was easing her forward again, gently this time, as if they were merely a couple holding hands as they walked.

You must be mad, she told herself. But she let herself be led on as if she were embracing the madness.

They seemed to be going up an incline or ramp of some sort, that spiraled, just like everything else in San Francisco. Twisting, turning, hilly. Her heart raced harder with each step. And she wasn't sure if it was the fear of the unknown place he was taking her to or the fear that she desperately wanted him to take her there—or anywhere.

There seemed to be people all around them. She almost wished there weren't. She almost wished he were leading her someplace dark and quiet and isolated. She almost wished—

"Don't open your eyes yet, love. Soon. But not yet."

He was standing so close that she felt his whisper on her cheek.

There were other people, but the brush of their bodies

against hers as they passed weren't as real as the warm
hand that held hers. There were other scents, but the only
one that mattered was the scent of him: spicy, like autumn
fruit, clean like an October wind. There were other sounds,
but the sounds of children's laughter couldn't compete with
the sound of her heart thudding in her ears.

And then a voice called—a woman's voice, sharp, clear,
authoritative—followed by the sound of running feet and
the feel of bodies passing so closely and swiftly that they
created a breeze. And then all was still and quiet.

"Open your eyes," he whispered into her ear.

She did. Her mouth fell open but she couldn't speak. All
she could do was watch as hundreds of fish swam in a
kaleidoscope of mad color all around her. It was dizzying.
Surreal. Like being underwater without getting wet.

"Beautiful," she whispered.

"Didn't I tell you?"

She tore her gaze from the swirling throng of color to
look at him. Reflections sparkling off the water in the tank
that surrounded them dappled his face with rainbows of
light. He looked like something magic.

And maybe he was.

"You like it."

His words were a statement, not a question. He clearly
already knew the answer.

"Yes," she told him anyway. "I like it."

He grinned and she forced her gaze away from him and
back onto the fish, stepping closer to the cylindrical tank
that surrounded them just as a shark moved past so close
to the glass that it made her jump back.

"Impressive, aren't they?"

She shivered. "Scary."

"Are you easily spooked?"

She gave him a look. "Only when I know there's obvious danger."

"But the sharks are behind glass. They can't touch you."

"The sharks aren't what I'm afraid of," she murmured. As soon as the words were out, she was sorry she'd said them.

He put his hand gently on her cheek and turned her to face him. "I won't devour you—unless you want me to."

The reflections of the water and the colorful fish shimmered on his face. His mouth was a soft temptation. His eyes were intent—for once without humor. His brows curved low over his dark eyes. His short, thick hair was windblown. Her fingers ached to touch it. His black T-shirt covered a chest that was well developed enough for Charlotte to know he could be very physical. His arms bulged enough for her to know he could be dangerous. But in a moment of pure clarity, which in itself surprised her, she knew it was only herself she was afraid of. Because she might very well want just that: She might very well want him to devour her.

He took a step closer to her. "Remember your promise?"

"My—uh—" She swallowed deeply, her gaze becoming fixed on his mouth. "My promise?"

"Uh-huh. If you liked what I showed you, you agreed to spend the rest of the day with me."

"I—" she gulped. "—I did?"

He grinned. "You did."

She made a feeble attempt to shake her head. "I don't think so."

He took another step closer and she was no longer at all sure if it was the swirling mass of fish and water surrounding her that was making her dizzy.

"I can show you a San Francisco that no guidebook will tell you about," he said in that soft, deep voice that made the breath catch in her throat. "Let me show you the city as only lovers can see it."

Was she going to faint? She suddenly felt hot. And more than dizzy. Dizzy was slightly nauseating. This was different. Her head had gone light, filled with some sort of soaring joy instead of a brain.

And clearly, she wasn't thinking with her brain. She was thinking with her body.

"Lovers?" she croaked, hoping she'd heard him correctly.

"Why not?" he asked, lifting her ringless hand up to his mouth and brushing his lips over it. "You're not married, right?"

"Uh, no."

"Attached?"

She shook her head.

"Then be mine while you're here."

She was stunned. Heat paralyzed her. The pounding of her blood was the only thing moving as she stared at him. And it was moving as fast as that fish she could see behind him. The one being chased by the shark.

But the fish didn't moan. Not like she did.

She'd never before made the sound escaping her lips. Plaintive. Needy.

His gaze fixed on her mouth and she knew by the look in his eyes that he recognized the depth of her need.

His hand cupped the side of her neck and slid back under her hair, but the pressure he exerted to bring her mouth to his wasn't really necessary. By now she wanted his kiss more than she wanted breath.

He wasn't gentle. Some part of her mind was surprised to realize that "gentle" wasn't what she wanted, anyway. She parted her lips and felt his tongue thrust into her mouth, searching for hers. The touch of it made her moan once again and thrust her hands into his hair, holding his mouth fast to her own. And then his other arm went around her waist, pulling her into his hard chest, before his hand moved lower to cup her bottom and thrust her pelvis up and into his own.

She gasped when she felt his arousal against the tight

denim that covered her. The sensation soared through her body and up to her breasts. Her nipples pounded while her mouth plundered. And she knew he was no longer doing the kissing. Nor was he causing her to move against him, to try to get closer to the hard heat of him. *She* was. And she couldn't seem to help herself.

Then, all at once, he pulled away.

She reached for him again but he merely took her hands in both of his as if keeping her at arm's length.

"Wha—" she began to ask dazedly.

But then she saw what had happened. A group of school-children filed into the observation tank. He'd heard them coming. She hadn't. She'd been so wrapped up in his mouth and his body, she hadn't heard a thing.

Mortification filled her. "Oh, no—" she whispered, tugging her hands from his and heading for the exit.

"Wait!" he called. But she was already running, threading her way through the crowd, hoping she would be lost forever in the sea of fifth graders.

HE'D LOST HER, DAMN IT. He shoved through the crowd but she'd taken off so fast he knew it was hopeless. Several busloads of children must have arrived at the same time, no doubt delayed because they'd been watching the dolphins being fed. Now they swarmed all over the place and there was no way he was going to find her in the throng. Not if she didn't want to be found.

He was still breathing hard, breathless from the heat of her kiss, when he pushed through the door of the science academy. How he wanted her. His body still pulsed with it. He hadn't felt anything like it in—hell, had he *ever* felt anything like it?

And where the hell had she gone? The trembling virgin had taken over once again and she'd fled from him as if he'd been the devil himself.

He started jogging down the steps of the academy. He had to find her.

AFTER AN HOUR OF wandering in the park, he'd stationed himself at the entrance, searching groups of people as they left. In vain, of course. The whole damn thing was ridiculous. He should go back to his hotel, take a shower, and forget he ever laid eyes on her.

Hotel. He snapped his fingers. That was it! He knew where she was staying. Sooner or later she would have to go back to her room—or leave it again. He would plant himself in the lobby and not leave until he saw her again.

THE DRESS WAS too short. And a little too low-cut. Plus Charlotte had never worn red before. She still had no idea who the dress belonged to. After a ridiculous telephone conversation with the airline, in which they insisted that if the suitcase was hers, so were the clothes, she'd given up trying to solve the mystery.

Charlotte turned this way and that in the mirror. Not bad. In fact, she looked pretty good. Or maybe she was just feeling reckless. Assaulting strange men in the middle of fish tanks probably had that effect on her.

She groaned and brought her hands to her face. "Lord, Charlotte, why didn't you just throw yourself to the floor and beg him to take you?"

Well, she might have done just that if it hadn't been for the schoolchildren filing in. That thought didn't make her feel any better.

She looked back at the mirror. The flush on her cheeks went well with the dress. She leaned closer, peering at her face. Maybe it was time to break out the bag of cosmetics she'd found in the suitcase that looked like hers, but obviously couldn't be. So far, she'd worn one of the lipsticks only. She studied her eyes in the mirror. Maybe a little shadow. Some mascara. The deeper lipstick.

She tugged at the low, deep V-neckline of the dress. Thank goodness it had long sleeves or she would feel totally naked. And weren't V necklines supposed to minimize breasts? Hers seemed to be right out there in front for all the world to see. She supposed it didn't help that the material was a body-hugging knit. She turned away from the mirror and picked up the discarded jeans from floor. Maybe she should just put them on again and order room service.

"No!" she said suddenly, tossing the denim aside. "You're going down to that restaurant and having dinner," she told her reflection. "And you're doing it in this red dress."

And as long as she was going to wear the dress, she might as well see what she could do with the cosmetics.

Half an hour later the maître d' was showing her to a table.

"And will madam be dining alone this evening?"

"Madam will most certainly be dining alone this evening," she answered emphatically, knowing that the maître d' was referring to her impromptu, outrageously underdressed lunch guest of the day before.

He bowed. "Very good. Your waiter will be over shortly. Enjoy your dinner."

She smiled and tried to relax. No one in the place seemed to take much notice of her. And why should they? For all they knew she dressed in red mini-dresses every day of her life.

The waiter had just left her a menu when he was back again.

"I'm sorry, I'm not ready to order yet," she said with an apologetic little smile.

"Of course not, ma'am. The gentleman wished me to ask you if he could join you."

"The, uh, gentleman?"

"Yes, ma'am. He's standing at the doorway."

She groaned and closed her eyes. Not again. That was

all she needed—something to make her even more con-
spicuous than the red dress. Although she had a suspicion
that the sudden tripping of her heart had nothing at all to
do with imminent embarrassment.

She opened her eyes, expecting to see the familiar black
T-shirt and ragged jeans of the man who seemed to be
haunting her every step.

He wasn't there.

Hard on the heels of her heart sinking came the question
of who else in San Francisco would want to dine with her?

She peered across the somewhat-dim restaurant to the
doorway, trying to make out who was standing there. But
all she could see was a pair of broad shoulders, draped in
what had to be pin-striped Armani, and the blaze of white
linen covering a decidedly male chest.

She wondered for a moment if the woman whose clothes
she'd somehow taken custody of had also willed her a male
model for the evening. Just as she was wondering why that
thought wasn't setting her heart a-flutter, the man in the
pinstripes stepped forward into the circle of light provided
by the tiny Tiffany lamp illuminating the table nearest the
door—and her heart more than fluttered. It seemed to soar
up toward her throat and hover there, making it almost
impossible to breathe.

She hadn't really thought he could get any better looking.
But the polish of the suit only made the man who'd kissed
her amid the sharks even more handsome. He inclined his
dark head toward her, the corners of his mouth lifting with
shadowed amusement.

"Madam?" the waiter was asking.

"No," she answered quickly.

"No?"

"No," she repeated. "Tell the gentleman that he may
not join me."

The waiter looked bereft. "Is madam sure?"

"Madam is very sure."

He gave a shrug and went off to do as she asked.

Charlotte picked up her menu but the words seemed to run together, unless the place really was serving ostrich *au chocolate*. Waiting for the other shoe to drop was robbing her concentration. She lowered the menu slightly to peer over the top of it. Had he really gone away without creating any kind of scene? And why wasn't she more relieved at the idea?

He didn't seem to be anywhere in sight. She craned her neck around the oversize menu but the area near the door was empty.

"Looking for someone?"

The menu almost flew out of her hands.

"No, of course not," she replied, trying to avoid looking at him. Which wasn't easy, considering he'd managed to secure the table directly across from hers.

"What looks good?" he asked.

She set her menu carefully aside. "Are you speaking to me?" she asked, busying herself with imaginary lint on the sleeve of her dress.

"Yes, love, I am."

"Well, since I don't know you," she said in her haughty tone, "I have no idea what might or might not look good to you."

"Well, love, I think you know me well enough to know that you in that dress look very, very good to me."

There was a distinct snicker from behind her and she resisted turning around for fear that the entire restaurant had heard his remark.

Her hand shook as she raised her goblet for a sip of water. When she brought it to her lips, water splashed gently over the rim of the crystal and she felt the cold trail of it in the open V of her dress.

Her eyes shot over to him.

"Nice," he mouthed, his gaze following the progress of the drop of water. She felt it course down her bare flesh and into her cleavage. And as she watched his eyes follow its progress, the water no longer felt cold but hot—as if the heat of his gaze warmed it.

"Does madam wish to order?"

"Yes," she told the waiter. "Yes, of course."

She picked up the menu again. "The medallions of pork with wild mushroom sauce," she said.

"With the angel-hair pasta," the waiter finished for her. "Very good, madam. An excellent choice."

After the waiter left, she fiddled with the stem of her water goblet, not daring to raise it to her mouth again.

"Did you enjoy the rest of your afternoon?"

There was no use pretending she didn't know he was talking to her. "Yes. Yes, I did."

"You left me so suddenly. Where did you go?"

The words sounded all too intimate and she cast a nervous look at the table next to her. The two elderly women seated there seemed to be waiting for her answer.

"I—uh—I went up to see the bridge."

"Ah, the Golden Gate."

"Yes, of course," she said defensively. "One can't come to San Francisco without seeing the bridge."

"No, I suppose not. But there are other sights far more romantic."

"Well, I'm not looking for romance," she said dismissively.

"What are you looking for?" he asked her softly, so softly in fact that she was surprised she could hear him. Had the place suddenly gone entirely too quiet? She resisted the urge to turn around, certain that every eye in the place would be riveted on her, every ear waiting for her answer.

She was saved by the waiter coming forward to fill her wineglass.

"I didn't order wine," she said uncertainly, not at all sure if she had or hadn't.

"The gentleman, madam."

Her gaze shot to his again. "Tell the gentlemen that I don't—"

"Tell the lady," he interrupted, his voice just loud enough to override her own, "that if she isn't looking for romance she has no business wandering around by herself in that dress."

"Oh, my," came words to her left, and she swung her head that way to find the two elderly women watching her.

"Accept the wine, my dear," said one of them. "Such gallantry should not be refused."

Her gaze went back to his to find that dark amusement in his eyes again as he watched her.

She took the wine from the waiter, raised it to her lips, and took a sip. The heat coursed down her throat and spread into her breast. Inexplicably, she took another sip and the room got hot enough to grow orchids.

But it might not have been just the wine.

"You look very beautiful tonight," he said.

She took another sip of wine.

"I thought you didn't wear that color?"

"I don't," she answered emphatically.

"Then you must have worn it especially for me tonight."

A retort was right on the tip of her tongue. Really it was. Her mistake was in looking at him before she started to speak. Her mind went blank. Or maybe it was just too busy shooting sparks throughout her body. Fireworks. Everywhere. From her forehead to her fingertips. If she looked at them she was sure they would be glowing. But she didn't look at them. She couldn't. His gaze held hers as if to look away would be to stop breathing.

"I want to be with you," he said, and she heard a gasp from somewhere in the restaurant.

"This is crazy. You don't even know me," she said.

"I know this. I know I want to touch you. I know that

when I kissed you this afternoon there was no one else in the world but us."

One of the elderly ladies to her left sighed and she couldn't help but grin. "Just you and me and a million fish."

His mouth quirked. His eyes danced. "Were there fish there? I didn't notice."

She had to laugh at that. "Is this your standard sweep-'em-off-their-feet procedure?"

He laughed softly and shook his head. "No, this is brand-new stuff."

"Oh? I'm flattered."

"Don't be," he said, his face suddenly sober, his eyes suddenly serious. "Just be mine for the rest of the evening."

Her heart stopped. The breath in her lungs grew still. Could this really be happening to her? This man who looked like something from a movie poster making verbal love to her from across the room?

The waiter came then and put her entrée before her. Then he went to her pursuer's table and set down an identical plate.

She watched him eat.

He watched her eat.

They sipped wine.

He asked her how she liked the hotel.

She asked him where he was staying.

He asked her how she liked the pork in wild mushroom sauce.

"Delicious," she told him. What did he think?

"I think it would be easier to dine with you if we were at the same table," he answered.

"He's right, you know, my dear," said one of the elderly ladies. "Why don't you let him join you for dessert?"

"Yes," he said with a subtle grin. "Why don't you?"

Chapter Four

Across the table from her he looked much more delicious than anything on the chrome-and-glass dessert cart. The prospect of a chocolate éclair dimmed considerably.

The waiter hovered. "And your choice, madam?"

She glanced at the cart again but the crème brûlée seemed to run together with the chocolate gâteau.

"Why don't you take the cart away for now? We'll decide later."

"Very well, sir." The waiter bowed and wheeled the cart away with remarkable silence.

"Why don't we skip dessert for now," he said. "I know a place in North Beach that has *tiramisù* from heaven."

"North Beach?"

"Yes. We can take a cable car to Washington Square. After that we can walk down to the pier. There's a club down there that—"

"Wait a minute. I said you could join me for dessert."

"Well, yes, but as long as we're in the North Beach area—"

"But we're not. We're here."

He settled back in his chair and looked at her, his eyes slightly narrowed, his mouth quirked. "Why do you fight this so hard?"

"Fight what?"

"You know very well fight what. If I touched you right now, your pulse would jump. If I took you in my arms again—"

"But you're not going to."

He leaned forward and picked up her hand from the table. "Why not? We're both free. We're both over twenty-one. We're both alone in one of the most romantic cities in the world. Why not see some of it together?"

His thumb was moving back and forth on the back of her hand. She wanted to close her eyes and go with the sensation. Was she that starved for her senses to be satisfied? Or was there something about this stranger across from her that made her want to do things she'd never done before?

"Are you afraid of me?" he asked softly.

She looked into his dark eyes. "No," she answered honestly. "I'm not afraid of you. Not in the sense you mean, anyway."

"You're only afraid of where it might lead?"

"But that's just it. It can't lead anywhere. I fly home on Monday—back to my life."

His thumb stopped moving. He raised her hand to his mouth and brushed her fingertips across his lips.

"Then we have a day and a half left," he said, the breath of his voice on her skin. "It could be wonderful."

Yes, she thought. Yes, it could. No future. No past. Just living in the now. And wasn't meeting a sexy man on vacation every single woman's fantasy? The only thing that ever marred that fantasy was the fact that you'd be waiting for an awful lot of long-distance calls before the relationship died a painful death. But that wouldn't be the case here. Not if they both knew it was only for here. Only for now.

"If we do this—" She had to stop and swallow; her mouth had gone completely dry. She tried again. "If we agree to spend time together, there would have to be some rules—''

He smiled. "Rules?"

She nodded nervously. "Yes. Rules."

"And who sets up these rules?"

"I—I do."

He chuckled deeply. "I thought so. And if I don't agree to any of your rules?"

"Then we can discuss it. Perhaps reach a compromise."

Still grinning, he shook his head. "Okay. Try me."

"No names."

"Wait—that doesn't work. I have to call you something."

She thought for a moment. "Okay. First names only."

"Deal," he said. "I'm Jacob."

She tried out his name in her mind. Yes. She liked it.

"And you're—"

"Char—" She started to say Charlotte but changed her mind. "Charlie," she said, switching to a childhood nickname that few people called her anymore.

"Charlie," he repeated softly, his eyes twinkling. "I like that. And rule two?"

"No history."

"Well, that's pretty rough, Charlie. Wouldn't history enter into just about everything we try to discuss?"

She frowned. "What do you mean?"

"Well, supposing I said I knew of a good jazz club?"

"Oh, I see what you mean. Okay, only trivial history. Nothing real personal."

He nodded. "I can live with that."

"And absolutely no exchanging phone numbers or addresses before I leave on Monday."

"I see. We know each other in San Francisco—and that's the only place we know each other."

She gave an emphatic nod. "Right."

"Is that all?"

She thought for a moment. The few points she'd made seemed to cover everything.

"Yes," she answered.

"Then, Charlie, you've got yourself a deal. Now let's get out of here and find our own San Francisco."

HE HELD HER HAND on the cable car. It wasn't quite dark and she felt the first of the night breezes on her face. They got off near Washington Square and he kept her hand firmly in his as they walked the few blocks to the café he'd told her about. They sat at a small table, steaming cups of cappuccino between them.

"Do you like to dance?"

She shook her head. "I don't dance."

"Then how am I going to get to hold you?"

He'd taken off his tie, unbuttoned a few buttons on his snowy linen shirt. If anything, he looked even more handsome. "Rakish" seemed to suit him.

"Do you practice being disarming?" she asked him, searching for some form of self-defense.

"I'm just stating the truth. I'd like to have you in my arms again."

"Really," she scoffed, while her hand shook too much to pick up her coffee cup.

He laughed. "There wasn't anything in the rules about body contact."

She looked at him, hoping to douse his amusement with a cold stare. But the opposite happened and she started to grin. "No, I suppose there wasn't."

"But we *were* supposed to have dessert."

"Yes, we were."

"Then let's split a piece of that *tiramisù* I told you about."

She laughed while he called the waiter over.

And it really was the best she'd ever tasted. Sharing a dessert with a man was a rather sensual experience—and it wasn't only because the *tiramisù* was cool and creamy on her tongue. The act of eating from the same plate; the comic sparring as he grabbed the last piece of dessert; the feel of his fingertip brushing a crumb from her lower lip. It was more erotic than she would have believed.

When he'd swallowed the last bite he rested his cheek against his fist, elbow on the table, and looked at her.

And kept looking at her.

"You're staring," she finally said, squirming a little in her seat.

"There was nothing in the rules about staring."

"Well, maybe there should have been."

"Too late."

She forced her chin up. "Not necessarily. We could attach an amendment."

"Not a chance, Charlie. If I've only got till Monday with you, I'm gonna look my fill."

She raised a brow. "I would think you've already done that."

"Not even close," he murmured.

She started to dip her head, to hide her embarrassment, or maybe just to hide from what was in his eyes. But something stopped her. These were new rules she was playing by. She didn't have to be the Charlotte Riesling who never had men look at her like this from across a table. She was Charlie. And she was wearing a red minidress. And there was no use pretending coyness. The man across from her, Jacob, had chased her all over San Francisco because he wanted to be with her. She had no idea why a man who looked like him, who was as carefree and confident as he was, would feel that way. But maybe the reason didn't matter.

Maybe all that mattered was that he was here—now.

"What's going on in that complicated mind of yours?"

"I think that's breaking the rules."

"Which rule?" he demanded.

"The one about no history. To answer that question would be to let you in on too much of my history."

He took her hand and squeezed it. "Then I propose a new rule."

"Do you?"

"Yes. A rule that says when you're with me you can't think such thoughts."

"And why is that?"

"Because it keeps me out. I want to be all you think of when you're with me, Charlie. All you see. All you feel. All you want."

The echo of his words hung in the air, thrilling her and puzzling her at the same time. "Wh—?"

He leaned closer and placed his fingers on her lips to stop the word. "That's another new rule. Never ask why."

His words were so low, so intimate—so *sure*. His eyes were dark as they looked deeply into hers.

"I want you in my arms right now. Badly," he murmured. "Let's get the hell out of here."

She heard the almost-violent scrape of his chair and then he was pulling her up and out of hers. He threw some bills on the table and pulled her to the exit. She felt the freshness of the night on her hot face.

"Charlie," he said, the sound of her name catching slightly in his throat. And then she was in his arms, his mouth on hers, the beat of his heart against her breast.

She'd never been kissed like this before. She couldn't think. Couldn't do anything but cling to him and let his mouth take her.

"I want you," he said when he'd pulled his mouth away. "You know that, don't you?" His thumb brushed her bottom lip, still sensitized from the raw passion of his kiss. "I want you, Charlie."

The words cut into her belly and spread—high into her breasts, settling into her nipples, making them throb; and lower, between her legs where there was another kind of throbbing. Her body was more alive than it had ever been before—alive like a bare electrical wire, and just as dangerous.

He put his arm around her shoulders and started to walk and the feeling stayed with her, this new feeling of life. And it seemed only natural to slip her arm around his waist as they walked.

They rounded a corner, skirting Washington Square, and came in sight of the twin spires of a church, illuminated against the darkening sky.

"That's Saint Peter and Saint Paul Church," he told her.

"It's beautiful. So graceful."

"It took fifteen years to build. Started going up in the early twenties."

She glanced at him. "You seem to know a lot about San Francisco. Do you come here often?"

He grinned. "Wouldn't that be breaking a rule?"

She smiled back. "Yes, I guess it would."

"Let's just say I find it a beautiful city worth knowing. Which is exactly how I think of you."

She felt his mouth in her hair and she resisted the urge to ask why again. The rules were, after all, her idea.

They wandered down more streets, music always faint in the background, passing restaurants that flooded the air with garlic and basil, bakeries with breads so beautiful they were like works of art gracing their windows, and a deli where Jacob insisted on stopping to sample cheeses and flatbread soaked in olive oil.

"I couldn't eat another bite," she told him when he tried to feed her a morsel.

"Go on, taste. There's nothing like it."

Laughing, she opened her mouth and let him feed her. The oil was smooth, laced with basil. The bread was fresh, the crust still crisp. "Mmm," she moaned, and he put his mouth on hers before she had even finished chewing, the oil mingling on their tongues like a shared experience.

They hopped a cable car and rode a few blocks and then they were walking again and she could smell the change in the air.

"Are we near the water?"

"Very near. I'm taking you to a club I know, close to the waterfront. The blues are hot, the beer is cold and there's barely a tourist in sight."

She laughed. "But we're tourists."

"Nope. Not tonight. Tonight the city is ours." He stopped walking and cocked his head. "Can't you feel it? She's embracing us."

Charlotte sucked in a piece of the night and closed her eyes. Yes, she thought, there seemed to be more than Jacob's arm around her at this moment. The feeling of new life he'd awakened in her earlier was still there, but it was no longer just sexual. It did almost feel that for this night only, more than just the man beside her belonged to her—so did the world.

They crossed the dark street diagonally and entered the dim and smoky club. The mellowing wail of a saxophone greeted them.

HE COULDN'T BELIEVE she felt so right under his arm, against his side. He loved the movement of her against him. The brushing that, by its very subtlety, became magnified, erotically charged enough to make the air glow. He hated to lose that contact long enough to get seated at the tiny table they'd managed to find in a corner. As soon as they sat down, his thigh was brushing hers again. He felt more than heard her gasp and his gaze shot to hers. Her eyes were wide. He pressed his thigh more firmly against hers and she drew in her breath enough to make her breasts rise. The sight stabbed him with fresh, urgent desire.

He picked up her hand and brought it to his mouth. He parted his lips around her finger, drawing it slightly into his mouth. She gasped again, but this time her eyes didn't grow wider. They nearly closed. He did it again and felt her almost-imperceptible jerk. She was feeling the same sweet tension he was.

He watched her face change as she caught herself, then straightened in her chair and pulled her hand from his.

He laughed softly. "You really shouldn't fight it, you know."

"No?"

"No," he said. "The progress of a vacation romance should never be fought against in any way."

"Is that a rule?"

"If it isn't, then let's make it one."

"And if the progress is much too fast?"

He leaned his head closer to hers, and took her hand again but only to hold it within his own. "We have only until Monday, love," he said softly. "By my calculations I should definitely be kissing you more often by now."

Her smile flashed and he kissed the side of her throat. "Like this," he murmured. "And this," he said again as he kissed the sweet curve where her neck became her shoulder.

She jerked away, but he had expected it. It gave him a chance to play with the ends of her hair.

"I'm, uh, not accustomed to necking in public."

He shook his head. "Charlie, Charlie—you didn't read the find print, did you?"

"Fine print?"

"Yeah," he said, trailing his fingertips over her jawbone, feeling the shiver that ran through her. "The fine print on the official *rules* sheet."

A faint smile quirked her wide mouth. "Never even noticed it. Why don't you tell me what it says?"

"It says that things otherwise not done, such as necking in public, are permissible on vacation."

"Permissible?"

Putting his arm around her, he leaned closer again and

nodded, the tip of his nose brushing her cheekbone. "Not only permissible, but actually encouraged," he whispered into her ear, close enough to feel the fine shudder as it hit her.

"Really?" she breathed.

"Really."

"Well, in that case—"

She turned her head suddenly and brushed his mouth with her lips.

It was all he needed. His lips parted before they took possession of hers. He felt a moment's hesitation in her, but he wasn't going to make it easy for her. He found her tongue with his own. It was then that he knew she'd surrendered to the kiss.

And she had. Charlotte felt something going out of her, something tight and careful. By the time his mouth left hers she was quaking with desire.

"I might be very fond of that small print," she said, her breath going deep and fast.

"I already know I am," he murmured just before he kissed her again.

She could barely think. Was she dissolving into a puddle on the floor? Was she disappearing entirely? Because this couldn't be Charlotte.

But then, it wasn't, was it? It was Charlie.

"Hey, you two, if ya want a drink ya gotta come up for air."

Their joined lips dissolved into laughter at exactly the same time.

"Want a drink?" he muttered, his lips still on hers.

"Maybe we'd better," she said, her voice as muffled as his had been.

They laughed together again, then pulled apart and turned to the waiter.

"Whiskey and cola," Jacob said, holding up two fingers. "Two times."

The waiter went away and she felt Jacob's hand stroking her upper arm.

She turned to find his eyes right there, waiting for her.

"Happy?" he asked her.

The question surprised her. When was the last time anyone had asked her that? Had anyone *ever* asked?

She smiled. "Yes, I think I am. Strange—"

"Happiness is strange for you?"

"Happiness with a stranger is."

"Maybe that's why it seems so perfect."

She nodded. "No past. No future."

He kissed her again—hard and quick. And then the waiter came with their drinks and the band came back from their break.

He kept his arm around her while they listened to the music. Charlotte wasn't accustomed to blues. She was surprised that it made her feel the same way a Rachmaninoff concerto did. Restless. Sexually restless.

Or was it just the man sitting so close to her that she could feel him against her even where he wasn't quite touching?

His hand slid across her back and up to her neck. It rested there, his fingers moving very lightly. She closed her eyes.

His whisper came to her somewhere underneath the music. "Do you want me?" he asked.

She moaned inwardly, feeling her lips part.

His other hand slid across her midriff and came to rest at her waist and she felt the moan escape her parted lips.

His soft laugh was a whisper against her cheek. "Is that a yes?"

She wondered at the audacity of her remark even as she heard herself say it. "How can I help but want you."

"Then let's get out of here."

He left enough cash on the table to cover the tab, all the while keeping his arm around her as they threaded their way toward the door. Outside the air was cooler. It smelled of the bay—a smell that was as earthy and natural as her desire for him. He took her deep into the pier area where fishing boats waited for morning, hulls creaking against their moorings.

In their shadow, he took her in his arms and pulled her close. Her arms went around his neck.

The beat of the music inside the club rushed through the damp air and into her veins. And then, suddenly, she no longer heard it—the beating of her heart was too strong as he slid his hand to her side, gliding it upward against the swell of her breast. The breath caught in her throat when his thumb found her nipple and brushed it to life.

"You like that?" he whispered when her mouth broke with his.

She kept her eyes closed and bit her lip, shaking her head, knowing that he already knew the answer.

"Tell me," he whispered. "I want to hear you say it. Do you like it?"

He moved his other hand from her back to her other side. And soon his thumbs were each brushing a nipple. Teasing. A hard brush that sent hot blood through her at a dizzying speed, followed by a touch so light she yearned.

He nipped her lower lip with his teeth and her eyes flew open almost as fast as the flash of desire flooding her body.

"Tell me," he demanded in a voice that made her want to obey.

She smiled slowly. This was a game. A game Charlotte couldn't have played. But Charlie knew all the rules.

"I like it," she said, keeping her eyes wide and looking into his. "And I want more."

He moaned. And then he pulled her roughly to him, his mouth plundering, possessing, his hands covering her breasts, kneading with a roughness that thrilled her and took away the last of her reticence.

She moved her hands from around his neck, skimming them, palms flat, down his chest. And lower still, forcing them in between their bodies, laying them flat against the hardness she felt behind his zipper.

He pulled his mouth from hers and buried his face in her neck.

"Don't," he groaned. "If you touch me like that I'm going to have to have you. Right here. Right now."

Some sort of power surged through her and she smiled. "That's not in the fine print?"

She felt his soft laugh as it rumbled in his chest.

"No. The fine print says something quite different."

"And what would that be?"

He pulled his head back to look into her face. "It says that the party of the first part wants to give the party of the second part a night to remember. And even more important, he wants to make sure that she leaves with no regrets—ever."

"So, you're a nice guy, too."

"Yes. I am. But if you don't move your hand right now, there will be no guarantees."

"Is that a clause?"

"Absolutely."

She laughed and pushed away from him. "I think I've had all the sweeping off my feet I can take for one evening."

"Then let's walk before I decide to amend that particular clause."

She laughed softly and his arm went around her shoulders, pulling her close again. Her arm went around his waist and they started to walk.

They hopped on a cable car halfway back to Union Square. In the shadow of the hotel doorway, he took her into his arms again.

"I want you to take me upstairs. You know that."

She couldn't seem to get any words out but something in her face must have betrayed her.

"I can wait, Charlie. We have tomorrow yet."

"Jacob, I think that—"

"That should be a rule, too. No thinking. Unless, of course, you think of this—"

His mouth took hers again and she knew she would think of nothing else.

SHE STARTED TO OPEN her eyes—slowly. The alarm clock the hotel provided was staring at her. Two o'clock.

Her eyes flew wide open.

Goodness, she'd slept half the day away. She rolled onto her back and stretched her arms above her head, feeling the slow smile spread across her face. Last night. Perfect.

She started to let her eyes drift closed again until a thought interfered.

Why hadn't he called her?

She flung the covers back and got to her feet, padding over to the window as if she were hoping to catch him crossing the street in front of the hotel, a bouquet of roses in his hand.

"Fat chance," she muttered to herself. She should have brought him upstairs last night. She shouldn't have counted on tomorrow. But he had said something about tomorrow, hadn't he? Bits and pieces of conversation ran through her brain but she came up with nothing useful, nothing that promised tomorrow. But her body was remembering plenty.

And it was very busy telling her mind that she shouldn't have passed up the opportunity to have a man like Jacob make love to her.

She was just about to throw herself, face first, back onto the bed when a knocking at the door stopped her.

She drew the crimson silk robe that didn't really belong to her over the black silk gown that also wasn't hers before she answered the door.

"Room service, ma'am," the waiter said.

"But I didn't order any room service."

"Seems to be a gift, ma'am."

Charlotte looked down at the cart. A flaky croissant shared a plate with slices of mango. She could smell the coffee in the silver pot. It made her mouth water. And then she noticed the flowers—a small porcelain vase full of tiny yellow roses. She picked up the note lying next to them.

Did you dream of me, love?

Glancing at the waiter, she quickly folded the note without reading the rest of it. She stepped back and he wheeled the cart inside. When he'd gone, she sat on the chair near the cart, broke off a piece of croissant to nibble and opened the note again.

Meet me in the lobby at eight o'clock. Wear something that shows off those legs.

Anger flared, surprising her. How dare he summon her like that! She picked up the croissant and took a bite. How dare he just assume that she had nothing to do on her last night in San Francisco. How dare he expect her to stand around in the lobby, waiting for him!

She seemed to have finished the croissant because there was absolutely nothing in her hand when she raised it to her mouth. She picked up a slice of mango. The juice dripped down her chin when she took a bite.

Cool. Sweet. Delicious.

She let her fingers trail over the tips of the tiny roses. They were so very sweet looking in their old-fashioned porcelain vase.

And who was she trying to kid? Anger at being summoned?

"You're lying to yourself, Charlotte," she said aloud around another bite of mango.

No, not Charlotte. It was Charlie. Charlie who wanted to

meet Jacob any damn time he summoned her. And it was Charlie who wondered if that burgundy velvet dress he'd chosen for her was still hanging in that shop in Haight-Ashbury.

Chapter Five

The elevator doors swished open and Charlotte stepped out. People were everywhere; coming back from dinner, leaving for dinner, relaxing in the Art Deco chairs that dotted the lobby, reading newspapers. An elderly couple seemed to be checking out. A millionaire seemed to be checking in, his matched leather luggage arranged in order of size and taking up half the lobby. She scanned a small crowd at the entrance for Jacob.

He wasn't there.

She whirled around, her thoughts on retreating to the elevators—she didn't think she could bear it if he didn't show up—and there he was, coming toward her, the crowd of people seeming to part to let him through, a look on his face as though he knew what he wanted. And what he wanted was her. There was a sensuality in his face, as if what he was seeing in his mind wasn't her standing amid a crowd in a hotel lobby, but seeing the two of them in an embrace that was hot, intimate, raw. The man coming toward her knew it was going to happen. And at that moment, Charlotte knew it, too.

He walked up to her and put a hand on her waist, drawing her closer to him. His mouth skimmed the corner of hers and kept going until she felt his lips move against her ear as he whispered, "I love that you wore that dress for me."

There didn't seem to be any point in denying it. The damned irresistible rogue had it exactly right. The look on his face when he pulled back was all she could have wished for when she'd stood in the mirror in the shop in the Haight trying on the vintage dress.

He studied her face, the sigh he emitted sounding like it was coming from somewhere deep inside him.

"The first time I saw you," he said, raising a hand to flick her hair back lightly with his finger, "I thought you were something special. But you seem to grow more beautiful every time we meet."

No one had ever called her beautiful before. And certainly not a man who looked like Jacob did in a tuxedo. His closely cropped hair looked darker for the black of his jacket. His skin looked more tanned against the white of his shirt. He was as handsome as the devil and far more dangerous. And he was calling her beautiful.

"It's…a… It's the makeup," she stammered. "It was in the suitcase and—" She went on, all the while telling herself to shut up and simply say thank-you.

He brushed the backs of two fingers from her cheekbone to her chin. "No," he said, his mouth curving into a gentle smile, "it's not the makeup. Not entirely, anyway. There's something…" He paused, his gaze searching her face, before he went on. "You're different, Charlie. There's something blazing in your eyes that wasn't there before, something softer in your mouth."

She knew very well what was blazing in her eyes. It was desire. But, no, *desire* was too calm a word for it. Too correct. There was nothing calm or correct about what her body was putting her through. Not desire—but *lust*. She wanted him with a fierceness that she'd never experienced before. Because she knew in that moment that if she had, she would have given in to it. It was too irresistible to deny.

The softness in her mouth was only because she wanted to be kissing him so badly.

"What do the rules say about kissing in hotel lobbies?" she asked in a confident, teasing voice that couldn't possibly be hers.

"The rules encourage kissing wherever and whenever the mood takes over."

"Then, now—I think," she said, placing her palms on his chest.

His smile was soft, slow. "The mood is taking over?" he asked.

"Mmm," she murmured, sparing just one brief moment to wonder at her audacity. "I am definitely a woman in the mood."

"How fortunate, because I am a man in the same kind of mood."

"Then kiss me," she whispered urgently when he just stood there, that gentle grin molding his mouth, his dark eyes intent yet unreadable.

"No." The negative movement of his head was nearly imperceptible. "You kiss me."

Anger flared fast and short inside her, replaced so swiftly by an absolute need to do his bidding that she wondered if the anger had been there at all. Because now, all she felt was total and consuming hunger.

Her hands slid to his neck and she brought his mouth to hers with a jolt that seemed to surprise him. Her mouth plundered his. Every nuance, every emotion she'd ever wanted to experience in a kiss she poured into this one. Her tongue swept his lips, delved inside to seek more. And when their tongues collided and swirled into a dance, the sound from his throat was a low groan that sent sexual power surging through her.

It didn't matter that people were skirting around them. It didn't matter that every time the elevator doors opened, the occupants' mouths dropped. All that mattered was his mouth—and how much of it she could devour.

"You have two choices," he whispered roughly when he'd pulled his mouth from hers.

"I—I do?" she croaked.

"Yep. Elevator to your right. Exit to your left. Which is it gonna be?"

She looked into his face, his chest still pressed to hers, and her whole being screamed *Right!* Take a right!

She opened her mouth. "Left," she said.

He chuckled and drew his arm around her shoulders, pulling her tight against him. "Then, come on," he said, urging her toward the exit. "The city is waiting for us."

They stepped out into the soft breath of evening and a limousine pulled up to the curb. The driver got out and came around to the passenger side to hold the door for them.

"Oh, my. I feel a little like Cinderella," she said.

"Ah, then I must be your Prince Charming. Our story will turn out a little differently, though."

"How so?"

"You aren't going to turn back into a scullery maid at midnight."

"I'm not? Then what will I turn into?"

He dipped his dark head close to hers. "You'll turn into my lover," he whispered.

And then he was helping her into the limo—a good thing, too, because her legs seemed to have lost their bones somewhere out on the sidewalk.

Was she going to turn into his lover at midnight? She had waited so long, wanting it to be right. Wanting it to be meaningful and special. And in all these years nothing and no one had come along to make her feel that way.

Not until Jacob.

IN THE LIMO JACOB simply held her hand. It was their last night together but somehow he didn't feel rushed. At the moment it felt like the night might last forever.

"I was right," he told her. "Your legs do look great in that dress."

Her sudden smile came as swiftly as the rise of color in her cheeks. It made her even more beautiful to him. The low scoop of the neckline bared just enough of her creamy, full breasts to make his loins ache. But it was the feel of her hand holding his that stirred his heart. She had the body of a temptress but her soft hand in his fluttered like a virgin's. Her wild pulse against his palm stirred a feeling that was new to him. It wasn't lust—although he certainly felt that for her. It was something more.

Protectiveness. She made his protective instincts rise. And that made him feel more masculine than ever.

Jacob, Jacob, he chided himself in his mind. *Next thing you know you're gonna wanna carry her off to your cave. Slay a few lions.* He laughed softly at the thought.

"Something funny?" she asked.

"Yeah," he answered. "Me."

She was looking a little worried so he raised her hand to his mouth and pressed his lips to the pulse in her wrist. "You've got me feeling things, Charlie. Things I haven't felt in a long, long time."

She smiled softly. "Well, it's only fair. You've got me feeling things I've never, ever felt before."

He pressed his mouth to her wrist again, then with his other hand he drew her head down until it rested on his shoulder.

What was happening to him? She could be his; he knew it. Right now, right here. He could have her in the back seat of the limo, fast and furious. And wasn't that the only kind of coupling he'd been interested in since Michelle? Fast, anonymous. Over almost before it began. But even with Michelle he hadn't felt this romantic, this protective, this...What? Hell, he didn't even know what. And he didn't know if he wanted to know.

"Where are we going, anyway?" she murmured.

"I'm taking you to a party on Nob Hill."

She lifted her head from his shoulder. "Really?"

"Yep. We're gonna dance in each other's arms high on the hill, the lights of the city twinkling below us."

"Hmm, sounds wonderful. But I told you I don't dance."

"You do tonight," he said.

The driver pulled to the curb in front of an enormous stone mansion, the ornate black iron fence surrounding it festooned with garlands of fresh flowers, the gates wide in welcome.

The driver held the door for them and Jacob helped Charlie out.

"Take the rest of the night off," he told the young driver. "I've got a hankering to take my lady home by cable car in the moonlight." He fished a bill out of his pocket and pressed it into the kid's hand. "Go on, get out of here."

"Thank you, sir!" the driver said, all smiles.

"Come on, love, I hear music."

She heard it, too. The sweet singing of violins, the melancholy strain of a cello. He led her by the hand up the walk. Beautiful people mounted the broad staircase to the enormous entrance where a man in tails and white gloves checked invitations.

"Hell," Jacob muttered beside her.

"What?"

"They're checking invitations."

"Don't you, uh, don't you have one?"

"Who would send me an invitation to a place like this?"

She gasped. "Then what are we doing here?"

"I wanted to treat you to a real Nob Hill party," he said as he pulled her off the walk and onto the grass.

"Where are we going?"

"Around back. Maybe we can sneak in from there."

"Sneak in? Are you crazy?" she hissed. "We can't sneak into someone's home!"

"Sure, we can. There's probably a patio around back and—"

She skidded to a halt. "That's not what I mean. I'm sure you know how to sneak into plenty of places, including the Saturday matinee when you were a kid. What I meant was there is no way I'm crashing a Nob Hill party!"

"Oh, come on, Charlie, live a little."

He tried to pull her along again but she broke her hand free and started back for the street, only to be brought to a complete halt when he caught her by the waist from behind.

"I thought you liked the idea of dancing with me at an exclusive Nob Hill house party."

"I did," she answered sharply, trying to ignore the feel of his fingers moving restlessly on her middle, trying not to imagine what the hard body pressed against her back would feel like holding her to the swell of violins. "But that was before I knew we'd be sneaking in like a couple of thieves."

"Not like thieves, love. 'Cause if we were acting like thieves we'd be sneaking out, too. And I have every intention of escorting you out through that front door when we leave."

She groaned. "I was afraid of that. You wouldn't be the type to sneak in, grab a dance, and leave."

He nuzzled her neck, one more thing for her to try to ignore. "Without having some champagne?" he asked.

"Oh, you are impossible!"

He spun her in his arms so fast she nearly lost her balance, but he was there, clutching her to the solid wall of his chest, covering her mouth with his in a kiss that left her shaking.

"Do it, baby. For once in your life, do something crazy. Do it with me."

"The idea that I'm here with you at all is about all the insanity I can handle."

"Bet it isn't."

She groaned again. That damned grin of his. That damned irresistible grin.

"One dance," she finally said.

"Two," he corrected.

She closed her eyes, knowing she was going to give in. "Okay, but no champagne."

"We'll see," he said, taking her hand and pulling her along again.

"What do you mean, 'We'll see'? Jacob—"

"Shh," he whispered. "You'll cause a scene."

"Me?"

He laughed as they rounded the side of the house to find a patio surrounded by a low stone wall. A few couples danced under the trees twinkling with fairy lights, but most of the sound spilled out from the two sets of open French doors.

"See?" she whispered. "There's a wall. We can't possibly—"

"Wanna bet?"

Suddenly his hands were at her waist, lifting her, and she found herself teetering on the three-foot wall, the low-hanging branch of a tree shielding her from the few people on the patio. "Are you crazy?" she hissed, grabbing on to the branch for support.

"You keep asking me that," he said as he hopped up next to her. "Haven't you figured it out, yet?"

"Yes, I have."

"And your verdict?" he asked her as he peered through the branches, waiting, she was sure, for the coast to be clear.

"Certifiable."

He gave her a quick look and she caught the gleam of his white teeth in the darkening evening. "And I think you like it, Charlie. I think you like it a lot."

"I do not!" she insisted.

He laughed softly at that then whispered, "They're going inside. Come on, here's our chance."

He leaped off the wall as if he'd had plenty of practice climbing and jumping down from them.

"Come on, love. Jump. I'll catch you."

She looked down into his outspread arms.

"Like I should trust you," she said with mocking disdain.

"What choice do you have? It's taking your chances with me on this side of the wall, or going it alone on the other."

Well, she thought, that was certainly true. The outside of the wall was just as far from the ground as the inside was. And inside, Jacob waited. An irresistible charmer who looked like something the devil sent in a tuxedo to lead poor, hapless innocents astray.

She'd never let anyone lead her astray before.

But then she'd never met anyone like Jacob before.

He was looking up at her, a wry grin on his face, his dark eyes waiting with a knowing, confident gleam. Oh, what the hell, she thought.

"Catch me," she said, and dropped right into his waiting arms.

He put her down but didn't let go. Instead he swept her into the shadow of the same tree that had shielded them on top of the wall, pressed her back against its trunk and taken her mouth with his.

She was limp in half a second.

When his mouth moved from hers she managed to say weakly, "Uh, I thought you wanted to dance."

"I do. Come on."

And then she was in his arms again, but with a difference

this time. One hand at her waist, his other hand holding hers, he moved her from the shadow of the tree out to the center of the patio with a smoothness that surprised her. It was easy for her to just move along with him.

"I thought you said you couldn't dance," he said.

She smiled. "You're a good dancer. You're making me look good."

"My mother would thank you for that. She insisted on lessons before the junior prom."

"Wise woman, your mother."

"Yes."

"And your father?"

"Has been gone too long for me to remember him—and aren't we on dangerous ground?"

"Dangerous ground?"

"Your rules. No past, remember?"

Yes, she remembered. But how was she to know that by the next day she would want to know so much more about him. Where he came from. Why he wasn't married. What kind of work he did. They were *her* rules. Surely she could break them if she had a mind to.

But did she have a mind to? Tomorrow she would be gone—and she would never see him again. The more she knew about him, the harder he would be to forget.

Who was she fooling? Jacob was going to be impossible to forget under any circumstances.

He held her lightly while they danced but she almost wished he wouldn't. She almost wished that he would press that hard body against hers, that he would touch her in places that ached for him. Instead he gently placed his chin against her cheekbone and waltzed her around the patio like a real gentleman.

"Are you hungry?" he suddenly asked her.

"A little."

"Let's find something to eat, then."

"Good, we're leaving."

But he didn't turn toward the wall as she expected.

"What are you doing?" she asked him as he headed for the patio doors.

"Going to find the buffet. These parties always have a buffet."

"Jacob, we can't!"

"I thought you were hungry."

"I am, but I'd prefer a hamburger I paid for to caviar on toast points that I stole."

"They throw out more food at these things than they use. Nobody is gonna mind if we spear a few shrimp."

Because it seemed easier, she let him lead her inside. "Okay, let's find the food and get out of here."

He smiled at her and she didn't like the gleam in his dark eyes—not at all.

"We should pay our respects to our hostess first, don't you think?"

"Absolutely not!" she hissed.

"Charlie, I'm surprised at you. Where are you manners?"

He put his arm around her waist and started for a tall, regally thin, silver-haired woman talking to a younger couple.

"How do you know it's her?" Charlie whispered frantically.

"I don't," he whispered back.

Her heart almost stopped, but by the time they were standing in front of the woman it had started up again—with a vengeance.

"Wonderful party," Jacob said.

"Oh, well, I'm so glad you're enjoying it, uh…"

"Jacob," he said smoothly.

"Yes, of course. Jacob. I'm so sorry."

"Hey, you can't be expected to remember all the guests' names when you're busy being such a wonderful hostess."

The older woman colored attractively. "How gallant of you to say."

"I don't think you've met my lady. Charlie, this is Mrs.—or may I call you…"

"Blanche. Yes, of course. Please call me Blanche. So glad you could come, Charlie. Have the two of you eaten yet?"

"No, we haven't."

"Then, please, allow me to show you into the dining room. We have a rather nice buffet set up, with plenty of champagne."

As the woman led them into the next room, Jacob winked at her and Charlie almost lost it. She should have known she wasn't the only woman who would be susceptible to Jacob's irresistible charm.

At the buffet, they filled an enormous plate with shrimp and crab and sweet lobster. From huge silver baskets they took crusty rolls, broke them open and drizzled herbed olive oil on the tender, fluffy centers.

"Wow, looks like we hit the jackpot," Jacob said when they stopped at a smaller table filled with tiny petits fours and tarts and truffles. He picked up a plate and piled several of each selection onto it.

"We're going to eat all that?" she asked him.

"Eventually," he answered with a grin. "Let me just grab an extra napkin—"

He did, stuffing it into his pocket.

"Now, some champagne."

Yet another table held several silver ice buckets with both opened and unopened bottles of champagne resting against the shiny rims.

Jacob bypassed the open bottles, snagged up a still-corked one, and said, "Let's go."

She followed him back through the crowd in the living room and out onto the terrace again where he led her to a stone bench set way in the back corner under the branches of another low-hanging tree.

Once they were settled, Jacob took two silver forks from his pocket and handed her one.

"Mmm." She sighed as she bit into a shrimp. "This is heavenly."

"So is the lobster. Here, try it."

He fed her a piece of cold lobster from his fork and watched her while she tasted it.

"I like the way you eat," he said.

She laughed. "It's one of the few things I do well. Obviously."

"Why obviously?"

She was a little taken aback at the question. Surely he'd noticed that she was no svelte size six?

"My, uh, figure..."

"Is enticing," he finished for her, popping another chunk of lobster into her open mouth. "You have the body of a goddess. And if you make love with as much passion as you have when you eat, then you're going to make me a very happy man."

A little stunned, she watched him for a moment while he bit into one of the crusty rolls. He ate with plenty of passion himself, she thought. And he was disarming as hell, saying things like that to her, then just casually turning his attention to the food.

Her mouth was suddenly dry and she reached for the bottle of champagne.

"Oh, we forgot the glasses." She moved to get up but he stopped her.

"We don't need glasses."

"No?"

"No. We'll swill it from the bottle like the bandits we are."

She laughed and he popped the cork, quickly holding the

bottle to her mouth as the champagne started to bubble up over the top.

She drank, feeling the champagne run down her chin, then watched as he tilted the bottle to his own mouth and drank deeply from it.

"Dessert?" he asked, holding forth the plate of delicacies from the dessert table.

She looked at them, knowing she should decline. But what the hell, she thought. A little chocolate wouldn't hurt. She chose a decorated petit four and bit into it.

"You like chocolate?"

"Mmm," she murmured as the cream filling exploded in her mouth.

"Another good sign. Chocolate is considered an aphrodisiac, did you know that?"

She looked at him skeptically. "No."

"Well, let's check it out, then. In the interests of science, of course."

He raised his hand and lifted her hair away from her face, leaned closer, and then she felt his tongue at her ear. She shivered.

"Mmm," he murmured. "It seems to be working."

"But how can we be sure it was the chocolate?" she asked him.

"Hmm, you're right." He picked up a lemon tart. "Here, let's try this."

She took a bite of it, the flaky pastry melting in her mouth, the tart lemon tickling her tongue. And then she felt his tongue at her ear again. This time she more than shivered. She nearly jumped.

"Interesting," he murmured, nuzzling her neck. "Lemon seems to work even better with the research subject. Let's try some of this."

He picked up the champagne bottle and held it to her lips. She drank from it, her eyes closed, the cool froth bathing her throat, heating her blood. This time when he nibbled her ear she moaned out loud.

"I think the research subject should be disqualified on the basis that she is a special case. Almost anything seems to arouse her."

She opened her eyes and looked into his. "Or maybe it's just you," she whispered.

His eyes never left hers as he said, "That hypothesis calls for private research, I think."

She swallowed. "Think so?"

Oh, Jacob knew so. Her obvious arousal was exciting him beyond anything he'd felt in far too long. Her face was flushed, her breathing deepened, her lips slightly parted as if they wanted to be kissed.

But he couldn't. If he tasted her now, he wasn't sure he could stop.

He forced himself to look away from her. He took another swig of champagne and handed her the bottle while he busied himself filling the extra linen napkin he'd taken with the rest of the goodies from the dessert plate. Then he folded it up and stuffed it into his jacket pocket.

"Come on, baby. Let's get out of here."

"Where are we going?" she asked as he pulled her to her feet.

"I'm taking you to my hotel so I can make love to you."

She gasped and he looked into her dark eyes. "It's what you want, isn't it, Charlie?"

She nodded. "I do... I just don't understand wh—"

He put a finger to her mouth. "Don't ask me why again," he said harshly. "Can't you feel it? It has no reason, no logic. It just *is*. Don't waste it, baby."

And then he took her mouth with his because he could no longer help himself. And she didn't resist. He felt her soft, full breasts press against him, felt her warm, wet mouth open to him. He slid a hand between them, gently brushing her breast, feeling her shake at his touch.

"Don't leave me tonight, Charlie," he murmured, his mouth still on hers. "Come home with me."

He felt her take a deep inward sigh, felt the light tremor that waved through her, saw it as it passed behind her closed eyelids, making her lashes flutter. And then she nodded.

"Say it."

She opened her eyes. They were darker than he'd ever seen them.

"Yes," she said. "Yes."

Chapter Six

His hotel was in North Beach. It was old, quaint, a little worn around the edges, but with an elegance that just didn't exist in the modern monstrosity where she was staying.

The elevator groaned and clanged and generally made more noise than the cable car had, but Charlie scarcely had time to wonder at it.

Jacob stood behind her, his arms around her middle, his face buried in her neck.

"I could stand like this forever, baby, just breathing the scent of your skin."

She moaned softly and arched her neck, closing her eyes when he started covering the side of her throat with kisses.

"Tell me how much you want me, love. Let me hear you say it."

His voice was a harsh, deep rumble against her skin and she moaned again at the feel of his hands sliding slowly down to cup her lower belly.

"I want you," she whispered, her voice nearly as harsh as his. She was so much in need that she grabbed his hands, tore them from her belly and placed them on her breasts. She would have said "please" if that was what it would have taken.

But it didn't.

Jacob knew what she wanted. And he gave it to her.

He found her nipples under the velvet and worked them with his fingers until she cried out.

"That's it, baby. Let me know how much."

She was sinking. Fast. Her entire being centered where his fingers teased and tormented. And the other place. The place no man had ever touched before. That place was burning for him. On fire.

By the time the elevator doors swished open, she was slumped back against him, her breath audible, her skin so hot that all she wanted to do was rip off her clothes and make him cover her with kisses.

He put his hand on her waist and she leaned against him as they went down the hall to his room. He swore softly as he fumbled with the key in the lock, then he was leading her inside where it was dark and cool and filled with the scent of him.

And then she was in his arms, his mouth devouring hers while he walked her backward until her knees hit the bed.

"If you want me to stop," he said, the words muffled by his mouth still moving on hers, "tell me now. Because I want you, Charlie. I want you here and now and hard and fast. If we start, that's how it's going to be. If you want to take a break—if you want me to—"

She could hardly stand it. "No!" she cried. "Now."

And then she couldn't speak at all, because his tongue was in her mouth and his hands were everywhere, ridding her of her dress, her slip. Standing there in his arms in her bra and panties, she wasn't embarrassed or ashamed. She didn't have time to be. She was too busy trying to tear his shirt off him. She wanted his flesh against hers. She needed it.

When she'd gotten him out of his shirt, he reached back and unhooked her bra and slipped it from her shoulders.

And then she felt the flesh of his chest pressed to hers, felt his breath as it rushed in and out of his lungs.

"Oh, baby, you feel good. I knew you would—I knew you'd feel like this."

She wanted to touch him. But she wasn't sure what to do, wasn't sure what would please him.

And then he took her hand and placed it over his hardness. He was solid, full, and she let her fingers explore while he kissed her throat, her cheek, her eyes.

"That's it, baby," he murmured.

"You like this?" she asked in a whisper.

His chuckle rumbled through his chest. "'Like' isn't the word, love."

His words gave her the courage to draw his zipper down and slip her fingers inside. She was surprised at the feel of him, so hard and yet so smooth. Like silk. He groaned when her fingers surrounded the thickest part of him.

And then, he suddenly pulled away. She thought she'd done something wrong at first and she opened her mouth to ask what. But he was busy tearing off his trousers, his sleek black briefs going with them as they sailed across the room. Her heart stilled as she looked at him.

His skin was lightly golden from the sun, his chest smooth and wide and hard looking, his waist tapered, his legs muscular and covered with dark hair. But her eyes kept returning to the hard part of him, the part she'd held in her hand, and the thoughts that raced through her mind surprised her in their boldness.

And then he was coming toward her, pulling her to him so she could feel the length of him all up and down her body. And his mouth was there again, on hers, in a kiss that went on forever. She lost all thought of anything but the need for him to be touching her breasts again.

And then he was. Cupping them, his thumbs brushed them to painful life again before his hands moved on, gliding around her to cup her bottom through her silk panties, pulling her up and in to him. She could feel the hard heat of him pressed against her. She could feel wetness spilling out of her. And then one of his hands moved to the front, low, and touched her.

Her head shot up and back. Her moan sounded desperate, raw.

"Baby— Oh, baby, I know. I know," he crooned as he lowered her to the bed.

And then he was stripping her panties off her and covering where his hand had been with his mouth.

She cried out and jumped, her arms flinging about for something to grab, something to hang on to before she drowned in sensation. Her hands touched his head and she shoved her fingers into his hair, gasping while his tongue worked her into something wild.

Something inside her was trying to burst free, something that caused her to buck her hips and hold his head more tightly to her. It was like riding the crest of a desire so fierce that her mind couldn't even grasp the idea that what she was doing was something she'd never done before, something she should not know how to do.

But she did—she knew how to do it. It was as if she was born knowing.

And then he pulled his mouth away and moved up her body and she instinctively arched her hips in offering.

He thrust inside and the pain was swift and hot, making her cry out in a different way.

He suddenly stilled, lifting his head so he could look into her eyes.

"Charlie?" he whispered, wonder in his voice.

She lifted a hand to his face, touching his lips with her fingers. He turned his head to press his lips to her palm.

And then he was looking down at her again, the expression in his eyes puzzled, his breath coming hard, his arms shaking with the strain of holding himself above her.

"Why didn't you tell me?"

"Does it matter?" she managed to ask.

"Of course it matters," he said harshly.

She swallowed hard. "You don't want me now?"

He closed his eyes and shook his head. "Baby, nothing could make me stop wanting you. But if I'd known, I would have been more…"

She placed her fingers on his mouth again. "But you're already perfect. Please, Jacob. Please, make love to me."

He stared at her for a long, painful moment. And then he smiled and started to move inside her.

"DO YOU THINK MAYBE WE could try that again?" Charlie asked.

Jacob laughed. "You like being on top, do you?"

The lady was a revelation. He'd never known a woman to respond to him as she did.

"Well, if you didn't like it—"

He looked down at her. Her head was cradled in the crook of his neck.

"I like anything and everything with you, Charlie. I especially like how you gave that little squeal when—"

She sat up. "Wasn't I supposed to do that?"

She was looking down at him, her silky hair rumpled, her face flushed, her full breasts moving with the motion of her breathing. Her nipples were still pink and hard. He reached out and brushed his fingertips across them, smiling when she closed her eyes and moaned.

"Yes, you were supposed to do that, love. That, and anything else you want. Sex should be two parts caring and one part exploration and adventure."

"Hmm…"

He laughed again. "Tell me what's going on in that insatiable head of yours."

"Well, I was just wondering," she murmured, her hand moving down his chest. "Well, I've never…I mean, I would like to…"

She slid her hand lower until she was touching him again, making him stir. Incredible, he thought. They'd al-

ready made love three times. He would have said he didn't
have an ounce of passion left in his body. But when she
touched him, her fingers fluttering and tentative, he felt
himself getting ready for her again.

He traced her wide, swollen mouth with his finger.
"What would you like, Charlie?" he murmured lazily.
"Tell me."

She was still stroking him. And if she didn't tell him
soon what it was she wanted, he was going to just take
what he was wanting more with every touch of her cool
fingers.

"Well, uh, you know what you did to me with your
mouth?"

"Yes."

"Well, I'd like to, uh, to return the favor. But I don't
exactly know how."

If he hadn't already been fully aroused, that halting re-
quest would have done it. The lady was something. How
had she kept all of this inside her for so many years?

"Oh, love," he whispered, grinning at her. "I'd be more
than happy to teach you."

JACOB WATCHED HER SLEEP. He hadn't been able to close
his eyes without his mind screaming thoughts at him—
thoughts he hadn't expected. So finally, he'd gotten out of
bed, covered her lightly with the sheet, and gone to the
windows to watch the approaching dawn.

A new day.

And there was no way Jacob was letting Charlie out of
his life—rules be damned.

He was in love with her. And he knew she must feel
close to that for him. Women like Charlie didn't give them-
selves lightly. And she had given herself—more than any
other woman he'd ever been with. She'd been an eager,
fast learner. She'd more than satisfied him. And not just
physically. His emotions were as raw as his muscles felt.

He didn't know for sure where it would lead. He didn't know anything about her—not the life she led, not her hopes, her dreams. He didn't know much more than the fact that, against all odds, he'd fallen in love with her and there was no way she was going out of his life forever.

She stirred in her sleep, the action causing the sheet to slip from one of her breasts. It made him ache all over again.

He went to her, slipping into bed beside her, kissing her still-swollen mouth until she opened her eyes.

"Again?" she murmured, her voice husky with sleep.

"Yes, Charlie. Again."

THE SUN BLASTED HIM in the eyes when he opened them. He squeezed them shut, remembering that he'd pulled back the drapes to the light of dawn just before he'd made long, slow, sweet love to Charlie one more time.

He rolled over to press himself to her back and found himself clutching a pillow.

He opened his eyes. She wasn't in bed.

"Charlie?" he called. But he already knew she was gone. He could feel the emptiness. After only two days with her, he could already feel the loss of her.

"Well, hell!" he muttered roughly, throwing the covers off and getting out of bed. She wasn't going to get out of that breakfast he had planned with her. The one where he fed her strawberries from room service along with the petits fours he'd filched from the party, and where he told her he loved her. He'd fallen asleep writing the script in his mind—and he wasn't going to waste it.

He grabbed a pair of jeans and pulled a T-shirt over his head. The only jacket he could find was the tuxedo jacket. He grabbed it from the floor and put it on. So maybe they wouldn't have breakfast in bed. There was always the restaurant in her hotel.

"Yeah," he said aloud, suddenly liking the idea of telling her there where he'd first laid eyes on her.

"WHAT DO YOU MEAN, she checked out?"

"Room 1822 checked out, sir, earlier this morning."

"Did she say where she was going?"

The desk clerk narrowed his eyes as he scrutinized Jacob. Damn, Jacob thought, he should have at least shaved and combed his hair. In his old jeans and a rumpled tuxedo jacket he must look like a madman.

But, hell, he was feeling a little mad, a little crazed.

"Are you an acquaintance of hers?"

Acquaintance? Hell, Jacob thought again, I'm her lover.

"Yes, of course," he forced himself to say calmly.

"But you don't know where she's going?"

"Well…no."

"And you don't know her last name?"

"No. You see—" Jacob stopped. What had he been going to say? *You see, we decided to have this short, hot affair, no questions asked. But last night I decided I was in love with her.*

The desk clerk, all done up in a conservative suit and striped tie, his hair cut perfectly for a young man who intended to make management some day, was looking at him expectantly.

"I don't suppose you could tell me her last name?" Jacob asked, wincing because he already knew the answer to that one.

The desk clerk looked incredulous. Jacob watched him open his mouth to answer and knew he was only wasting his time.

"Forget it!" he said as he headed for the exit and out onto the street.

There was a short line of cabs waiting. He chose the first one in line, whipped the door open and slid inside.

"San Francisco International," he said. "And hurry."

The cab crawled through the Monday-morning traffic and Jacob cursed himself for agreeing to any damn rules. Cursed himself for falling asleep. But she'd worn him clean out.

"Can you speed it up a little?" Jacob asked impatiently.

The cabbie shrugged. "If I got a good reason."

"How about fifty bucks and my lifelong happiness?"

"Ooo-weee, you got it bad, Mac," the cabbie jeered, stepping on the gas and pulling into the fast lane. "And that ain't good."

Jacob snorted. No, maybe it wasn't good. But it *could* be—if she felt the same way. It could grow and...and what? Hell, he didn't know. He only knew he had to find her before she got on a plane and flew out of his life forever.

"Which terminal, Mac?" the driver asked.

"What?"

"Terminal? What airline your lady usin'?"

"I don't know," Jacob admitted dully. He hadn't even thought about the fact that he had no idea where to start looking for her.

The cabbie threw his head back and laughed. "Oh, my goodness. I'm startin' ta feel like I'm in a movie."

"Well, I hope to hell it has a happy ending."

"Me, too, Mac. Me, too. I'm all for love."

The cab pulled up to the terminal building. Jacob fished a large bill out of his pocket and handed it over, then got out.

"Good luck, Mac. Yer gonna need it."

"Tell me about it," Jacob muttered as he strode inside, heading for the nearest white courtesy phone.

"Not possible," the woman on the other end of the line said.

"Oh, come on. Why can't you page someone without a last name?"

"Sir, you said the name was Charlie?"

"Right."

"Well, if I simply page Charlie, no last name, no airline, no known destination, have you any idea how many men are going to go running for the courtesy phones? Some of them will miss their flights. We'll get so many complaints that I'll lose my job."

"Come on, lady. Haven't you ever been in love?"

"Sir, I don't see what that has to do with—"

"I love this woman. And I have absolutely no idea where she lives, how to find her. I have to talk to her before she leaves San Francisco."

There was a silence on the other end of the line, then: "Sir, is this some kind of joke?"

"Joke? This is my *life*, lady!"

Oh, hell, he thought, he was just wasting time. He slammed the phone back into its cradle and started to run. He wove in and out of clusters of people, past concessions, restaurants, bars. Ghirardelli Chocolates and sourdough bread blurred with miniature Golden Gate Bridges and postcards as he aimlessly ran on, dodging people, checking faces, looking for a head with shiny dark hair, a body that could send him to the moon, and a face that gave that sudden smile that could drive his heartbeat into overtime.

He chose a concourse at random, skipped to the head of the line for the security check.

"Hey, buddy, get in the back of the line," yelled the guy he'd jumped in front of, but he was already emptying his pockets. Along with some loose change, he fished out the crumpled linen napkin. The sweets from the party. The ones he'd planned to feed to her while he told her he loved her. He flipped open one corner of the napkin. The tiny cakes were crushed and crumbled.

"Hey, buddy," the guy behind him said. "I thought you were in a hurry."

He shoved the napkin back into his pocket and hurried through the metal detector.

He didn't bother picking up his change—just started running again, scanning faces at every gate he passed, not stopping until he had nearly knocked a small child down.

He bent over, breathing heavily, his palms on his knees as he tried to catch his breath. He looked ahead of him, at people hurrying, pulling their suitcases along, at people reading newspapers, at people with cell phones to their ears. Hundreds of people.

Who was he trying to kid? He would never find her. Not without a clue as to where to start looking.

She was gone.

NAIL POLISH. THE SMELL of it hit Charlotte as soon as she opened the door to the reception area at WEND. Carrie, who not only answered the phones but seemed to be able to handle anything anyone threw at her while giving herself a perfect manicure, sat behind the half-oval reception desk, fanning a nail while she talked into the telephone receiver cradled in the crook of her neck. The speakers that piped WEND programming into the offices and reception area were off, but Charlotte heard a muffled beat pounding out from behind the door to her office.

She frowned at the door. She'd come directly to the station from the airport seeking refuge in the music. The sound coming from her office offered no refuge.

"What's going on in there?" she asked Carrie.

Carrie hung up the phone. "Charlotte! You look fabulous!" she cried, wiggling her fingers out in front of her to dry the polish as she came out from behind the desk. "The new hairdo—it couldn't suit you any better if I had picked it out myself!"

Charlotte was dubious about that statement. Carrie believed in big hair. Her glossy blond locks were permed and teased and sprayed to the point where Charlotte was surprised they didn't protest and fall out just for a rest.

Carrie gave her one of her quick hugs, and Charlotte noticed that the polish glistening on Carrie's nails was the same silver as the shadow on the lids of her gray eyes.

It should have looked preposterous. But when you're five foot eleven, blond and beautiful in that all-American, swimsuit-ad kind of way, Charlotte figured you could get away with anything. Even silver eye shadow.

"And," Carrie said as she walked on her three-inch heels back to her position behind the desk, "I knew that color green would look gorgeous on you when I—"

Charlotte's head shot up when Carrie stopped speaking mid-sentence.

"Uh-oh," Carrie muttered as she sank back into her chair.

"When you what?" Charlotte asked, narrowing her eyes. "When you packed it in my suitcase?"

Carrie grimaced. "Oh, me and my big mouth."

"You? You're the one who stole my clothes?"

"Well, I didn't exactly steal them," Carrie said with a huff. "I mean, they're over in my apartment, safe and sound. Although why you'd want them back at all is beyond me."

"Because they're mine!" she nearly shouted.

Carrie flapped her hand. "Oh, all those long skirts and baggy sweaters. You look much better the way you're dressed right now."

Charlotte opened her mouth but she knew this time she really would be shouting. So she closed it, took a breath, and tried again.

"Carrie, you knew I was going out there to confront J.J. Tanner. What ever made you think that I'd want to confront him in a *red—knit—minidress?*" By the time she'd finished the sentence, her jaw was tight.

Carrie grimaced. "You're really mad, huh?"

Charlotte didn't even trust herself to answer.

"Well," Carrie rushed to add, "red is a power color. I figured it would help you deal with J.J. Tanner. You know, put you in a position of power."

"Carrie," she began with the air of long-suffering, "you wasted your money. The way some of us look in a minidress does not exactly put us in a position of power."

Carrie laughed. "Well, you couldn't find J.J. so there was no harm done. And you know I never pay full price for anything. Besides, you needed a new look. And it prompted you to get the new hairstyle, so even though you're mad, I'm not sorry I did it."

Charlotte had it on the tip of her tongue to tell Carrie what had really prompted the new haircut. But she wasn't ready to share what had happened to her yet. She didn't know if she ever would be.

Outside of Melinda, a distant cousin who worked as a part-time sales manager at WEND, and Carrie, Charlotte didn't have many women friends. The women she'd known from high school and college were all married, raising children or having babies. She hadn't known Melinda well while she was growing up, but they'd gotten closer since Melinda's husband had been killed five years ago. But even though Melinda no longer had a husband and didn't seem interested in other men, she had three incredibly energetic children who kept her busy.

Carrie was ten years younger than Charlotte but in the five years she'd been working at WEND they'd become pretty good friends. Charlotte knew about the farm in northern Wisconsin that Carrie had escaped by marrying too young. And she knew Carrie had come to Madison so she could slowly work on an MBA. Besides being the chief right hand to everyone at the station, she bartended at a trendy café where she made more in tips than her WEND salary netted her. She was gutsy and smart, knew what she wanted and went after it.

And what she had apparently recently wanted was for Charlotte to change her style of dressing.

"What made you do it?" Charlotte asked her.

"Oh, a couple of things," Carrie answered vaguely.

"Like?" prompted Charlotte.

Carrie hesitated, then blurted out, "Like you dress like a frump and I didn't want you to confront that arrogant J.J. Tanner looking like one."

"Gee, thanks," she muttered. But Carrie's words weren't exactly a surprise. She'd been after Charlotte for over two years to do something about her wardrobe.

"Come on, Charlotte, don't be angry. I just wanted to give you a little edge. Besides," she added with a grin, "I thought you might consider a small holiday fling with a bellhop or something."

Charlotte quickly turned away. She had no intention of going down that particular road. "Is that Barnabas in my office?"

"Yes."

"What on earth is he playing?" she asked as she headed that way.

Not waiting for an answer, Charlotte opened the door. Barnabas was reclining in the black leather chair that used to be his, his blue eyes staring at the ceiling. One of his elegantly crossed legs and his head, its mane of silver hair brushed back from a high brow, were keeping time with the beat of the rock song that filled the office.

"I thought this nonsense wasn't starting for two more weeks," she scoffed as she entered the room, giving the door a push so that it closed with a whack behind her.

Barnabas lazily turned his narrow, patrician head toward her, his blue eyes quietly resting on her as if he knew she'd been there all along.

"It doesn't," he replied with a serene smile. "I'm listening to PowerCord's tape again."

Charlotte groaned. "You mean that Peter Pan that J.J. Tanner talked you into hiring?"

Barnabas laughed, the sound deep and rich and making her feel like she'd come home despite the fact that the air was filled with the wrong kind of music.

"J.J. tells me that PowerCord Baker is usually popular with the ladies."

"Not this one."

"I see he's failed to win you over in the time that he's been here."

"It doesn't show, does it?" she asked with mock innocence.

"Well, I like him. And I love his..." Barnabas moved his hand in an elegant gesture while his mind searched for the word. "You know, his *rap*."

His rap? Who on earth had taught her grandfather such phrases? Who, indeed, she thought sourly. J.J. Tanner, who else. She sighed. "Barnabas, PowerCord Baker is a forty-year-old boy who thinks if he never cuts his hair it'll always be 1976."

"But women love him, Charlotte, women who are exactly the age of our target audience. J.J. says that in order to—"

Charlotte sighed. "Barnabas, in less than a week I'll have to deal with the man in person. I've already heard every word he's ever said to you more than once. I just got back from a wild-goose chase to northern California. I'm going to be the man's boss and he has so far managed to avoid exchanging more than a few words with me."

Barnabas's eyes twinkled. "Ah, but the words, Charlotte, my dear. Enough heat to melt the snow on the roof, come January."

Nobody had to remind her of that, Charlotte thought as she ruffled through a small stack of messages on her desk. She remembered only too well the brief but loud telephone exchange. Tanner had merely mentioned the idea of WEND

promoting rock-revival concerts sometime in the future and
Charlotte, visions of aging, beer-bellied ex-rock stars who
could no longer hold a tune dancing in her head, had gone
ballistic. It wasn't one of her finer moments, she thought
dryly.

"And speaking of heat, Charlotte, my dear, the weekend
in California must have been good to you."

Charlotte's head shot up. "What do you mean?" she
demanded, wondering if there were outward signs of her
holiday fling.

"Just that you have some sun in your skin and a new
hairdo." He narrowed his blue eyes and tilted his head to
the side. "And I believe we have a new wardrobe, as well."

She was back in the jeans, wearing them this time with
an emerald-green satin shirt that was embarrassingly form-
fitting.

"These clothes aren't mine," she hastened to tell him.

Barnabas tilted his head even farther to the side. "Not
yours," he stated. "A pity."

"Why do you say that?"

"They're most becoming."

She put the sheaf of papers down that she was flipping
through and went around the desk to stand behind the
leather chair. Bending, she put her arms around her grandfather's neck and pressed the side of her face to his.

"And you're a sweetheart to say so."

"Only the truth, my dear," he said, patting her hand.
"You have the body of a woman—I've never thought you
should hide it. A man likes a woman with a little flesh
covering her bones. Not like your mother who keeps herself
so thin she could—"

"Float," Charlotte finished for him. She'd heard it all
before, of course, and she loved him for it. But the fact
was that most men—

She became still as her usual line of thinking took a little
turn. Most men might prefer women with waists they could

put their hands around. But not all. Most certainly, not all. Jacob had taught her that.

The thought of him flooded her body with heat, her mind with longing. She had done her best to avoid thinking of him on the flight back. Resolutely refused to think of him as she drove up to Madison from the airport in Milwaukee. And now here she was, her arms around her grandfather, remembering how Jacob had felt under her fingers, how he'd looked rising above her, how he'd smelled, tasted, sounded.

She slid her arms from Barnabas's neck and quickly turned to the window behind her desk. The view from the window usually calmed and reassured her. But at the moment the quaint church spire and the color of the autumn leaves illuminated in the dusk by the soft glow of a street-lamp couldn't seem to penetrate the sensory overload she was experiencing.

Jacob. She mouthed the word silently and a small circle of condensation appeared on the window. With her finger she wrote the letter *J*.

"Is something bothering you, Charlotte?"

She quickly rubbed out the *J* on the window and turned back to her grandfather.

"The same thing is bothering me, Barnabas, that has bothered me from the start."

Barnabas sighed and stood, the old chair wheezing in relief.

"If we are going to get into one of those discussions about the merits of classical music, I am going home."

"Oh, Barnabas—"

Barnabas put up his hand. "Charlotte, I know the merits of classical music. I know the importance of tradition. But I also know that this place will go under if we don't make a change. And there is no point, Charlotte, in debating the issue once again."

"I know that."

"Then let's not. Instead why don't you come out to Maple Bluff with me. We'll get Sarah to fix us an omelet while we sit in the library and catch one of Anthony's last shows."

Anthony had been the evening announcer at WEND for as long as Charlotte could remember. He had decided to take retirement rather than have to spin requests for oldies by yuppies.

"You know Sarah doesn't approve of you eating eggs."

"I know. Infernal woman watches my cholesterol closer than she watches that soap opera of hers. We could save breath by dropping the word *house* from her title and merely call her my keeper."

Charlotte laughed, but the truth was, Barnabas wouldn't know how to make a peanut-butter sandwich—not that he would ever eat one, of course. He would be lost without Sarah.

"I think I'll skip the omelet—and Sarah's lecture. I'm going to head home and unpack."

"Very well," Barnabas said, slipping into his long dark coat. "But don't sit here all night and pine, my dear. Time marches on for all of us. Best to accept it."

"Good night, Barnabas," she said, kissing him on the cheek. "And don't worry about me."

"I'll try not to, my dear. And you keep wearing that shade of green. It's most becoming."

When Barnabas had gone, she flipped the switch to open the speaker that piped broadcasts into her office. Anthony was playing Debussy. "Clair de lune." The piano had a sweet, melancholy sound. Simple, yearning. She'd always thought of the piece as equally a beginning or an ending, depending on what was going on in her life at the time.

She went to stand once again at the window, looking for the moon. If it was out at all, it was hiding from her. Moonlight—the end of a day—or the beginning of a night.

This night was beginning so very differently from the last.

She should be working, going over some final notes for her first confrontation with J.J. Tanner. She should be answering letters that needed answering. She should be stopping by the studio to visit with Anthony on this, his last week.

But instead she stood at the window and remembered the man who had changed her life even more than J.J. Tanner was going to.

Jacob had awakened something in her. Set something free. And she had absolutely no idea what she was going to do with it.

"Well, one thing you're not going to do," she muttered, "is stand at this window mooning over a man you're never going to see again. Go home, Charlotte," she told herself. But just as she turned out the light and shut the door it came to her that tonight "Clair de lune" had sounded more like an ending.

SHE PARKED HER CAR in the garage and walked around the side of the house and up the front-porch steps. A few years ago, against Barnabas's wishes, Charlotte had bought the house on west Washington Avenue, just two blocks from the State Capitol building. It was a big old duplex, in a long row of big old duplexes, and it ate money, but Charlotte loved the huge screened-in porches that fronted the first and second floors. And she liked the idea that the upstairs apartment would generate income for as long as she owned the house. Madison was Wisconsin's capital, but it was also home to the University of Wisconsin. Thousands of students poured in every autumn to swell the population, and the upstairs apartment hadn't been empty since the new paint had dried.

But the real reason she'd bought the house rose up into the night two blocks away. The dome of the State Capitol

building lit up a piece of the darkness just as it always had.
Tree-lined Washington Avenue sloped upward toward Capitol Square and all Charlotte had to do was step outside her
door to see the gilded bronze statue *Wisconsin* glowing
from its perch on top of the dome. The dome itself was
granite. Solid. Constant. She'd been able to see its glow
from across Lake Mendota from Barnabas's house in Maple
Bluff all the while she was growing up. When she'd decided five years ago to finally get out from under her grandfather's loving protection, she liked the idea of owning a
house with a view of one of the few things that had always
been there during her childhood.

The State Capitol Building, Barnabas and WEND.

And now she was losing one of them.

The screen door slammed shut behind her as she entered
the porch. It smelled of the bushel of apples she'd bought
the week before. It looked as if her current tenants, three
girls all studying political science, had been helping them-
selves to the McIntoshes while she'd been gone.

The house felt chilly when she let herself in.

And empty.

She couldn't recall having had that feeling ever before.

"Damn him," she muttered as she set down her suitcase.
She'd accustomed herself to a life alone. She'd built it into
something meaningful and productive. She loved what she
did. But soon she would no longer be doing it. Oh, she
would never leave the station, she knew that. But she would
also never fill the air with the music she loved but had
never been able to learn to play.

And now even the refuge of her quiet, ordered life was
being taken away from her. Because all she could think of,
all her mind would allow inside, was Jacob. And the idea
of him was making her restless in a way she'd never felt
before.

She picked up her suitcase again and hauled it to her
bedroom. Throwing it onto her bed, she unzipped it, flipped

it open and stared down at the clothes that she now knew had been put there by a well-meaning but misguided Carrie.

Except for the dress.

It lay on top, its velvet folds glowing like rich red wine in the light of the bedside lamp. She ran her hand across it then picked it up, slipped it onto a hanger and hung it on the back of the closet door. She wanted to be able to see it whenever she opened her closet. To tease herself with it. To torment herself with it. She would let the memories come for two days, she vowed to herself. And then she would hang the dress way in the back of her closet, slipping the memories back there with it.

She didn't plan to wear it ever again.

Chapter Seven

The blue jeans were another matter entirely, thought Charlotte a week later. She was biking to work as usual, breathing deeply as she pedaled up the two-block rise that led from her house on Washington Avenue to the State Capitol building. Her skirt flapped in the breeze, sending chilly October-morning air up her legs. And then there was always the danger of getting her skirt caught in the chain. The remembered comfort and freedom of the jeans she'd worn in San Francisco had been pretty tempting this morning when she'd gotten dressed. Or maybe she was just dwelling on the memory of how it felt to wear blue jeans because it was one of the few memories from that weekend that she allowed to come freely into her mind.

And that, she thought as she took a right at Carroll Street, was getting into dangerous territory. The weekend in San Francisco was off-limits to her brain. Even the blue jeans were off-limits—especially today. Today of all days, she didn't need the added stress of wondering what her fanny looked like if she had to bend over to pick up a paper clip.

Today was J.J. Tanner's first day at WEND. And there was no way she was meeting him for the first time with only tight blue denim between her fanny and the world.

She rounded one last corner, then hopped off her ten-speed, bumped it up the curb, and used it to push the door open to the old brick building that her grandfather owned. WEND, occupying the top floor of four, shared the space with a dentist, a handful of lawyers and a CPA or two. The marble-and-oak main entrance area was large and empty save for a bike rack that held an odd assortment of pedal-type transportation.

Charlotte wheeled her ten-speed over and locked it to the rack. Then she punched the elevator button. The doors slid open and she stepped inside.

Carrie was standing there when the doors swished open again on the fourth floor.

"He's here!" she squealed in a strangled voice.

"Tanner?" Charlotte whispered, hating the alarm she heard in her own voice.

"Yes! And you should see him, Charlotte. He's absolutely—"

Charlotte grabbed Carrie and hauled her into the elevator car.

"For heaven's sake, Carrie," she hissed as she gave a quick glance up and down the thankfully empty reception area before she pressed the button to close the doors. Once they were safely inside, she slumped against the paneled elevator wall. "It would be just like him to get here before me today," she muttered.

"It seems he and Barnabas had breakfast together this morning."

Charlotte bit her lip. "You're kidding?" she asked warily, wondering why her grandfather would choose not to include her, then quickly deciding that it was just as well. She didn't relish the idea of dealing with J.J. Tanner while worrying about the possibility of egg yolk on her chin.

"No kidding. They've been at the station for almost half an hour already."

Charlotte glanced at her watch to make sure she wasn't late. And she wasn't. She'd given herself plenty of time that morning to get in and get her bearings before she had to meet the enemy. And now it seemed the enemy had stormed the gates while she'd been eating her granola.

Well, she conceded, not exactly "stormed." Barnabas had obviously escorted the tune-spinning conqueror right into the fortress.

Carrie was busy fanning her face with a well-manicured hand. "Charlotte, I have never in my life seen such a babe."

"Oh, come on," Charlotte scoffed in annoyance, knowing that Carrie had dated every eligible bachelor in Madison, many of whom she'd declared certified babes.

"It's true! He is gorgeous. And nice..." Carrie dragged out the last word like a swoon.

Charlotte wrinkled her nose. "Nice? Don't tell me you've gone over to the other side already?"

"Well, gee, Charlotte, he really is nice," Carrie said defensively. "And those dark eyes..." Again, the last word was drawn out as though the elevator was going to need a fainting couch any minute.

Charlotte rolled her eyes. "For heaven's sake, Carrie. Get hold of yourself."

"I'd rather get hold of him," Carrie murmured dramatically.

"Oh, please," scoffed Charlotte as she pressed the button to open the elevator door. Carrie had become an instant J.J. groupie and Charlotte obviously wasn't going to get any information out of the woman that would be of any use.

Instead she decided that she'd rather not run into him for the first time in the elevator or the hallway. It would be better if she hung up her coat, smoothed her hair and collected her wits about her first.

"Where are they now?" she whispered as she left the elevator and skirted the reception area in front of her office.

"They're in your office."

She'd actually had her hand on the knob when Carrie

had answered. "My office?" Charlotte croaked, looking at the solid wood door in alarm.

"Uh-huh," Carrie nodded.

She shook her head. "Oh, swell. Why the heck didn't Barnabas take him to his own office?"

Although her grandfather didn't come in to the station every day anymore, he kept a small office down the hall from Charlotte's so he would have somewhere to hang his hat, when he felt the need to be a part of the operation.

"I think Barnabas is really taken with him, Charlotte. He's really eager for the two of you to meet."

"Oh, good," Charlotte muttered. "Yet another J.J. groupie."

"You're going to like him, Charlotte. You won't be able to help yourself."

"Oh, yes I will," she mumbled as she took off her jacket and handed it to Carrie. "Hair okay?" she asked.

Carrie studied her. "Just a minute," she said as she smoothed a strand into place. "There."

Charlotte pulled her long, bulky sweater down over her olive challis skirt—her Monday outfit for autumn—then reached again for the doorknob to her office.

"Okay, here goes," she said to Carrie.

"Good luck," Carrie mouthed as Charlotte opened the door and went inside.

He was standing at the window—*her* window—his back to the room.

"Charlotte!" Barnabas beamed handsomely. "You're a little early. I was just about to show J.J. around. But now that you're here, let it be my pleasure to introduce you."

Barnabas held out his arm to her and Charlotte went, feeling a little steadier when her grandfather pulled her close to his side.

"J.J., this is my one true love, my granddaughter, Charlotte."

J.J. turned from the window and smiled—and Charlotte had to cling to Barnabas to keep from sliding to the floor.

Because it was worse than she had even expected.

Of all the thoughts she could have been thinking, what flashed in her mind was that he looked different somehow. This wasn't the man in the torn T-shirt and battered jeans who'd bullied the maître d' into seating him at her table. Nor was it the man in the dark tuxedo who'd danced with her under the stars.

No, this was a man in a crisp white shirt, the cuffs rolled up to his elbows, and a pair of pressed khakis.

The clothes were different, but there was no mistaking him. J.J. Tanner was the irresistible rogue who had stolen her heart high on a hill in San Francisco.

J.J. Tanner was Jacob, the holiday lover she was never supposed to see again.

But not only was she seeing him—because there he certainly was, standing at the window in her very own office—but she was also going to be his *boss*.

She watched him as a slow grin started to curve the corners of his mouth. That same mouth that had—

Oh, what was she thinking?

He was coming toward her, his softly sculptured mouth opening, and she suddenly knew for sure that the rules they'd made in San Francisco had to be followed.

She moved from the protective weight of Barnabas's arm and held out her hand.

JACOB DIDN'T WANT TO LET GO of her hand. Now that he was touching her skin again—something he thought would never happen—he just didn't want to let go.

But if holding her hand was this good, holding her in his arms would be even better. Trying to rein in the silly grin he knew was plastered on his face, he started to pull her toward him.

And then she opened her mouth to speak.

"Good morning, Mr. Tanner," she said in a voice that couldn't possibly be from the same woman who had begged him for more the last time he had touched her. "Welcome to WEND."

He narrowed his eyes, watching her. Looking for any sign of warmth—or perhaps even irony. There was none.

While his heart was thumping from the absolute miracle of having found her again, he became aware all at once that Charlie had every intention of sticking to the ridiculous rules she'd laid down in San Francisco.

He let go of her hand and inclined his head. "Ms. Riesling. Pleased to meet you at last."

The old man flung back his head and laughed richly. "Never thought I'd hear you being so formal, J.J. Come on, you two," he said, putting an arm around each of them. "Surely you're not going to continue the animosity that started with that one, unhappy phone call? Come, Charlotte, we've been waiting for you. I thought it only appropriate, since you are to be his boss, that you should escort J.J. to his new office yourself."

"Yes," J.J. Tanner said. "Why don't you show me to my new office, *boss?*"

He thought he saw some uncertainty flicker across her face. But all too quickly she collected herself, every inch the haughty woman he'd glimpsed more than once in San Francisco.

"Of course," she replied, turning toward the door. "Are you coming, Barnabas?"

"I'll be along in a minute. You two go ahead."

He thought she would protest, but she didn't. "Very well," she said as she continued to move toward the door.

In the hallway he thought surely she would change, become his Charlie.

But she didn't.

"That is my grandfather's office," she said, indicating a door next to her office as they passed it. "Yours is right next to it. The studios are down the hall on the other side of the reception area. You've met Carrie. She handles paperwork and phone calls for all of us.''

He followed behind her, listening to her rather formal speech. Her dark, shiny hair moved slightly as she walked. He remembered how it felt under his hands. His gaze moved lower, down to the skirt that fell almost to her ankles.

He knew what was under that skirt. He knew the soft, seductive woman's body that she was trying to hide with the baggy, bulky sweater pulled down over her hips. He knew the feel of it, the scent of it, the taste of it. His body stirred restlessly while the memory of that last night in San Francisco fought its way through anything else that was in his mind.

And her, damn her, all she apparently had on her mind was letting him know how to work the phone system.

''I'm sure you'll want to meet with your star boy as soon as possible. As far as I know, he's staying at The Inn on the Park until he finds an apartment.''

''PowerCord's here already?''

She didn't look at him when she answered. ''Yes. He apparently likes to get a feel for the city he's working in before he goes on the air.''

Jacob and PowerCord Baker went way back. They'd been pioneers at an underground radio station back in their college days. It had been the age of disco and polyester and they'd mocked the whole concept while searching out obscure bands—hoping for a find that would give them both enough clout to write their own ticket in the world of rock radio.

PowerCord had done it long before Jacob had, immersing himself in the standard drugs, sex, and rock and roll. Jacob, who had married and become a father fairly young, had made a slower, but as it turned out, steadier climb. When he'd negotiated his contract with WEND he'd made it clear that he would only come on board if PowerCord could come with him. His old friend had been out of the big markets for a while, but Jacob knew PowerCord still had what it took to be a hell of an afternoon drive-time jock. As it was, he'd been way underused on his last two gigs.

"I've scheduled a meeting for this afternoon for you to meet with the two other disc jockeys you've approved. And then later this afternoon, you're scheduled to interview the candidates for internship in the news department. Then—"

Jacob had had enough. If she thought she was going to be able to ignore what they'd shared together, she was wrong. He stared at her head, bent over the schedule she'd placed in the center of his desk. He needed to touch her again—badly. He lifted his hand toward her hair.

"Well, I see Charlotte has taken you under her wing, J.J."

At the sound of Barnabas Riesling's voice, Jacob let his hand drop. It was on the tip of his tongue to say that he would much rather be under Charlotte's *skirt*. Instead he said, "She's been filling me in on my schedule for the next few days."

"Good. Good." Barnabas came into the office, tapping a long finger against his mouth. "You'll want to meet with the disc jockeys about the playlist—"

"He knows that, Grandfather," Charlotte interrupted impatiently.

Barnabas smiled lovingly at her. "Of course he does, my dear. But you know me, WEND has always been my child and I'm bound to poke my head in now and then, whether it's needed or not."

"For the record, Barnabas," Jacob said, "your head is welcome to poke into this office any time you get the urge."

"I appreciate that, son," Barnabas replied. "I can't wait to see you and PowerCord working together. It's going to be, uh," The old man seemed to be grappling for the word.

Then his face lit up, his blue eyes sparkled. "*Awesome,* I believe, is the word."

A faint choking sound came from Charlie's throat. Jacob grinned.

"Something wrong, my dear?" Barnabas asked her.

"I was just thinking of all the other words that might apply here," she answered wryly. "Now, if you gentlemen will excuse me," she added, making her way toward the door, "I have some calls to make."

"Of course, Charlotte. But don't forget, the three of us are meeting PowerCord at The Top of the Park for lunch."

Charlotte froze with her hand on the knob. *Thought you were home free, didn't you, love?* Jacob said to himself.

"We, uh, we are?" she asked, her back becoming even more rigid.

"Carrie made reservations for noon. I thought we'd all walk over there together. That way we can give J.J. a little tour of the immediate area and—"

Charlotte whirled around. "No!"

"No?" Barnabas repeated.

Jacob couldn't help but notice the change in the old man's voice and demeanor. The guy could look patrician and formidable as hell when he wanted to. Jacob almost had it in him to feel sorry for Charlotte, who was on the receiving end of that blue gaze as it became more piercing, but he was enjoying her discomfort at the situation too damned much.

"Charlotte, you *are* going to join us for lunch?"

Jacob figured he was even more interested in the answer to that than the old man was.

"Ms. Riesling, I assure you that both Mr. Baker and I will be most bereft if you don't," Jacob said formally, all the while trying not to grin when Charlie turned a look his way that was almost as piercing as her grandfather's.

"Yes, of course," she said reasonably. "I only meant

I'll have to meet you there. I have some outside business to take care of first.''

Barnabas made a graceful gesture with his long-fingered hand, his eyes twinkling once more. "Good. Good. Now, I suggest we get out of our new program director's office so he can get down to business.''

Charlotte didn't need further prompting. She was out the door almost before Barnabas had finished his sentence.

Why him? she thought as she rushed down the hall in an effort to avoid talking to her grandfather. She didn't want to see anyone right now. All she wanted to do was be alone to think about what had just happened. To ponder this latest catastrophe that had become her life.

She reached her office, zipped inside and shut the door. The decisive click sounded like rescue to her ears.

"Rescue?" she muttered, slumping back against the solid wood door. Even if by some miracle no one came to her office, lunch was looming closer by the minute. She looked at her watch. Who on earth had decided to put the noon meal at noon, for heaven's sake?

And how on earth was she going to break bread with J.J. Tanner now that he had turned out to be her rogue holiday lover?

"Jacob," she whispered as if to torment herself further. "Jacob." And with the sound of his name escaping her lips came the heat. The same heat that had flooded her body over and over again that night in his hotel room. The same heat that made her body long and yearn. The same heat that made her mind think crazy thoughts.

She wasn't supposed to ever see him again. That had been the plan.

But despite the fact that she'd finally put the burgundy velvet dress in the back of her closet, she'd never quite succeeded in putting Jacob in the back of her mind. Just last night, lying sleepless in bed listening to the branches of the big ancient oak in her front yard restlessly scraping her bedroom window, she relived every touch, every word, marveling anew at how free she'd been with him. How womanly. How wanton. And one of the reasons she'd finally let go like that was that she knew she would never see him again. Of course, the other was that he was the most desirable man she'd ever laid eyes on. Desirable and sexy and just plain irresistible in his seduction. In her real life, he would have been dangerous, but in San Francisco—when she wasn't even wearing her own clothes—it had felt safer to give birth to that other side of herself. After all, she would never see him again.

And now here he was, just down the hall.

And not only that, she thought, as panic turned to anger. Not only was he here, in her life, where he wasn't supposed to be; but he had acted as though he had absolutely no idea who she was!

Well, he wasn't going to get away with it! She was going to march right back down that hallway and ask him what he thought he was doing. Pretending not to know her, for heaven's sake! Acting like they'd never—

Her phone started to beep. She strode over to the desk and picked it up.

"Carrie, I really don't want to be bothered now."

"Well, you're about to be, whether you want it or not. Mr. Merriweather is here and I think you'd better deal with him."

Charlotte groaned. Macon Merriweather of Merriweather's Fair Weather Florists. Just who she didn't need to talk to at that moment. But she really had no choice. Merriweather had sponsored one of WEND's most beloved hours, *Bach in the Morning.* Charlotte and Melinda had been working on him for weeks, trying to convince him not to pull his advertising completely, but to give them a chance to find an alternative he could live with. Like maybe an hour of Elvis. Or one of the new happy-talk shows that were in the works.

She sighed, wishing Melinda were here to take this meeting. But Charlotte couldn't afford to drop the Merriweather ball now. "Okay, Carrie, send him back."

She went to the door of her office and opened it. Macon Merriweather was already standing just outside.

"Charlotte, we have to do something," he said, striding into her office. "I can't have my flowers pushing that rock and roll. We survived the sixties without going over to the other side. I don't see why we have to now."

His clothes had survived the sixties too, Charlotte thought to herself. Pushing seventy, Macon hadn't renewed his wardrobe since just after World War II. His clothes were clean, in remarkably good condition, but he looked as though he should be in a black-and-white movie.

"Macon, I understand your feelings perfectly," she soothed, gesturing him into her office and over to a chair. "But what you don't seem to realize is that WEND is changing its format because we need a larger share of the audience in order to survive. And, Macon," she said gently as she slid into the leather chair behind her desk, "if we get a bigger share, so do you."

It seemed as if she'd been explaining this to Macon Merriweather for an eternity.

"But I won't have my flowers pushing that awful music, Charlotte. I just won't stand for it."

Macon Merriweather had been a good-looking man in his day. *Dapper* would be the word for him. He'd kept the trim figure on his medium frame. Indeed, thought Charlotte, if he hadn't, he would have had to buy new clothes. His nose was still narrowly regal and jutting. His hair was still thick. Yes, thought Charlotte, he would still be a handsome man—if he didn't have an obsession with using self-tanning lotion all year-round and dyeing his hair a shade of black that made him look as though he wore a dead crow on his head.

This morning his skin was incredibly dark, leading Charlotte to believe that Macon had given himself a new application just yesterday. She noticed that he'd missed a wrinkle under one eye. Of course she wouldn't say anything; she never did. And neither would anyone else in Madison. Macon, a wizard with flowers, was the most popular florist in town, so he was left to be as he was.

Charlotte tried to reassure him one more time. "And neither would I, Macon. Now, what I propose is that I sit down with the new program director and try to come up with some alternatives you can live with."

"Well, I certainly hope you can, Charlotte. We've supported WEND ever since my father opened the shop in the twenties, and he'd climb out of his grave if he knew we were helping to put that stuff on the air. You trust this man?" Macon asked.

"Of course I do," Charlotte lied. "Barnabas and I have every faith in him."

"TRUST. FAITH," Charlotte muttered to herself as she turned the corner onto Carroll Street. She was becoming far too adept at shoveling it. Because the truth was, she wouldn't trust the new program director with an old transistor radio, let alone a whole radio station.

The idea! Pretending not to know who she was!

Well, she thought, shoving her hands into her jacket pockets, she had done the same thing, hadn't she? She gave herself a moment to wonder why she wasn't glad that Jacob had followed her lead. Did this mean that with one little sign from him she would have been more than happy to run right into his arms?

That thought made her remember what it felt like in his arms. Her skin grew hot. That dull ache started in her lower belly.

She bit her lip and gave a few fast shakes of her head. Those feelings belonged to another time, another place. By now they were supposed to be nothing more than a memory.

"I've got the luck of the damned," she muttered, as she turned onto Main Street. The "memory" had come alive again—was alive and kicking. And he was working just down the hall from her.

Nick's Candy Store occupied a red brick storefront, halfway down the block from the corner of Carroll and Main. It was Charlotte's destination late that morning, just as it had been on many days all through her life when she was troubled, anxious, happy—or just plain hungry.

"Hi, Nick," she said when she'd pushed the door open and went inside. "Got a cherry soda for me?"

"That I can do," Nick said. "Sit on down. I'll bring it right over."

"Where's Katherine?"

He jerked his head toward the back of the store. "Got a batch of candy going. She'll be out in time for the lunch crowd."

Nick's Candy Store had been a fixture on Main Street since the early twenties when Nick's father had immigrated from Greece. It was prohibition, and soda fountains and candy stores had sprung up all over Madison—the perfect place to take your girl on a Saturday night.

Over the years, shops surrounding Capitol Square had come and gone. But Nick's Candy Store was a survivor. Charlotte suspected it was due not only to the wonderful hand-dipped chocolates on display in the glass case that lined the right side of the front of the shop, but also to the warmth of Nick and his wife, Katherine.

Nick presided behind the counter that lined the wall opposite the candy cases, dispensing sodas from an old-fashioned soda machine and ladling homemade hot fudge and caramel sauce onto sundaes.

"Looks like you could use more than a cherry soda,

Charlie,'' Nick said as he set the classically shaped glass down in front of her.

Charlie. Nick was one of the few who still used her nickname from her childhood. She was Charlotte to everyone but Nick and Melinda and her children. And now, of course, Jacob. Jacob had called her Charlie.

Charlotte shook off the thought. ''You know, I think you're right, Nick. Bring me something sinfully fattening and utterly huge.''

''You'll spoil your lunch,'' Katherine said as she came out of the back of the shop carrying a tray of freshly dipped creams.

''I think a Happy Thought sundae would strike just the perfect note for lunch today,'' Charlotte said.

''Don't be silly, Charlotte. You're having lunch at The Top of the Park today.''

Charlotte groaned. ''Good news travels fast, I see.''

''Your granddaddy was in this morning for his usual quarter pound of maple creams. He said you're lunching with the new director and disc jockey today—Top of the Park. You don't want to spoil your appetite for that.''

What appetite? thought Charlotte. The prospect of sitting across from a man she'd spent a night in bed with doing—well, doing *everything,* wasn't exactly making her feel like digging into a Caesar salad.

''Maybe I need the fortification,'' she mumbled.

''That new deejay was in here yesterday,'' Nick said. ''Seems like a card.''

''And very handsome, too,'' Katherine added, pursing her lips.

Nick shook a finger at his wife. ''Now don't you go giving me any trouble or I won't let you out in front again.''

Katherine flapped her hand. ''Oh, pooh! Like a young Turk like that would give the likes of me a second look.''

''If he doesn't,'' Nick said, scooting behind the candy

counter to give Katherine a pat on her backside, "he'd have to be blind."

Katherine's laughter filled the shop.

Where did people find love like that? Charlotte wondered. Those two had been together forever, their love spilling over to anyone who came in for chocolate-covered peanuts or a cream phosphate. The booths way in the back of the narrow shop were perfect for holding hands, or splitting a Lover's Delight sundae. More than one marriage proposal had been made here. Legend had it that a state senator who had gone on to become a bigwig in Washington had proposed to his wife over a banana split, then taken her right next door to the jeweler's to pick out the ring.

Charlotte had loved all the stories she'd heard when she would come into the shop after school. Ah, to be a grown-up, she'd thought as a ten-year-old, and find romance.

Well, she was a grown-up now and so far, the only slightly romantic thing she'd ever experienced was when she'd gone steady in her junior year. He'd been a student at the university. Tall and awkward. A wannabe poet dressed in black. That entire autumn, she'd listened to him endlessly read his poems. As Christmas loomed, she'd been so bored with his self-absorption and so tired of watching his Adam's apple as a diversion, that she'd broken up with him.

And that had been the only romantic thing that had ever happened to her.

Until San Francisco.

Suddenly she really needed that sundae.

"Nick, make me a Happy Thought."

How many times had she said that line? It had been the summer of her eleventh year when she'd come to stay with Barnabas for good. But for years before then, her parents had shipped her to Madison whenever life got "complicated," as her mother put it. Which meant, Charlotte had figured out before she was seven, that her parents were fighting again. Sometimes it would be a week. Sometimes a month. Once it had been an entire winter. In the early evenings she would stand in the window of her grandfather's Maple Bluff home from where she could see all the way across Lake Mendota to the comforting glow of the State Capitol dome. In those days it had sometimes seemed like the only thing that could make her feel safe.

Well, that and one of Nick's Happy Thoughts sundaes.

DAMN! SHE WAS GOING to be late! It was already ten past twelve when she shouted a hurried goodbye to Nick and Katherine and several of the regulars who stopped in every lunch hour. It was just a short way down the street to The Top of the Park, but she would have to duck into the rest room of the hotel lobby first to try to get the sundae sauce off her sweater.

A lot of good having that sundae had done her. There was no way any of her present thoughts were happy.

She trotted across Carroll Street in front of The Inn on the Park, where the restaurant commanded the eighth floor. She was only a few feet from the curb when the roar of a motorcycle caught her attention and she pulled up short. A good thing, too, because if she hadn't heard it, it would have run her down. Instead, it rumbled to a stop right in front of her. She gasped, wondering how the huge machine could possibly have fit so precisely in the few feet between her and the curb.

"Hey, sweetheart," the driver said.

"Are you crazy? You could have killed me!"

He reached up and pulled off his helmet. "Never, sweetheart," he drawled. "I'm much too good."

Her mouth twisted. "Well, if it isn't PowerCord Baker. Maybe they should have nicknamed you Hell on Wheels."

He laughed. "Already taken, sweetheart, or it would have been mine."

She snorted. "You drove that thing the two blocks from the station? Don't they walk where you come from?"

"Sure they do. Just wanted to give the chicks on campus a drive-by."

The University of Wisconsin was down at the other end of State Street from the State Capitol. "I'm sure it was a thrill for them," she replied dryly.

"Be nice and I'll give you a ride sometime."

"No, thanks," she said, starting to skirt around him and the huge bike. Using his feet he walked it forward to block her way.

"Aw, you don't like my Harley?"

She gave him a mock sympathetic smile. "Let's just say I like it almost as much as I like you."

Instead of getting angry, he laughed. "Hey, nothing like a mouthy chick. Let me get the Harley valet-parked and we'll go up to the restaurant together."

She had it on the tip of her tongue to refuse, then thought better of it. Arriving with someone would be easier than arriving alone. Even if that someone was a man with a name like PowerCord.

"Okay, I'll wait," she said.

He nodded, got off the Harley and wheeled it over to the valet.

"Be nice to her," he said, giving the kid a bill.

"Aren't you going to kiss her goodbye?" Charlotte asked innocently.

"I would but I don't want to mark the chrome," he said, giving her a lopsided grin.

Katherine was right; the new deejay was good-looking. His blond hair, brushed back from a high forehead, fell past the collar of his leather jacket. He had the sideburns to go with the jacket, giving him the look of someone who wouldn't mind getting into a fistfight now and then. His eyes were the color of caramel, his mouth a thin, hard line above a squared-off chin. His body looked compact and solid, in his tight, worn jeans.

"Come on, sweetheart," he said, holding the door for her. "We'll miss the cocktail hour."

"At lunch?"

"You bet," he said, giving her a wink as they crossed the marble floor of the lobby.

She couldn't help but notice the reaction of the desk clerk, a young girl probably working her way through the university. The girl's eyes followed them all the way to the elevator. And why not? thought Charlotte. He was clearly a maverick. And didn't mavericks always stir a woman up?

Well, most women, anyway, she amended in her mind as they rode the elevator up to the eighth floor.

"After you, sweetheart," PowerCord said, when the doors opened.

She smiled and shook her head. "I haven't heard the term 'sweetheart' used this much since I watched my last Humphrey Bogart movie on late-night television."

Baker laughed. "Not working on you, huh?"

"Nope," she said as they walked down the hall to the restaurant.

"Hmm, you must have it bad for some other guy."

She laughed the remark off. "What an ego."

But when they got to the entrance to the restaurant she stopped. There he was, across the room, sitting at Barnabas's favorite window table.

The "other guy" she had it bad for.

Chapter Eight

The restaurant had a spectacular view of the State Capitol building. Jacob sat at a window seat and looked down on men and women in business suits hurrying along, dodging young women with strollers and teenagers on in-line skates. "Watch checkers," Jacob had always called them. It was one of the reasons he'd gotten into radio. It tended to be a little more laid-back and unpredictable.

Except you wouldn't know it, to look at Barnabas Riesling sitting across from him. The old man was checking his watch once again.

"It's not like Charlotte to be late."

Yeah, he wanted to answer. *I know.* She'd been right on time that night he'd picked her up in the lobby of her hotel. That night she'd knocked him out by buying the dress he'd chosen for her. That night she'd surprised him in more ways than one.

"Ah, here they are now."

Jacob's gaze swung to the entrance of the restaurant. Well, well, he thought. Yet another surprise. Because Charlie hadn't arrived alone. PowerCord Baker had his hand at the small of her back, leading her over to the table like he'd done it all before. It made Jacob's eyes narrow and his brow furrow—that is until he caught himself. PowerCord had a taste for younger women, ripe twenty-year-olds with long blond hair and legs up to their— Well, Charlie did have great legs. At the moment, Jacob was feeling relieved that she had them well camouflaged.

"Charlotte, there you are," Barnabas said, rising to his feet to kiss his granddaughter on the cheek. "And how refreshing to see the two of you arriving together."

"I tried to get her on my hog, but nothing doing," Baker said, pulling out a chair and throwing himself into it.

"She doesn't look like the kind of woman who would take a chance, Baker. Better give it up," Jacob said, his gaze on Charlotte. The look she gave him told him to drop dead. The only thing was, he liked it. It was exactly the kind of look she'd given him in San Francisco. In the beginning. Before…

"We've just been discussing the new advertisers J.J. is bringing on board," Barnabas was saying.

Charlotte, who'd been focusing her rapt attention on the linen napkin in front of her since sitting down, jerked her head up. "What new advertisers?" she asked sharply.

Barnabas patted her hand. "Why don't we order first, my dear. Then we can discuss it while we wait to be served."

Jacob thought she was going to refuse. He saw a slew of emotions cross her face, but she held them in and took the menu the waiter handed to her.

"I'll just have a salad," she said, after a quick glance at the menu.

"Come, Charlotte, you need more than that to sustain you until dinner."

"I'm not all that hungry."

Jacob's mouth quirked. "I imagine that hot fudge sundae you just had spoiled your appetite."

Her gaze shot to him across the table. He inclined his head toward her sweater. She looked down and squeezed her eyes shut for a moment, biting her lip. Then she sat up straighter.

"It wasn't hot fudge," she said as if she was discussing something far more serious. "It was a Happy Thoughts sundae."

He grinned. "And did it work?"

She continued to stare at him. "It did until I just heard that you're bringing advertisers on board yourself."

"Well, I wasn't exactly idle my last week in San Francisco," he said, lowering his chin and mustering up the kind of intensity in his eyes that usually worked for him with the opposite sex.

It didn't seem to be working now.

"I don't imagine," she said, raising her chin, "that you're idle anywhere, Mr. Tanner."

So cool, he thought. But it was impossible to look at her, even in that damn bulky sweater, and not remember a time when she hadn't been so cool. Not remember her body thrashing under his. Not remember her voice crying his name. And the sound of it hadn't been cool at all. Not at all.

He would bet if he reached out at that moment and touched her, he could have her trembling in an instant. Even in the crowded restaurant.

He lifted his hand, but quickly dropped it again. Hell, he was the one who was trembling.

Shrugging with an indifference he was far from feeling, he picked up his napkin and shook it out, hoping no one had noticed the tremor of his fingers. "Not unusual," he said casually, "for a program director to build his own advertising base. I am, after all, in charge of setting the tone of the station. We're changing formats. That means changing advertisers. Our target audience will be different." He paused deliberately, hoping to unnerve her, a little. "I'm sure you have enough experience to know that, Ms. Riesling."

"My experience isn't in question here, Mr. Tanner. What *is* in question is the fact that you are not in charge of wooing advertisers. At the moment I'm working with some of our old sponsors to see if we can come up with programming ideas that might fit their needs and—''

Jacob stopped grinning. "Wait just a minute. *You're* working with the sponsors? Since when is it the station manager's job to come up with programming?''

"Mr. Tanner, we are a small station, everyone does double duty. I've known some of these people since I was a child and—''

"And,'' he interrupted, "that would make you a pushover, Ms. Riesling, for anything they might suggest.''

"How dare you!''

"Oh, I dare very easily. There can only be one program director. And I'm it, lady. When I came on board I was promised complete control—''

"Not by me you weren't!''

"This will never do,'' Barnabas bellowed.

Baker, slumped nonchalantly in his chair, gave a bark of laughter. "I was finding it rather entertaining, myself,'' he drawled.

"But hardly productive,'' Barnabas said in a tone of voice that could put him on the stage doing Shakespeare. It was formidable as hell, effectively shutting Charlie's mouth for the moment. Even Baker, Jacob saw, had suddenly sat up straighter in his chair.

"Now,'' Barnabas continued, "we have a part-time sales manager—''

"Part-time? He'd better start putting in more hours for the time being,'' Jacob said.

"It's a she,'' Charlotte said. "And she can barely handle the hours she has now.''

Jacob stared hard at her. "Then why do you keep her on?''

"We keep her on because she's a second cousin who was widowed very young and—''

"Oh, brother! See, this is just the kind of thing I'm talking about! You can't run a successful station if you're giving jobs to every out-of-work relative in the state.''

"Are you implying that my position at WEND is based on nepotism?"

"I don't know, Ms. Riesling," he replied with a dangerous calm. "Is it?"

She held his stare for so long, he thought that he was going to have to be the first one to look away. In the depths of her dark, glowing eyes he saw anger—and something more. Hurt. He'd hurt her. And badly.

"Look," he began in a gentler tone. "I think—"

"I think this meeting is over," she finished for him and made as if to rise from her chair.

"Keep your seat, Charlotte," Barnabas said sternly. "The meeting is over when I say it is."

"But—"

The old man raised his hand. "Hear me out, my dear. You are both partly correct in this matter. J.J., my granddaughter has worked very hard with her cousin to build an advertising base for WEND. True, some of that will have to change since, as you say, the target audience will be different. And it's true that we've taken on cousin Melinda as a favor—Lord knows, the girl really is better at raising children. But the same isn't true for Charlotte. She's been a very fine manager and she's virtually taken over the sales department, as well. Melinda usually works out of her home and is mainly clerical support.

"Now, what I propose is that we combine J.J.'s new list of advertisers with those of our regulars who are willing to discuss program changes. For that, you will have to work together. *If* you can handle it."

Jacob felt like the old man's blue eyes were pinning him to the wall. He was formidable, all right, and smart. He had to be if he was willing to go to the lengths he was to save his station. And Jacob had known all along that, given the size of the station, he would have to work closely with the station manager. And he'd been willing to do it. Until, that is, he'd seen who the station manager was.

How the hell was he supposed to reason with a woman that he was in love with when she was pretending she'd never laid eyes on him before?

Baker leaned forward in his chair. "Look, you two, he's right. Let's all play nice."

Jacob looked at his old friend. "You're just worried that if I get tossed out on my ear, you'll be right behind me."

Baker laughed and shook his head, glancing at the old man. "He knows me too well."

"Which is why you're here, PowerCord," Barnabas said. "J.J. has told me that the two of you make quite a team and that you've pulled stations out of the basement before."

"We have," PowerCord said.

"Well, now you have one more on your team. You have Charlotte." Barnabas looked pointedly at Jacob. "Do I hear any objections?"

Jacob wasn't one for squirming in his seat, but the old man was pushing him close to it. Barnabas looked at every one of them in turn, then smiled the peaceful smile of a man who was used to getting his way. "Good. Ah, here comes our food. I suggest we eat."

JACOB SLAMMED THE DOOR to his office. Man, he hated this! It wasn't like him to lose control. He liked things simple, loose.

He paced to the window, looking down on the street. Madison, Wisconsin. What had ever made him come here? He was used to bigger markets, more progressive people. He'd been a fool to take this job. What had possessed him?

But he knew what had possessed him. Gaby. He wanted Gaby to grow up in a place like Madison.

The phone on his desk rang and he reached from the

window and snagged up the receiver. "Yeah?" he barked into it.

"Mr., uh, Tanner?" croaked a nervous male voice.

Jacob rolled his eyes to the ceiling and rubbed the back of his neck. Making his way in this town wasn't going to be helped by barking at unknown people on the phone.

"Yes," he said, making an effort to sound more friendly, "this is Jacob Tanner. What can I do for you?"

"Well, you don't know me, but my flowers have been helping to bring beautiful music to this town for several decades. I met with Charlotte and she assured me that I wouldn't have to sponsor any of that rock-and-roll stuff. Well, I got out my Benny Goodman and Frank Sinatra records and, well, I thought…"

CHARLOTTE RAPPED THE TIP of her pencil on the desk— tap, tap, tap—while she brainstormed ideas for Macon's show. She'd already thought of a name: *The Flower Power Hour.* Now she was trying to think of a category of music that would fit with it—one that both J.J. and Macon could live with.

Maybe sixties "flower child" stuff? Her visit to San Francisco had piqued her interest in the era. There was a lot of feel-good music floating around then. Of course, she doubted that Macon Merriweather had ever been a flower child, but he probably wouldn't find anything to object to in the music she was considering. So far her list included such innocuous groups as The Partridge Family, The Lovin' Spoonful and The Beau Brummels. She searched her brain for a catchy slogan to tie it all together, scribbling hearts and flowers on the edge of her legal pad as she did so.

She was so absorbed that when the phone on her desk started ringing, she jumped and blinked, forgetting for a moment where she was.

On the third ring, she picked up the receiver. "Charlotte Reisling."

"Charlotte, I never thought it would come to this."

"Sherman?" She recognized the voice of Sherman Clark, the man who'd been current-affairs commentator on WEND since Charlotte had been a teenager.

"Yes, Charlotte, it's Sherman. And I would think that after the loyal service I've provided this station for years, the news would at least have come from you if not from your grandfather."

"What news?" Charlotte asked warily.

"The news that I'm fired, Charlotte. That's what news!"

Charlotte caught her breath. "Fired?"

"Yes, fired! That P.J. or C.J. or whatever Tanner your grandfather hired, just informed me."

Charlotte pinched the flesh in the middle of her forehead. "There has to be some mistake. We agreed that we would find a place for anyone who wanted to stay on."

"Tell that to that...*Californian!*" Sherman Clark said the word as though it was something nasty.

By the time Charlotte could think of anything to say, the dial tone was buzzing in her ear.

She slammed down the receiver. "Of all the nerve." Barnabas might have promised J.J. Tanner full control, but if he thought he was getting away with this, he was dead wrong. She pushed her desk chair back and got to her feet. Barnabas had gone home after lunch and J.J. Tanner was going to have to deal with her without that particular buffer. She couldn't wait to tell him what she thought of him!

She stormed over to her office door, threw it open, went into the hallway—and ran smack into J.J. Tanner.

"What do you think you're doing?" they shouted in unison.

"Me?" they parroted again, a parody of a wacky, out-of-sync chorus.

"How dare you fire Sherman Clark!" she said.

"What's the idea of telling Merriweather he could host an hour of Frank Sinatra?"

"What?" they both said again.

"You didn't tell Macon Merriweather that he could sponsor an hour of big-band sounds?"

"I did not," she replied firmly.

"Well, I didn't fire Sherman Clark, either."

She wrinkled her nose. "You didn't?"

"No, I didn't. I gave him several options, but the old windbag refused to even discuss them."

She was about to open her mouth to defend Sherman, but, realized, when all was said and done, he really was a windbag. More than half of Madison had tuned him out years ago. His show mainly rehashed everything that went on under the Capitol dome and received the lowest ratings of anything WEND offered.

"What kind of options?" Charlotte asked.

"A cheap-eats kind of restaurant-review show, for one."

"Cheap eats?" she repeated.

He seemed to bristle. "Look, we're going after the young yuppie crowd and the aging baby boomers. More taste than money. Media across the country are doing shows that feature reasonably priced restaurants. But," he added, sarcasm lacing his words, "I suppose a highbrow like you wouldn't stoop to—"

There had been too many misunderstandings. "That's not it," she said, shaking her head. "It's just that Sherman Clark hasn't eaten anything but baby food in years. His show is generally peppered with references to his gastrointestinal troubles."

Jacob rolled his eyes. "Oh, great. And I suggested he might want to start with several Mexican places in town to tie in with one of the new sponsors, Alfie's Flour Tortillas."

"Alfie? No kidding? I love those things."

Jacob grinned. "Me, too. I put everything but the kitchen sink in 'em."

"Have you tried scrambled eggs?"

"Absolutely. With green pepper and onion—"

"And lots of salsa," she finished for him.

He nodded. "Yep."

"One time I even—" She stopped. Was she going to stand here and discuss tortilla filling options with the enemy? Where was her mind?

Well, she knew where her mind was. Right now it was focused on Jacob Tanner's inviting mouth. She hadn't seen the kind of smile he was giving her now since San Francisco. She was a little surprised to realize how much she'd missed it.

"I guess Sherman Clark wouldn't see the beauty of Mexican food, would he?" Jacob asked softly.

Her gaze went from his mouth to his eyes. He was watching her with a wary kind of intensity that forced her to swallow hard. "No, uh, I don't think he would." She licked her suddenly dry lips. "Uh, what other suggestions did you offer him?"

"A show that would involve covering events at the university, interviewing students—"

"He'd hate that. He hates young people."

"So he told me," Jacob said, raising his hand to brush a strand of her hair off her cheek.

She swallowed again, trying to ignore the sensation the nearly imperceptible touch of his finger was causing. "Wh-what else?"

"The art beat."

"The, uh, art beat?" she asked, aware that his fingers were moving slightly on her skin.

He nodded, his eyes studying her mouth. "There are a lot of innovative artists in this town. Marketing shows an upsurge in original-art purchases within the demographics we're trying to attract."

She nodded back. "Good idea. But Sherman's idea of modern art is Norman Rockwell."

The corner of Jacob's mouth quirked. His fingers trailed

down her to chin. "He informed me of that," he said, "just before he said that he quit."

"He quit?"

"Uh-huh," he nodded.

"You didn't fire him?"

He shook his head and looked back into her eyes. "Nope. And I wouldn't have—not without talking to you or Barnabas first."

"Oh." She felt like the wind had been totally knocked out of her sails. It wasn't only that she'd been wrong about him, it was the sensation shooting through her body from the simple touch of his fingertips. Somehow, her entire face had become an erogenous zone.

"And you didn't tell Merriweather that he could have Sinatra?" he asked her softly.

She shook her head. "In fact, I've been making notes ever since lunch on an alternative programming plan for him."

"Such as?"

He took his hand away from her face and she gulped in air and tried to clear her mind.

"Well, I was thinking of sort of a flower-power hour. You know, the feel-good music from the late sixties, early seventies. I've been racking my brains for names of groups that could provide a core playlist."

She could have bitten her tongue as soon as the word was out of her mouth. This was the most civilized they'd been with each other since that morning. She braced herself for an onslaught of new venom for stepping into his area of expertise.

Instead, he surprised her by saying, "Show me."

She searched his face for a moment, looking for a possible ambush, and found none. "All right," she answered.

He followed her into her office and shut the door.

JACOB STOOD BEHIND HER desk chair, looking over her shoulder at the notes she'd made for the new Merriweather

Fair Weather Florist spot. At the moment, he was busy wishing he'd taken the chair opposite her desk. He wouldn't have been able to smell her hair from over there.

He watched her hands as she gestured toward what she'd written on the legal pad. Quick movements. Fluttering fingers. His gut tightened remembering those fingers moving on his flesh. She'd been eager to learn and in their one night together he'd been a more-than-willing tutor. But he'd learned from her, too. He'd learned that his body could quicken at another woman's touch; could feel at home in another woman's body. Not since Michelle had he felt that combination of arousal and homecoming.

The memory made him want Charlie—right here, right now.

He cleared a too-dry throat. "And you think Merriweather might go for this?" he finally asked, simply because he had to do something. Because if he didn't get his mind off the curve of her neck he would go crazy.

"I think there's a good chance. Worth a try, certainly. Fair Weather Florists has been a fixture in this town for generations. If they still have a voice at WEND, it could pave the way for some of our listeners to stick around long enough to see what we're doing."

"Makes sense," he replied as he teased his nose by leaning in a little closer. Citrus. Her hair smelled like lemons and oranges. But he would have known that even if he hadn't moved nearer. His senses remembered everything about her. Every scent, every feel, every taste.

He had to get out of here before he threw himself on his knees and begged her to let him touch her once again.

He straightened. "Well, I've got calls to make. You deal with Merriweather on this."

"You sure?"

At the door he paused. "Yeah. He's used to you. See what you can do."

She gave him a tentative smile that set his loins on fire. He was getting out of here—now. He threw open the door, and had one foot poised to walk out.

"One more thing—"

He gritted his teeth, refusing to turn around to look at her again. "What's that?"

"Sherman—"

"I'll try to smooth it over with him."

"No."

Her unexpected response finally did make him turn around. "No?"

She was shaking her head. "Let him go. His were the worst numbers in the book."

He stared at her for a moment, wondering if he should gloat a little, fire her up again. But he didn't have the stomach for it. He would only be torturing himself in the end.

He nodded. "Right," he said, then finally stepped over the threshold and shut the door behind him.

An hour later he was still wondering how she could do it. How she could be so close to him and not feel anything. How she could have forgotten the time they'd shared in just one short week.

To him it had been one of the most memorable two days of his life. It had changed something inside him. Made him want something for himself again. Something that had nothing at all to do with being Gaby's father.

When Charlotte had slept beside him in the early hours of dawn last Monday, he knew he'd been blessed for the second time in his life. Blessed with finding a woman he loved and wanted. When he'd woken to find her gone, he'd thought not ever seeing her again would be the worst thing that could ever happen to him.

Now he knew he'd been wrong. Being this close to her, working with her, and having her totally ignore what they'd shared was far worse.

CHARLOTTE COASTED THE last block down Washington Avenue and made a neat, soundless turn into her driveway. It wasn't yet five o'clock but she'd left the station early, knowing she would get no more work done that day. She hadn't seen Jacob again since their talk in her office, but she knew he was out there, just down the hall from her. Every time she heard a door shut or the sound of footsteps outside her door, she became still, holding her breath, alternating between hoping it was Jacob coming to see her about something, and hoping whoever it was would pass by her door so she could be alone to wallow in her thoughts of him.

In the last two hours she'd wallowed enough for a barnyard full of piglets. *Enough,* she'd finally declared, and had gathered up some files to work on at home and practically tiptoed down the hallway to avoid running into Jacob again.

Propping her bike against the side of the house, she went around to the front and let herself in through the front screened porch. She could smell apple-and-spice potpourri as soon as she opened the front door. She had small baskets of it in every room. Autumn was her favorite season and she liked bringing the scents of it inside.

She took off her jacket and hung it on an antique coat-tree in the tiny entrance hall then walked into the living room. This was the one room in the downstairs flat that was what she considered completed. The oak floors had been refinished, the natural woodwork had been stripped of old varnish. Both glowed warmly in the late-afternoon sun streaming in the tall narrow side windows that were adorned with simple yellow café curtains. A larger window at the front of the house looked out on the screened-in porch and the odd assortment of antique wicker furniture she'd been collecting since she was a little girl.

The overstuffed, French country sofa was covered in a blue and yellow plaid, the throw pillows tossed in the corner done in the same blue-and-yellow floral pattern as the wing chair that sat at right angles to the sofa. The coffee table was an old oak kitchen table that she'd found at a rummage sale. She'd cut it down and refinished it, liking the fact that it was big enough to hold books and magazines without looking cluttered.

The rest of the downstairs flat was still a work-in-progress. But she was in no hurry. She'd redone the upstairs flat first, wanting it to be in good shape before she rented it out.

The soft comfort of the sofa was inviting and she couldn't wait to flop down on it. But before she did that she wanted a pot of tea at her side. Tea after work—one of the habits that she enjoyed the most.

The kitchen was old-fashioned, but pleasant. No cupboards but a long narrow pantry with shelves from floor to ceiling. She'd made a curtain to go around the old-fashioned sink to match the curtains hanging in the window above it and the windows in the small alcove that held another oak table with mismatched chairs.

While the water boiled, she filled a plate with shortbread, selected a tea bag from a canister and set everything on a blue-and-yellow floral tray. Once she'd poured the steaming water into the pot she carried it into the living room.

"Heaven," she breathed, sinking into the sofa and curling her legs under her. She had never really thought that she would be able to make a sanctuary for herself that would equal Barnabas's house in Maple Bluff. But she had. This was home to her now. She smiled to herself as she heard running footsteps overhead, heard someone shout, then the faint ringing of a phone.

The homey sounds of the three girls who lived upstairs only added to her feeling of security and belonging.

The place was *hers*. And it meant a lot.

She was just pouring the steeped tea into a flowered cup when she heard a honking coming from the driveway.

"Oh, no," she moaned to herself. With the amount of

noise the engine was making, it could only be cousin Melinda arriving for a visit. And wherever cousin Melinda went, her three children followed.

Giving her tea one last, longing look, she put the cup back on the tray and got up, hoping to head the kids off at the porch, where they would do much less damage.

She heard them before she saw them. By the time she reached the porch, the threesome was pounding up the steps and arguing about who was going to open the door.

"Come on, children. Make up your minds or Mommy will simply open it herself," Melinda said calmly.

Melinda did everything calmly. It was a mystery to Charlotte how she accomplished that with the brood she was raising all by herself.

Amy finally yelled the loudest, so she got the honors, swinging the door open with such force that it banged against the side of the house. Hard to believe that a three-foot-tall golden-haired "angel" could make that much noise.

"Aunt Charlie," the little girl yelled, swooping toward Charlotte with her arms outstretched.

"Hi, angel. You giving your brothers orders again?"

"She sure is," growled Matt, who was seven and didn't like the idea of being bossed around by a five-year-old. "Bossy baby," he snarled—well, as much as a little boy with freckles and hair sticking up all over his head could snarl. Matt had been blessed with the same strawberry hair and freckles as his mother.

"Am not!" Amy defended herself, making a comical picture with her fanny stuck out, her little fists on her hips and her lower lip protruding a good half-inch.

"Kids! Don't make me sorry I brought you over here," Melinda said calmly.

Sam was the last to enter, dawdling on the steps in that distracted way he had. He was darker than the other two, in coloring and spirit. At six, a real middle child—the most artistic, the most introverted.

Amy and Matt more than made up for him. They swarmed over the screened porch, picking up the pumpkins Charlotte had scattered artfully among the furniture, plopping them down into inappropriate spaces, and then examining every apple in the bushel for the biggest and brightest.

To Charlotte they seemed to multiply before her very eyes. Creating much more noise and disorder than any three children possibly could.

"Sit down, Melinda," Charlotte told her. "You look exhausted."

"Thanks," she said, sinking into a wicker rocker.

"I was just having some tea—"

"I'd love some. Absolutely love some."

"I'll help!" Amy yelled, scampering into the kitchen alongside Charlotte.

With Amy's brand of help, it took a little longer to pour juice for the kids, find another cup and add chocolate-chip cookies to the plate of shortbread. But soon they were all back on the porch, the kids content for the moment with their snack, and Charlotte and Melinda sipping fragrant tea and nibbling shortbread.

"You make the best shortbread," Melinda said around a mouthful. "Mine never turns out like this."

"Probably because of your helpers," Charlotte said dryly.

Melinda laughed. "Well, that's probably so. Too many cooks…"

With no makeup on her freckled face and her long red hair tied into a ponytail, Melinda looked barely old enough to be a student at the university, let alone the thirty years of age she was. But Melinda had never wanted to go to college. She'd been an indifferent student. Having met her husband, Tony, when they were in high school, she'd known what she wanted all along—to be Tony's wife and the mother of his children.

She'd gotten what she wanted, waiting until Tony had finished his four years in the service to start a family. But fate—the same fickle fate that had brought them together in the first place—had dealt them a cruel blow. Tony, who had run his own contracting firm, had been killed in a freak accident on the job when Melinda was pregnant with Amy. Besides the huge empty space in his family's lives, he'd left debts from his fledgling business and a wife with almost no work skills.

"I got a call from your new program director this afternoon," Melinda was saying.

Charlotte swallowed her tea and set the cup down before asking, "And?"

Melinda made a face. "And he's not very pleased with me."

"What did he say?" she asked her cousin carefully.

"You mean after he told me it was about time I started coming in to work every day?"

"Of all the nerve," Charlotte almost growled.

Melinda laughed. "Well, the man has a point, Charlotte. I don't do much to earn my salary."

"But you've got three kids to raise!"

"So do a lot of women."

Charlotte could feel her blood boiling hotter than the tea. Jacob had left her office on a positive note that afternoon, which was one of the reasons Charlotte had decided to leave early, get out while the going was good. But it seemed that J.J. Tanner's tentacles were going to reach her wherever she tried to hide.

"What else did he say?" she asked through a tight jaw.

"He wants me to come in for a meeting tomorrow."

Melinda studied her for a moment, her green eyes scrutinizing Charlotte uncomfortably. "I must say," she finally said, "I'm looking forward to meeting the man."

"Why on earth?"

"To find out what it is about him that gets you in such a state."

Charlotte picked up her teacup again and sipped, turning her attention to the children who were busy rolling apples all over the porch.

"No comment?" Melinda prodded.

"The man has an ego the size of California, for starters," Charlotte said, her voice sounding testy even to her own ears.

"And looks to go with it, I hear."

"You've been talking to Carrie."

"Uh-huh. She told me about the clothes, too."

"Before or after the fact?"

Melinda laughed. "After. But I would have helped her pick them out if she'd told me before."

"Traitor," Charlotte snapped.

"Oh, she meant well, Charlotte. She was hoping you'd get a new outlook along with the new clothes. Maybe have a holiday fling."

Charlotte choked on a crumb of shortbread and had to take a big swallow of tea.

"Raise your hands like this, Aunt Charlie," Amy said, demonstrating.

"Want me to hit you on the back?" offered Matt.

"No—I'll be fine," Charlotte managed to answer.

When she felt fully recovered, she looked at Melinda. The expression on her cousin's face was speculative as she studied her.

"What?" Charlotte asked.

"Hmm, I was just wondering if maybe Carrie's plan hadn't worked, after all."

Chapter Nine

"What time is Melinda's meeting with Tanner?" Charlotte asked Carrie the next morning.

Carrie tapped a finger on her appointment book. "Nine this morning."

"Figures. He wouldn't take into consideration that she has three kids to get going in the morning. What a jerk. Just when I was starting to—"

She caught herself before she could finish the sentence. Because she'd been about to say she was just starting to see glimmers of the man who'd stolen her heart in San Francisco. And saying that to Carrie wouldn't do at all. It would cause questions, questions that would lead to more questions. Before she knew it, the whole San Francisco episode would be invading her real life. It was bad enough that the rogue was turning her radio station upside down. She wasn't about to let him turn her life upside down, too.

And it wasn't only that Charlotte hated upheaval and distrusted change. Since she'd bought the duplex, she had settled into a life she liked. To let the San Francisco Jacob into her Madison life was to let hopes and dreams in again. And anyone could see just by looking at him, whether he was Jacob or J.J., the man wasn't the type to stay in one place long enough to make those kinds of dreams come true.

"I've got some calls to make," she said as she started down the hall to her office. "Then I think I'm going to insist on sitting in on the meeting between Melinda and Tanner."

"Wait a minute, Charlotte. There's someone—"

"Not now, Carrie. I'll check with you in a few minutes."

As she opened the door to her office the peaceful strains of Beethoven washed over her. The concerto had been one of her favorites as a child. Closing the door, she shut her eyes and leaned against it, remembering herself as a little girl, sitting at her grandfather's desk in this very office, letting the music take her away even then.

She opened her eyes and gave a start.

There was a little girl sitting at her desk. The desk that used to belong to her grandfather. Charlotte blinked, thinking that she'd conjured up the image from her memory. But when she opened her eyes again, the child was still there.

"Hi!" the little girl said brightly.

So it wasn't an apparition after all.

"Hello," Charlotte said, coming farther into the room.

"This music is pretty," she said.

"Very," Charlotte agreed.

The little girl smiled, showing dimples on either side of her small, full mouth. Her dark hair was cut short and shaggy, like a pixie's. Her eyes were large and dark, her complexion rosy.

Charlotte smiled. "Do we have an appointment?"

The child's hand flew to her mouth and she giggled. "No! Is this your office?"

"Yes, it is."

The little girl jumped off the chair to her feet and skipped out from behind the desk. She was wearing jeans and a hooded sweatshirt and what looked like brand-new sneakers.

"I didn't touch anything," she said with a seriousness that came and went suddenly.

Charlotte looked around. "No, I can see that you didn't."

"Daddy told me to stay out of trouble so I didn't touch a thing!"

"Good for you. Where is your daddy?"

The girl shrugged. "I got tired of waiting for him."

"So you decided to borrow my office?"

She giggled again. When she did, her face lit up brightly and quickly. "Sort of." With a look of determined concentration, the little girl scanned the room. "What do you do here?" she asked.

"I run the radio station."

She nodded, then began to study Charlotte with an almost-comical gravity.

"What's your name?" she finally asked.

"I'm Charlotte. And who are you?"

"I'm Gaby," she said. "It's short for Gabriella. Do you have a short name for Charlotte?"

"Well, some people call me Charlie."

"Oh, I like that. Charlie." The little girl tried it out, then giggled again. "Can I call you that?"

"Yes, I suppose you can."

Who was this enchanting child? When she'd first seen her at the desk she'd thought she was a ghost—perhaps even the ghost of herself haunting the place because of the upheaval that was going on all over the station. But this little girl, except for a possible interest in classical music, wasn't anything like Charlotte as a child.

Charlotte had been far too shy to have carried on a conversation anything like this one with a complete stranger.

"Are you here with your daddy?" Charlotte asked.

Gaby shook her head. "Nope. My Grandma. She takes care of me. I think we're here to get a playmate for me."

"Really?" Charlotte doubted that. "Where is your grandmother now?"

Gaby shrugged again.

"Maybe we should find her?"

"Okay."

Without hesitation, Gaby took hold of Charlotte's hand. For some reason, the childish gesture of immediate trust and acceptance got to her. She felt a lump rise in her throat. It was crazy, but there was something so sweet about the feel of the little girl's hand in her own.

"I have school this afternoon," Gaby said.

"You must be in kindergarten, then," Charlotte said.

"Right! I'm almost six!"

Six. The age Charlotte had been when her small, shaky world really started to fall apart. It was the age she'd been when her parents had stopped taking her on most of their trips, when she'd started spending more and more time with Barnabas.

"Okay, Gaby who is almost six. Let's see if we can track down your grandmother."

Gaby covered her mouth and giggled again.

Charlotte opened the door and led her out into the hall-way. As soon as they came within sight of the reception desk, Gaby yelled, "There she is! See? She isn't lost!"

The woman who'd been talking to Carrie turned around.

"Gaby! Where have you been?"

"In Charlie's office. We had a meeting!" She giggled.

"A meeting, is it?"

"Yes!" Gaby yelled, suddenly seeming to be in motion everywhere at once. She was behind the desk, under the desk, in front of the desk, her big dark eyes taking in everything. "Charlie runs the radio station," she stated when she'd had enough of exploring the reception area. "Can I use this phone?" she suddenly asked.

"And who would you be calling?" her grandmother wanted to know.

"I'll have Daddy paged."

"Oh, no, you won't."

The child's grandmother grabbed her and swung her

away from the phone, making her squeal. "Your father has work to do."

Gaby stuck her lower lip out. "Well, then where is the little girl I can play with?"

"She'll be here soon. Let's go outside and wait for them. You can run off some of that energy."

Without saying goodbye, Gaby ran to the elevator and pushed the button.

"That child is gonna run me ragged."

"You look like you can handle it," Charlotte said. And the woman really did. She was short, trim in a pair of jeans and a wool blazer, with salt-and-pepper hair cut much like Gaby's. Charlotte figured the woman was somewhere in her mid-fifties.

"Thank God for those aerobics classes," the woman said.

"Elevator's here, Grandma!"

"I'd better go or she'll leave without me."

Charlotte laughed as she watched the woman slip into the elevator just as the doors were starting to close. She was just about to ask Carrie who they were when she heard a door open down the hall.

She turned to see PowerCord coming out of Jacob's office. Good, she thought, Tanner was free. She had a few choice words to say to him, starting with the orders he'd given Melinda about spending more time at the office.

"Morning, sweetheart," PowerCord drawled.

"Huh!" she retorted, breezing past him and thrusting Jacob's door open without knocking.

JACOB LOOKED UP FROM the paper he'd been studying on his desk.

Man, she was a sight this morning. Her face was flushed, her dark hair a little windblown. He'd heard she rode her bike to work, which would account for the flushing and the hair. And it also would account for those firm muscular legs he remembered. When she'd wrapped them around him in San Francisco, he'd wondered—

"You're out of line, Tanner," she accused.

Jacob started. Had she been reading his mind? If so, then she also knew what his thoughts were doing to his body at that very moment.

He pushed his chair back and stood, skirting the desk and walking toward her. "I don't think so," he said. It was about time that someone made her remember that she'd been a very willing partner in San Francisco. It was about time that he touched her again.

Looking a little nervous, she stepped back a pace. "Well, I do."

"Maybe I like getting out of line," he said, taking back that one pace she'd just stolen. "Maybe you do, too."

That seemed to startle her. "We—we've always had an understanding with Melinda."

He furrowed his brow. "Melinda?"

"Yes. Her children need her. Insisting that she come into the office more often is both overstepping your position here and being insensitive to the needs of her and her children."

So this was about Melinda. She'd worked herself up into a fine head of steam over the situation. He'd managed to rile her that morning without even trying.

He shoved his hands into his pockets where they would be safe. "Maybe you haven't taken some of Melinda's needs into consideration."

"What are you talking about?"

He shrugged. "Just that you might not know what's best for her."

"She's my cousin! You haven't even met her."

"Which is why I might be able to see the situation more clearly than you do."

She folded her arms in front of her. "And just what do you think the situation is?"

"She has three children, two of them in school all day. She's a young woman who should get out in the world a little. She's got an opportunity to work with some of the best in the business—"

"Oh, right. You and PowerCord, I suppose?"

"Yes, me and PowerCord. She can learn a lot. Besides, WEND needs a hands-on sales manager."

"And what about Amy? She's only in afternoon kindergarten. What should she do with her? Bring her to work mornings and hang her on a hook?"

Jacob laughed.

"Oh, you would think that was funny! A rogue like you with no ties wouldn't know the first thing about what it means to be a parent. Or to lose a partner like Melinda has. Her life is hard enough and now you want to make it even more complicated by insisting—"

Jacob felt his jaw tighten and his heart break a little. "Look, lady, you don't know a damn thing about me."

"I know you're insensitive. That you can't imagine what it would be like to be a single parent after having loved someone so much that—"

Jacob couldn't let her finish. "You know nothing, lady, nothing at all about me. Except—" he said, putting his hands on her waist and jerking her close until she was almost touching his chest. "Except…what we shared in San Francisco."

His gaze was riveted on her eyes but he heard her soft gasp.

"That was San Francisco," she said in a voice barely above a whisper.

He was pushing her, and he knew it. But he was hurting, and he was wanting. Being close to her like this for the first time since that night he'd become her first lover, his body more than stirred. It ached. He thought he saw the same ache in her eyes. "And this is Madison," he murmured. "And I still want you. And you hate that you still want me, too."

"Don't be absurd," she said haughtily.

She tried to pull away but he held tight. He knew his hands were hard on her waist but he didn't care. He wanted her mouth under his again.

"Charlie," he said, his voice sounding thick and needy. But he couldn't hide it anymore.

"Don't," she whispered. "Jacob, don't."

He shook his head almost imperceptibly and then he brought his mouth down on hers.

He didn't want it to be gentle and it wasn't. He'd lost sleep last night over her and he wanted to pay her back for the tossing and turning he'd done in his brand-new, too-empty bed. But even more, she tasted so good, so right. And he couldn't get enough. Not with his lips, not with his tongue, not with his teeth.

He felt her fingers curl into his shirt, felt her mouth become slack, pliant under his, and then he just lost himself in the kiss, the way he wanted to lose himself in her body.

Behind them, the door to his office opened.

"Oh, my goodness!" he heard the startled voice of a woman say, followed by a flurry of commotion in the hallway.

"Girls, wait outside for a minute," the voice said again.

This time Charlie heard it, too. She pushed him away from her and moved quickly to the window. Her back was rigid, her shoulders shaking slightly with her labored breathing. Jacob was having a little trouble catching his breath himself.

"Carrie said to go right in or I wouldn't have—"

"No problem," he said, wiping his mouth on the back of his hand. "You must be Melinda."

The woman had a sweet smile to go with her tangled strawberry hair.

"Yes," she said, "yes, I am. And you must be J.J. Tanner."

"Right. Thanks for coming in on such short notice."

"Well, once your mother called and made her offer, it suddenly got easier."

At the window, Charlie swung around. "His...his mother?"

Jacob tried to stifle a grin. "I do have one, you know, Charlie."

"And a very nice one, too," Melinda added.

"Oh," Charlie said.

"In fact, she's right outside now with the girls. They wanted to come in and say goodbye. But when I saw—"

"The girls?" Charlie croaked.

"I didn't have time to call you this morning, Charlotte, but J.J. called back last night and when I found out his daughter is in Amy's class and that his mother would be happy to sit a few mornings a week, well," Melinda said, with a girlish laugh, "I could suddenly see the benefits of coming in to work more often."

"His daughter?" Charlie asked nonplused.

"She said you've already met, Charlotte," Melinda replied.

"We—we have?"

"Yes." Melinda laughed again. "Claimed she had a meeting with you in your office this morning."

She closed her eyes briefly before asking Jacob. "Gaby is your daughter?"

"Yes."

"And her mother?"

"Died when Gaby was a baby. Making me a single parent who knows about the loss of a partner."

With that, he walked to the door, opened it, and let the two little girls and his mother inside.

"No calls," Charlotte hurriedly told Carrie as she practically ran down the hall to her own office.

Although, she thought as she closed the door and collapsed against it, *slink* would be a better word for how she should be moving. Slinking like a snake. Slithering right down the hallway to the hole where she belonged.

She groaned. "Of all the sanctimonious," she moaned. Because that was what she had been. Sanctimonious and self-righteous and insensitive. And just plain wrong.

Jacob Tanner knew exactly what it was like to be a single parent who had lost a partner he'd loved: because that was what he was.

And now she owed him an apology.

Never mind that he was still arrogant, had still overstepped his bounds—she still wished she'd never ever uttered those words to him.

Because not only was he aware of what Melinda had gone through, he'd also been sensitive enough to find her a baby-sitter so she could come in to work more often.

And the more Charlotte thought about it, the more she could see that he had a point about Melinda's needs. She not only needed to get out into the adult world occasionally, she also needed to be able to develop skills to earn a good enough living to keep shouldering the increasing expenses of raising three children on her own.

Why hadn't Charlotte realized that? Why hadn't Charlotte done anything about it? She knew Melinda had refused financial help from Barnabas. But Charlotte could have found a sitter and helped out with that. It could have been an expense of the station. Lots of companies supplied day care for their employees.

Not that WEND could afford an expense like that now. After all, that was why Jacob was here in the first place. As much as Charlotte hated the idea, WEND needed him. And she was going to have to learn to work with him.

And the only way she thought she was going to be able

to do that was by avoiding him as much as possible. But first, she owed him an apology.

She started for the door. Then stopped.

No. Not in person. She couldn't possibly face him in person again so soon. Not after that kiss.

Damn it! Why did he have to go invading her life again? He was supposed to remain a memory, a Prince Charming who had disappeared after the ball was over. He wasn't supposed to turn into someone's father, someone's son.

She went to her desk, sank into her chair and stared at the phone. In fact, she sat motionless, staring at it for so long that when it rang she almost jumped out of the chair.

"Hello?" she said after finally coming to life on the fourth ring.

"Hi."

She squeezed her eyes shut and swallowed. Oh, Lord, it was him.

"I'm sorry," she said.

"I'm sorry," he said.

"What?" they both said at the same time.

"What do you have to be sorry about?" she croaked.

"I shouldn't have sprung it on you like that. It was pretty crude and I apologize."

She didn't know what to say.

"Charlie? Still there?"

"Ye-yes. I'm—here."

"Then do you forgive me?"

His voice sounded too much like the voice she'd heard in her ear in the aquarium in Golden Gate Park. Tempting, wanting. Or maybe it was just that her eyes were closed as they had been then.

She opened them.

"I'm the one who should be apologizing. Jacob, I had no idea."

"Of course you didn't, Charlie." His voice was kind—

kinder than she deserved. "How could you know? It would have been against the rules to tell you."

Those damn rules, she thought. They'd done nothing but backfire on her. And now here he was being nice to her when he ought to be angry. Couldn't he do anything right?

"I looked for you."

She looked at the receiver. "What?"

"I went to the airport that morning, looking for you."

"You...you did?"

"Yes. I didn't want you to go, not until I knew how to find you again."

"But we agreed—"

"I know we did. But we were wrong."

"Wr-wrong?"

"Last week was hell, Charlie. I couldn't sleep. I wandered the streets hoping for a glimpse of you—somewhere."

"Jacob, I don't think—"

"Good. Keep it that way. Don't think. Just tell me to come down the hall to your office so I can have you back in my arms where I want you."

She suddenly couldn't breathe. He was just down the hall. Her irresistible-rogue lover. The man she'd been shameless with. The man she was never supposed to see again.

Phone still in her hand, she stood abruptly. "No," she said aloud.

"No? Come on, Charlie."

His voice was caressing, not quite begging but certainly getting there. And she wanted to say yes. *Yes. Come to my office. I'll lock the door. You can take me in your arms again, drag me to the floor. Make love to me again. Anything. Anything.*

But she couldn't say yes. She couldn't because this wasn't Jacob, her rogue lover from San Francisco. This was

J.J. Tanner, the new program director who had come to turn her world upside down.

And he was doing it. Oh, he was doing it, all right.

"We're not in San Francisco anymore, Jacob," she said, forcing her voice to remain steady. "We're in Madison and we're work colleagues. Anything else would be inappropriate at this time."

"Inappropriate," he repeated without inflection.

"Ye-yes."

"At this time."

"Right."

There was a slight hesitation on the line, then: "You mean like that moan I heard coming from your throat when I kissed you in my office this morning was inappropriate?"

She swallowed hard and prayed to the ceiling for a voice. "Right," she croaked. She quickly cleared her throat. "I'm glad you agree that it was."

"No, actually, *boss*,—" he emphasized the last word coldly "—I thought it was a very appropriate response to a kiss from a woman that I've made love to. A woman who—"

"Jacob, I'm hanging up now."

"No, *boss*. I think I'll be the one hanging up."

And he was. With such force that Charlotte had to rub her ear to stop it from ringing.

And that was that—she thought. Until an hour later, when Melinda poked her head into the office.

"Got a minute?"

"No."

Melinda laughed and came in, shutting the door behind her. "You didn't think you were going to get away with it, did you?"

"Get away with what?" she asked, trying to make her voice sound casual and disinterested while she pretended to read a report.

Melinda grabbed the paper from her hand. "Get away

with kissing J.J Tanner without me asking what is going on?''

"I wasn't kissing J.J. Tanner! He was kissing me. A totally unwelcome kiss. That's all I'm going to say on the subject, Melinda.''

Melinda laughed again. "You sound just like your father.''

"Good, you were always a little afraid of him. Now give me back my report and get out of here so I can get some work done.''

"Yes, sir!'' Melinda saluted smartly, turned on her heel, and marched for the door. Just before she opened it, she turned. "Just one more thing.''

Charlotte sighed. "What?''

"Is he a good kisser?''

Charlotte picked up a paperweight and gestured as though she would throw it right at her cousin. Melinda laughed and scooted out the door.

Chapter Ten

"So how was the first week at your new school?" Jacob asked his daughter on Saturday morning while he buttered her a slice of toast.

Gaby threw her hands up into the air. "Great!"

Jacob laughed. Everything always seemed to be great with Gaby. He had his mother to thank for that. After Michelle had died, she'd moved right in, arranging her hours at the beauty shop where she worked to accommodate Jacob's still-uncertain career in radio.

He'd been doing a night shift then, creeping quietly into the apartment in the early hours of morning, often carrying Gaby to bed from where she'd fallen asleep in her grandmother's lap. When Jacob had started to get better gigs, he'd persuaded his mother to quit her job, giving her the chance to become the full-time "mother" she'd never been able to be when Jacob was a baby. His own father had bowed out of the scene early, and far too thoroughly. Looking at Gaby, Jacob had no idea how anyone who helped to create such a wonderful thing as a child could possibly just walk out of that child's life.

He'd been lucky to have Mary Tanner on his side as a boy, and he was just as lucky to have her on his side now. She'd been lovingly nonjudgmental when he'd buried himself in work after Michelle had died, quietly creating the kind of firm foundation for his daughter that Jacob was incapable of doing in those first, shaky years. And she'd had a gentle way of reminding Jacob, and probably Gaby, too, that Jacob was the father. She would bring Gaby down to whatever studio he was under contract with for lunch, or stop by in the middle of the afternoon to show off a new dress or doll. And three times a day, Gaby, with her grandmother's help in the early years, called him on the phone just to say hello, or to tell him which cartoon she was watching, or whom she'd played with at the park that day. It had been his mother's way of keeping the relationship alive for both Gaby and himself while he healed from his loss.

Gaby was older, Jacob was wiser and they no longer needed Mary in the same way that they once had. But when he'd decided on the job at WEND, there had never been any question that his mother wouldn't come to Madison with them.

For the past year, he'd known that he needed something more in his life. When Barnabas Riesling had invited him to save WEND, he'd welcomed the new challenge. And had felt the move to Madison would be good for all of them.

Jacob cut the toast diagonally the way Gaby liked it and put the small plate in front of her.

"Cin-mon! I wanted cin-mon toast!" she cried, raising her arms into the air again.

Jacob clutched his heart dramatically and fell to one knee beside Gaby's chair.

"I would rather my heart burst out of my chest and drop to the floor before I would displease you, Lady Gabriella," he wailed dramatically.

Gaby's peal of laughter filled the room with the sunshine that was missing from the sky that morning.

"Yuck! I don't want your heart on the floor, Daddy!"

"Neither do I," his mother said, coming in from the

living room. "It would make a mess and then I'd have to clean it up."

"Yeah!" Gaby agreed.

Jacob clutched his heart again and struggled to his knees, his movements that of a wounded man.

"Alas, romance is dead. The ladies in my life think only of mops and brooms."

"And cin-mon toast," Gaby added.

Jacob laughed. "Okay, Pumpkinhead, you win. Cinnamon toast instead of bleeding hearts."

He took the plate back to the cupboard and sprinkled cinnamon sugar from a big glass shaker onto the buttered toast.

"Can I watch cartoons while I eat?" Gaby asked.

"Sure, Pumpkinhead. Don't make a mess," Jacob called after her as she ran from the room.

"You didn't sleep well last night," his mother said when Gaby had gone.

"Nope."

"Worried about the job?" she asked him again as she poured coffee into a large white mug.

"No. Yes. Well, not the job, really."

His mother handed him the mug and laughed. "Is the station manager still giving you trouble?"

"It will work out," he said out loud. But in his head he was thinking *Oh, yeah. All kinds of trouble.* The kind that kept a man tossing and turning at night. The kind that got him out of his bed to roam a still-strange apartment by the light of the moon.

He sipped coffee from his mug and wandered into the living room, looking at the boxes of his belongings. He wasn't even interested in unpacking his books, his music collection. Nice as the apartment was, it didn't feel permanent, didn't feel like a home.

He went back into the kitchen. "I think you should start looking for a house," he said.

His mother looked up from the paper she'd been reading at the kitchen table.

"A house? I thought you said we wouldn't be here that long? You must be liking Madison more than I thought," his mother said from behind him.

"Maybe," he muttered.

He braced his hands on the counter in front of the sink and looked out the second-floor window. Madison was a beautiful little town. One of the highest rated in the country. And the idea of building up a radio station again was exciting. It would take two years, he'd thought, when he'd decided to come.

But that was before Charlie. Now, everything had changed.

He turned from the sink. "Even if we don't stay, we'll just sell the house when we go. I want Gaby to have the security of a home, Ma. I want her to have a yard, maybe a swing set."

His mother took another sip of her coffee before saying, "Everything you didn't have."

He went to her then. Hunkered down beside her chair and took her hand. "Ma, you gave me everything I ever needed. And you did it alone. I'm grateful I don't have to. If it weren't for you..." He let his words trail off. It had all been said before.

"Let's get a house, Ma. I want to make a home here."

His mother looked at him with that same tenderness he'd always seen in her eyes. Then she smiled. "Okay. I'll start looking tomorrow."

"What's wrong with today?"

She laughed. "My. You are eager."

Jacob stood. "Maybe a little."

"Well, I've signed Gaby and me up for karate lessons this morning."

"Karate?"

"Yeah!" Gaby said, running back into the room. "We want to be able to protect us, don't we, Grandma?"

Mary nodded emphatically. "That's right."

"And we wanna wear those cool white suits!"

Jacob laughed. "I suppose you're planning on becoming the terror of State Street, striking fear in the hearts of all men."

Gaby giggled. "Well, maybe not all men."

"Oh?"

Gaby turned pink and dipped her head.

"It seems," his mother said when he threw a questioning look her way, "that a certain little girl thinks a little boy named Sam is extra cute."

"Grandma!" Gaby squealed as she took off once again. "Don't tell *him!*"

Jacob laughed. "Melinda's Sam?"

"Right. I never saw her so quiet as she was when she met that boy."

"Crush?"

"Her first. They're so cute together."

His mother rinsed out her cup and left the room, calling for Gaby to find her shoes so they could get going, while Jacob stood in the tiny kitchen of the apartment he didn't want to live in, hoping that Gaby's crush was going to work out better than his was.

DESPITE THE ENDLESS drizzle coming from the gray skies, Jacob didn't feel like being cooped up in the apartment. He'd planned on going into the station that afternoon, but suddenly he didn't feel like waiting. With his mother and Gaby gone, it was too quiet.

He grabbed a denim jacket and put it on over his old black T-shirt, then headed for the door.

He'd forgotten until he reached the street that his mother had the car. The drizzle was light and fine. The steel gray of the sky with its fast-moving puffs of dark cloud fit his restless mood. He decided to walk.

The apartment was close to the university and despite the drizzle the sidewalks were teaming with students, biking, walking, in-line skating. He strolled down State Street, stopping to browse at outdoor stalls set up in front of shops that sold silver jewelry, used CDs and books. Saturday morning in Madison was as good as a street fair, he mused, as he walked on toward the State Capitol building. The parade was even thicker here and some sort of street fair really did seem to be going on.

Ah, he thought after a closer look, this was the farmer's market that surrounded the Capitol every Saturday until November. Hands in his pockets, he walked past a girl dressed in a long black cape, playing a violin. Squirrels chattered and scampered across the sidewalk, nearly running over his feet before chasing each other up huge, vibrantly colored trees on the Capitol lawn. The stalls were a kaleidoscope of goods. Everything from expensive jams and jellies put up by ex-hippies who had become gentlemen farmers to real Wisconsin farm people selling winter squash and bushels of apples from their ancient trucks and vans.

He bought a bag of fresh-roasted peanuts and sank onto one of the stone benches that lined the street. The rain had stopped, the dark, fast clouds overhead breaking up to show blue sky.

He threw peanuts for the greedy squirrels and wondered if he would be here next autumn. Or the next. Why had he told his mother to start looking for a house? True, he wanted it for Gaby, to give her a real home. Was he feeling the need to settle down—finally? After nearly five years of moving around from market to market, station to station? Why on earth now? he wondered. And why on earth this place? But he knew the answer.

Charlie.

Charlie, who pretended that she'd never laid eyes on him before.

Charlie, who made him lose sleep.

Stubborn, uptight, beautiful Charlie.

He tossed the last of the peanuts to two quarreling squirrels and stood.

He started walking, then stopped abruptly, narrowing his gaze toward one of the farmer's stalls. Was that her?

CHARLOTTE HAD A CRAVING for a caramel apple. She usually made her own, but she wasn't in the mood that day. And she'd needed to get out of the house. Try to clear the cobwebs out.

"One caramel apple, please," she told the stall vendor.

"Make that two," said a voice behind her.

She closed her eyes and groaned. But something inside her was refusing to cooperate. Something inside her—that thing that had broken free in San Francisco—was soaring up through her chest, pounding at her throat, and trying to come out of her mouth in a smile.

She had to bite her lip to fight it.

"Two?" the old woman asked.

"No," she said.

"Yes," he said.

Raindrops flew from the woman's plastic rain bonnet as she looked from one to the other of them. "Well, land's sake, decide."

Behind her, Jacob laughed. "Okay," Charlotte said. "Two. And the gentleman will pay for them."

She grabbed her caramel apple and took off down the street. With any luck he wouldn't have the right change—and neither would the woman in the rain bonnet.

Halfway along the block, she slowed down enough to take a bite.

"How do you expect me to catch up with you if you walk so fast?"

"I don't," she said with a full mouth.

"Then how can we spend the morning together?"

"We can't."

He skipped ahead of her, dodging a boy on in-line skates.

"Why can't we?" he asked, walking backward in front of her.

"Because I don't want to," she answered.

"Liar," he said.

The grin on his face when he said the word was almost too much. To keep from laughing—which would be conceding something, wouldn't it?—she took another bite of apple.

"Good, huh?" he asked her, chewing on his own.

"Go away."

"Is that any way to treat your newest employee?"

"We're not at the station now."

"No," he said, halting in front of her. "We aren't."

She started to go around him. He sidestepped in front of her.

"Show me Madison," he said.

"You're looking at it."

"No, I mean, show me where you went on your first date. Where you got your first kiss. Where you used to take your boyfriends parking."

"I didn't do that kind of stuff," she said, brushing past him and walking faster.

"A shame," he called after her. "You're so good at it."

She closed her eyes, hoping for invisibility, hoping that he wasn't going to keep following her.

She paid close attention to the rest of her caramel apple, feeling as if all eyes in the street were on her. They couldn't possibly have heard what Jacob had said, could they? And if they had, would they know what he was talking about?

"Good at it, indeed," she muttered.

"That's what I said," came the voice from behind her. She stopped short and turned around.

"Will you stop following me?" she said, a trifle louder than she'd planned. She looked sharply around to see if anyone had heard her.

"Sure. All you have to do is walk next to me."

"That would be a little too much like walking *with* you."

He grinned. "Exactly. It'll be painless. Before you know it, we'll be spending the day together."

She laughed. She couldn't help it. "That's what I'm afraid of."

He stepped closer to her. "Why afraid?"

She looked up into his dark eyes and the rest of the street disappeared. She was back there, back in San Francisco. Hoping to never see him again. Hoping he would show up again around the next corner.

He raised his hand and brushed back a strand of her hair. How many times had he done that? Enough times for the feel of it to be familiar. And that was a very scary thought, indeed.

She jerked her head back from his touch.

He frowned. "Hey, you really are afraid, aren't you?"

She pushed her chin up. "Of what?"

His dark eyes scrutinized her, making her feel suddenly warm despite the fact that the drizzle had started to turn into rain. "That's what I'd like to know," he said in a voice that was far too soft. Far too caring.

"Oh, nonsense," she scoffed as she backed away from him, nearly stumbling on a crack in the sidewalk.

"Careful. You'll fall," he said.

I already have, she thought. *I already have.* She turned away from that dark gaze and started walking again. As fast as she could without running.

By the time she reached Nick's Candy Store, the rain had started again.

"Well, look what the weather blew in," Nick said when she burst in the door.

"Hi, Nick. I need a chocolate soda—fast."

"Go on to your usual booth. I'll bring it right over."

Charlotte took off her fleece jacket. She'd given in to wearing the blue jeans today, along with her usual Saturday sweater. They'd been just too tempting to pass up on such a chilly, rainy October day.

"There you go, Charlie," Nick said, sliding a tall fountain glass in front of her. "Enjoy."

"Thanks, Nick."

The straw was stuck to the condensation on the side of the glass, as always. She peeled it off, stripped off the paper and plunged it into the foamy head of the soda. The first sip was heaven. By the time she finished it, she would have forgotten all about Prince Charmings who were supposed to get lost after midnight.

The bell over the entrance jingled.

"Well, if it ain't the new man on the block," Nick said.

Charlotte looked up. He was coming in the door, shaking the rain out of his hair. A lot of good drinking a soda was going to do to make her forget him if he was going to follow her right into the shop.

"How's it going, Nick?" he asked. "And where's the beautiful Katherine?"

"It's going," Nick said. "And Katherine's in the back. She'll be out as soon as she knows you're here, I expect."

"Meanwhile, I'll join the second most beautiful woman in Madison."

He snagged a straw from the old-fashioned dispenser on the counter and sauntered toward her booth.

Sliding in next to her, he ripped the paper off his straw and plunged it into the fountain glass next to her own.

"What do you think you're doing?"

"Sharing a Saturday-afternoon soda with my girl," he said. "Midwestern small-town tradition, I hear. According to Nick, a chocolate soda can lead directly to a proposal."

"Well," she muttered, "I don't think he had your sort of indecent proposal in mind."

Jacob laughed. "But you haven't even heard my proposal yet, love. So how do you know it'd be indecent."

She snorted. "It's coming from you, isn't it?"

After taking a long gulp of her soda, he gave her a considering look. "The ice cream isn't the only frigid thing in here. Pity, since I know the kind of heat you're capable of."

"Shh," she hissed, looking toward the front of the shop to see if Nick had heard. Thankfully, he seemed absorbed in polishing chrome at the moment.

"Oh, don't mind Nick," he said.

"And that's another thing. When on earth did you have time to ingratiate yourself with Nick and Katherine? You act like you've known them forever."

"Not everyone in this town is as unfriendly as you are, love."

"Then why don't you go follow some of the friendlier inhabitants around?"

"'Cause I'm right where I want to be," he said, his dark eyes fixed on hers while he lowered his head to the straw. "Start sipping," he said, "or you're not going to get your share."

She glared at him, but when she heard the sound of his straw sucking up her soda, she put her mouth to work.

Their heads were far too close together, but the game had become a challenge and she wasn't giving up. Never mind that she could smell the rain in his hair. Never mind that the scent of his cologne was conjuring up images that had everything to do with indecent proposals. In her mind, giving in to him on the soda would be too much like giving in to him on everything else.

Their eyes locked. The slurping became louder. She watched his mouth sucking on the straw and wondered why she was torturing herself this way. The point she'd been trying to prove was fast becoming lost in the sensation of being so close to him again, in the sound of noises that were far too close to other noises they'd made together.

Still, she didn't want to give in.

He gave one last final slurp, then pulled his mouth away. "I believe you got more than your share, Charlie."

"Of course," she said with an offhandedness she was far from feeling.

"You're one stubborn woman, aren't you?"

"When I have to be."

"Well, you don't have to be."

"Because the station is already changing, you mean?"

"I'm not talking about the station, Charlie."

His voice had gone softer. More intimate.

"The station is all you and I have to talk about."

She made as if to get up, but he put his hand on her arm, holding her there. "No, it isn't, lady. Not by a long shot. We've got San Francisco to talk about—and those silly rules you made up."

"The rules stand."

"Why? I still want you. Every time I see you I want you."

She stared at him, her heart hammering in her chest like it wanted to break free. And if it did, she knew what it would do. It would go right into the irresistible rogue's hand.

"That's crazy," she finally said.

He snorted. "Tell me about it. Crazy is how I'm feeling these days. How I've felt from the moment I woke up that morning to find you gone."

"But we decided—"

"No. *You* decided. I want out of the agreement. I want to take you to bed again."

My God, she thought, how could such simple straight-forward words make the blood in her veins heat with such swiftness? But hadn't he always been straightforward? Elemental? Hadn't that been part of the attraction? Pure lust. Sex with no strings.

She wanted it again, too.

But this was Madison, where she lived. And she was this man's boss, like it or not. There could never be anything pure about it. Any involvement between them now came with built-in strings.

She gathered her jacket. "That can never happen again," she said. Then she slid out of the booth and headed for the door.

Jacob was right behind her. Once outside, he took hold of her shoulders and pressed her to the bricks of the building.

"You know, Charlie, when I found you again, when you pretended that you didn't know me, I was angry enough to turn bitter. It was a struggle not to. Then I remembered that I'm not the bitter type. I'm the type that goes after what I want. And, lady," he said, his finger caressing her chin, "I'm coming after you."

He pressed closer then and she thought for a moment that he might kiss her, right there on Main Street with the horse-drawn hay cart clopping by, advertising rides for a dollar a head. But he didn't. He let his body rest lightly against hers for only a moment, then used his hands to push away from her. And then he was gone, sprinting across the street, leaving her alone in the autumn rain.

Chapter Eleven

He didn't know why he hadn't thought of it before. If he'd succeeded in seducing her once, he could seduce her again.

He sank into his desk chair and buried his hands in his hair. After he'd left her at the candy store, he'd come up to the station. WEND was making the changeover on the air a week from that coming Monday. There was still plenty to do. There were playlists to build for each show, ad spots to produce. And he still needed to fill the early-afternoon slot. The way things looked, he was going to have to take over that slot himself—at least until they could find a dee-jay who would work for what they could afford to pay. He'd done it before, earlier in his career. The program director often did double duty in smaller markets. But he'd hoped to spend more time with Gaby this time around.

"How the hell am I supposed to seduce her when I barely have time to be a father?" he muttered to himself.

"Easy, use the kid as bait."

Jacob jerked his head up to find PowerCord lounging in the doorway.

"Gaby as bait?" he asked.

PowerCord shrugged and came into the office. "Sure, man. Why not? All's fair, right?"

"All but children, friend."

PowerCord slumped into a chair and stretched out his

legs, crossing his booted feet at the ankles. "Hey, might as well put them to use. Hell knows they don't serve any other purpose."

Jacob refused to rise to the bait. The two of them had been over the subject of children, and PowerCord's monumental dislike of them, during more than one late-night session.

"So you think I should just dangle Gaby in front of the lady and reel her in once she latches on?"

"Why not, man? Charlotte Riesling is mother material if there ever was any. Hell, the lady's even got the body for it."

Jacob sat back in his chair and frowned. "Charlotte?"

PowerCord laughed. "Who you trying to kid, man? Charlotte's the one. The tension between you two is strung out like a fishing line caught in a propeller."

Jacob's mouth quirked. "You've been in the Midwest less than two weeks and already you're sounding folksy."

"Laugh, my friend, but something's gotta give. 'Cause if that line snaps, it's gonna cut deep."

Jacob grimaced. "It's that obvious, huh?"

PowerCord nodded. "Yep. It's also obvious that the lady doesn't chomp on the hook easily. Bait it with Gaby, you might have a chance."

Jacob shook his head. "You're unbelievable, you know that? I can't use Gaby like that."

PowerCord shrugged again. "I saw them together the other day. They already like each other."

Well, thought Jacob, that was no surprise. Gaby was a lovable kid. And Melinda had told him that Charlotte was great with her three kids. But to actually set it up? Naw, he couldn't do it.

"Sorry, buddy. Guess I'm just not as ruthless as you are."

The deejay stood, shaking his head sadly. "Gotta use all your resources in the hunt, man."

"Hey, Gaby isn't a resource. She's my daughter."

"You're gettin' soft, man. But then I guess you always were softer 'n me."

Jacob watched PowerCord move to the doorway. When he got to it, he paused and turned around. "I hear Charlotte takes a bike ride every Sunday afternoon through the campus." He grinned wickedly. "Hasn't Gaby been wanting a bike?"

AN HOUR LATER, JACOB stood in the drizzle in front of a bike shop, staring at a black ten-speed. Gaby was too young for it, but it would be perfect for himself. Maybe he could get one of those seats put on the back for her. And a little helmet for her to wear. She would look so cute. Almost irresistible.

"Oh, boy, what are you doing?" he muttered at his reflection in the rain-streaked window.

There was no way he was using his daughter as bait to seduce a woman, he thought angrily as he turned away from the shop and started to walk, telling himself to forget the whole idea.

As he walked bikes kept whizzing past him. He started to count them. By the time he'd gone a block the count was up to fifteen.

It seemed that people in Madison had a near fetish about riding bikes. Even in the rain. Why shouldn't he have one? Besides, Gaby would love it. It would be a great way for them to spend more time together.

And if they ran into Charlie—quite by accident, of course—what would be the harm?

He turned around and started to jog back to the bike shop.

CHARLOTTE HATED TO MISS her Sunday-afternoon bike ride. She stood on her screened porch, sipping coffee, watching the rain splash onto the walk. Big, noisy drops.

She peered at the sky, looking for even a small patch of blue.

In the living room behind her, the phone rang.

Taking her cup of coffee with her, she went to answer it.

"Good morning, my dear," said Barnabas. "Did you go into the station yesterday?"

"Uh, no, I didn't." She'd been going to—had every intention of it—but that was before she'd run into J.J. Tanner at the farmer's market. She squeezed her eyes shut, trying to block out the memory of his mouth around that straw, the memory of his dark eyes watching her while she slurped.

"I intended to, but..." She let the words trail off.

"No matter. I was just wondering if J.J. had shown you the T-shirt samples."

Charlotte frowned. "T-shirts?"

"Yes, my dear. For promotion."

Charlotte groaned. "We're in the T-shirt business now?"

"Well, not exactly, my dear. We won't be selling them, but giving them away. J.J. says it's quite common. Little contests. You know, the fourth caller on the third Beatles song. That kind of thing."

She rolled her eyes toward the ceiling. "Yes, Grandfather, I know."

"And you don't approve."

Barnabas had been wise to make it a statement and not a question. He knew very well she didn't approve of anything about J.J. Tanner.

She sighed. "Barnabas, are we going to be showing up at supermarket openings anytime in the near future?"

"If we need to, Charlotte, we will."

"I was afraid of that."

Barnabas's laugh was smooth, untroubled. "You can be an enormous snob, Granddaughter, dear."

"You raised me."

"Yes, but your first five years, the years the experts say are the most important, were spent with your father and mother. Both of whom far outsnob me."

She could hear the smile in his voice as he said it.

"You're enjoying all this, aren't you?"

"Of course, I am. What is the alternative, my dear? Close WEND for good? Sell to some network that will throw canned music out into the air? Change is inevitable, my dear."

"Well, I don't like it."

"You never have." Barnabas sighed. "Which is a pity since change can be very life affirming and exciting."

"Then why did you never change the station before?"

"I didn't need to, my dear. And I still wouldn't if I had the choice. But I don't. The only choice I have about this entire venture is my attitude toward it."

"And you're choosing to enjoy it?"

"Yes. And so should you. Take a look at the T-shirt samples on Monday. I'd like you and J.J. to make the final choice together."

She said goodbye and hung up the phone before she could tell him that she didn't want to do anything at all with J.J. Tanner. Even pick out T-shirts.

She took her coffee cup into the kitchen and poured the now cold coffee into the sink.

Barnabas was right. She was being stubborn and she was only hurting herself. But if WEND had to change why did the man who'd been hired to change it have to turn out to be her rogue holiday lover?

The thought made her want to run. Even if it was only as far as the screened porch again.

She let the door slam behind her, wondering if she should call Melinda and see what she was doing for the day. But the thought of Melinda's children only made her think of Gaby. And Gaby only made her think of—

"Oh, hell," she muttered. "I'm going for that bike ride even if it is raining."

She put on the jeans and a pair of hiking boots, threw a bulky sweater over her turtleneck, flung a small backpack over her shoulder, and wheeled her ten-speed down the porch steps.

By the time she'd pedaled across to State Street, the rain had stopped and her head was feeling a lot clearer. She took State all the way to the University of Wisconsin campus and quickly lost herself in ivy-covered walls and tradition.

On Sunday, the campus was peaceful. Not deserted by any means, but the students and faculty traveled less hurriedly along the walks. The clouds overhead had dispersed enough to allow patches of crisply blue autumn sky to blaze overhead. The trees, laden with rust and gold and orange, dripped from the rain.

She tried not to think of T-shirts or playlists or impossibly irreverent deejays. And most of all, she tried not to think about J.J. Tanner.

And she was doing okay with that. She really was. That is, until he pulled up next to her at a stop sign.

"Marvelous day we're having."

She turned her head to look, mostly because she couldn't believe her ears. But it was him, all right, wearing jeans and a fisherman's-knit sweater that was doing way too good a job of bringing out his tan and his playful dark eyes.

"Are you following me?" she asked.

"Of course not," he said with an angelic look on his face. "How could I possibly know where to find you in the maze of the campus?"

She gave him a skeptical look. "I expect the impossible from you, Tanner."

"Good," he said.

"Good?" she repeated.

"Yep. Then you won't be disappointed."

She opened her mouth to speak, but couldn't think of a thing to say. All she could think of was how his hair was blowing in the wind, and how sexy he looked even straddling a ten-speed.

"Charlie!"

She'd just been about to tell Tanner to stop calling her that when she realized that the high, little-girl voice couldn't possibly have come from him.

"I get to wear a helmet! See?"

She tore her gaze from Jacob's widening grin and looked behind him. Gaby was there, strapped into a child's seat.

"Well, hello, Gaby. That helmet makes you look like a superhero. All you need is a cape."

"Yeah!" the child yelled, raising her small fists into the air. "A cape! Daddy, I want a cape!"

"Okay, Pumpkinhead, maybe for Halloween."

"Yeah!"

Charlotte laughed at the little girl's enthusiasm. Clearly, no one had constantly told her to be quiet the way Charlotte had always been shushed.

"Nice to see you again, Gaby," she said, and started pedaling.

At the next stop sign, they pulled up beside her again.

"Gaby wants to ride with you," Jacob said.

"Oh, I'll bet," she muttered under her breath.

"Can we, Charlie?" Gaby asked.

The little girl had a beatific smile on her face and a hopeful look in her root-beer-colored eyes. To refuse would make her seem a complete ogre.

"Of course, you can. Come on, I'll show you the campus."

For the next half hour she did her best to wear Jacob out. His riding skills weren't bad, but it was obvious he hadn't been on a ten-speed in years. She chose the steepest streets but he kept up with her, the sound of Gaby's laugh-

ter filling the autumn air when they would coast down a
hill and Jacob would put his hands out like he was flying.

Every time they stopped at an intersection, Gaby would
prattle about her new teacher, her new bedroom and, of
course, Sam. Every time she mentioned the boy's name,
she would hide her face behind her pudgy little-girl fingers
and giggle.

Finally Charlotte succeeded in wearing herself out, even
if Jacob wasn't, so she led them down to Lake Mendota
and the terrace the students used to study and picnic and
endlessly discuss whatever students discussed these days.

The three of them sat on the wide concrete steps that
descended to the lake and Charlotte took a small plastic
bag of old bread from her backpack and showed Gaby how
to feed the ducks swimming nearby. Gaby sat between her
legs on the step below her, leaning against her chest. The
little girl's thick dark hair stirred in the breeze and the
sound of her delighted calls rode into the air over the faint
music coming from someone's radio.

"Look, Charlie! There's one with a green head! It's so
pretty."

"Yes, it is. That's the daddy duck," she explained.

After a moment, Gaby asked, "Where's the mommy
duck?"

"That's her right next to him, the one with the brown-
and-white markings."

"Oh." Gaby sounded disappointed. "She isn't as pretty
as the daddy."

"Well, she's pretty, but in a different way. In a special
way."

Gaby squirmed around until she was looking into Charlotte's face. "Why is it special?"

"She's colored that way so she won't be noticed as easily as the daddy duck. That way she can keep her babies
safer."

"Really?" Gaby asked.

"Uh-huh. Other birds are like that, too. It's nature's way of protecting the species."

Gaby scrunched up her nose. "The what?"

Charlotte laughed. "The different kinds of animals, Gaby. See that bird over there?"

"Uh-huh."

"Well..."

"YOU'RE GOOD WITH HER," Jacob said when Gaby's curiosity about how mommy birds protect their babies was satisfied.

Charlotte watched her skipping up and down the wide steps a few yards down. "She's a great kid," she said. "You've done a good job with her."

"My mother's done a good job with her, you mean."

"You must have had something to do with it," she replied, surprised that she was so sure this must be true. "You get along so well. There's a bond that couldn't exist with neglect."

Jacob placed his elbows on the step behind him and leaned back, watching Gaby skip up the steps and wander around the picnic tables above them, examining students and skateboards and in-line skates. His crisp dark hair ruffled in the breeze off Lake Mendota. His eyes squinted against the sun but his softly molded mouth held a tenderness that she hadn't seen before.

And she had seen him tender. Oh, in San Francisco he'd shown her just how tender he could be.

But this was different. This was a look that only a very lucky child would receive from a parent. Charlotte knew, since she had never been that lucky.

"What happened to Gaby's mother?" she asked.

Jacob turned his head toward her. "Ovarian cancer. It was quick and terrible. Before Gaby turned one, she was gone."

"I'm sorry," she murmured.

He shook his head. "Sometimes it seems like another lifetime. One that I've left behind. That's what I was doing that last week in San Francisco. I was saying goodbye."

She sensed she'd entered even more dangerous territory. This was personal. This was against the rules. But she asked the question anyway. "Saying goodbye to your wife?"

"Her—and the city. We'd gone there on our honeymoon, loved it enough for me to look for work there. It wasn't the same for me after she left. I buried myself in work. Became the success she always told me I'd be. When Barnabas offered me the job here, it seemed like it was time to move on. I packed my mother and Gaby up, sent them here to find an apartment, with the idea that I'd spend that last week visiting the places Michelle and I had loved, saying a final goodbye."

He looked away from her, picking up a stone from the step below him and skipping it across the water. "It didn't work out that way."

His gaze focused on her again, facing away from the sun, and she could see the tenderness in his eyes now, as well as in the way he held his mouth.

She swallowed hard, knowing she should keep quiet, knowing it was safer to back away. But she couldn't. "Go on," she murmured.

"Michelle was no longer there in all the places we'd known together, as I expected her to be. So I went to other places, places that were only mine. And I found you."

She thought her heart would stop at those words. Frozen by them, she was vaguely aware of his hand coming up to brush a strand of hair from her face and tuck it behind her ear. The gesture was familiar. A memory she'd already made with him, despite her reticence.

Who was she trying to kid? She'd already made lots of memories with him.

"And you helped me find another San Francisco. One I knew existed, but I'd neglected for far too long."

He moved closer, his dark eyes focusing on her mouth.

"No," she whispered.

"No what, Charlotte? No, I don't want you? It's too late. I already do."

And then his lips were touching hers in a kiss that was so sweet, so poignant that it couldn't possibly make her blood stir.

But it did. The cool breeze from the lake burned her heated cheeks as his lips stayed on hers, barely moving. His eyes were open, delving deep into her where no man had ever reached. Where no man had tried to reach. She wanted to close her eyes for protection, but somehow couldn't; somehow she'd become paralyzed on the outside from the feelings quaking her insides.

Wasn't it enough that he'd been the first inside her body? Did he have to be the first inside her soul, too?

"Daddy!"

The sound of Gaby's voice brought life to her muscles again and she jerked her head back, away from his kiss—and his eyes.

The little girl was standing two steps above them, her hand covering her mouth, absolute delight in her eyes.

"You were kissing!" she gasped through her fingers.

"No—" Charlotte began.

"Yes, you were, I saw you!" The laughter broke loose from her then. It bubbled up right out of her throat into the October sky.

"Come here, Pumpkinhead, and I'll give you a kiss, too," Jacob said.

"Pumpkins!" she shouted, skipping down the two steps to her father's waiting arms. "Some big kids up there are cutting faces into pumpkins, Daddy. Can I do that? Please? I want a pumpkin, too. Where can we get one?"

"I've got several pumpkins, Gaby," Charlotte said,

grabbing on to the change of subject. "I'd be happy to give you one."

"Really? Now? Can we go get one now?"

"Well, they're at my house—"

"Oh, goody. Then let's go to Charlie's house right now, Daddy. Can we?"

Jacob looked at her, one dark brow raised in question. "Can we?" he echoed his daughter's question.

Charlotte looked from his dark, knowing eyes, to his daughter's dark hopeful ones. What could she do?

"Yes," she said. "Let's go to my house and carve a pumpkin."

"DADDY, YOURS LOOKS scary!"

"Think so, Pumpkinhead?"

Gaby giggled. "You can't call me that anymore."

Jacob drew his head back and feigned surprise. "I can't?"

Gaby shook her head. "Nope. Not with these real pumpkin heads here."

"Oh." Jacob made a show of considering that. "Hmm, maybe you're right. With Halloween so close we don't want to risk someone sticking a candle in your mouth, do we?"

"Oh, Daddy," Gaby said with that exaggerated patience she sometimes showed him when she thought he was being way too silly.

"When do I get to see your pumpkin, melon head?"

The peel of laughter he heard from his daughter's throat was that special one, the one that warmed his heart no matter what else was going on in his life. But right at that moment, his heart was feeling pretty warm already. Warm and cozy.

Charlie's kitchen was big and old-fashioned. Comfortable as a pair of old sneakers—and far more colorful. She'd put pots of autumn-colored chrysanthemums on the deep windowsills and bright yellow-and-white-checked curtains at the windows. A colorful woven rug covered a good part of the worn linoleum floor and there was a white-painted rocking chair with a blue and white cushion in one corner.

But it wasn't only the warmth of Charlie's kitchen that was making him feel this inner contentment. It was watching Charlie and his daughter together that was filling him with peace.

"You can't see our pumpkin till we're done with it. Can he, Charlie?"

"No, he can't," agreed Charlie. She didn't look up at him but he saw her smile. Placidly and beautifully. It made him wonder if she was feeling anything like he was.

"And maybe never!" Gaby added dramatically, pushing out her bottom lip.

"Never?" He did his best to look flabbergasted. "Aw, how come, melon head?"

"'Cause I don't wanna be called melon head!"

Charlie laughed. "Guess she told you, didn't she, Tanner?"

"She did, indeed. Maybe it's not such a good thing after all to let the two of you get together."

Charlie looked up at him then, her eyes dancing, a small smile on her lips. "Oh, I think Gaby can take care of herself without any input from me."

He grinned at her. "I think you're right."

He managed to hold her gaze for a few moments. As he did so, he felt the grin on his face fade. Something else was taking over.

Her hair was tumbled, her skin was free of makeup as were her big brown eyes and her wide, expressive mouth. She had the sleeves of her sweater pushed up and there was pumpkin on her arms and hands.

And she looked so damned beautiful. As he held her gaze her skin flushed, her smile faded as his had, and he knew she must be feeling something of what he felt. She had to be. He couldn't possibly want a woman as much as he wanted her at that moment without her feeling something. Could he?

She cleared her throat and her eyes skittered away from his. "I'll see if I have some candles."

She went to the sink and rinsed her hands, then started rummaging in kitchen drawers.

"Can our pumpkin be a girl pumpkin, Charlie?"

"Sure. Our pumpkin can be anything you want it to be."

Gaby nodded with the certainty that only a child can feel. "Then it's a girl."

She frowned for a moment before her face brightened again. "She needs lipstick," Gaby announced.

Charlie was coming back to the table with the candles. "Lipstick?"

"Yeah! How else will we know she's a girl?"

Charlie laughed. "You're absolutely right. And I just happen to have a very red shade that someone bought for me and I never wear."

"Cool," Gaby said.

"I think it's in my bedroom. I'll go get it. Here," she said to Jacob, handing him the candles. "You take care of these while I'm gone."

Jacob watched her leave the room, wishing he could follow her into her bedroom. Wishing he could lie on her bed and have her come to him, willingly, sweetly.

"She's nice, isn't she, Daddy?" Gaby whispered when they were alone.

"Yes, she is," he replied, as he fit a candle into his pumpkin.

"You like her?"

"Of course, I do."

Gaby nodded. "Do you like kissing her?"

Jacob laughed. "I like it very much."

"I think she does, too."

"And why do you say that, Pumpkinhead?"

Gaby sighed and rolled her eyes dramatically. "Daddy..."

"Oh, sorry. Why do you say that, Gabriella?" he asked as he started to work on Gaby's pumpkin.

"Because she looks at you like the ladies in the shows Grandma watches look at the boys they always kiss."

Jacob's mouth quirked, and the knife stilled in his hand. "You think so?"

Gaby nodded again.

"Hmm," Jacob said. He wanted to say more—hell, he wanted to go down on his knees at his daughter's side and ask for every little detail. How many times had Charlie looked at him like that? When? Where? He wanted to grill Gaby like a high-school freshman would grill a buddy who had passed a love note to him from a girl.

And maybe he would have, but Charlie came back into the room just then.

"Found it," she said, holding up a slim, gold tube.

He sat down on one of the scarred old oak kitchen chairs and drank in the sight of the two of them. Their dark heads were bent together, with twin frowns of concentration on their faces as they painted a mouth on the pumpkin, Charlie taking it all as seriously as his little girl did.

If he didn't already love her, he knew he would have fallen for her at that moment. But he didn't, because he was already there. He'd fallen and it looked like he was staying down.

"There," Charlie said.

"Yeah," Gaby added.

"Can I see it now?" Jacob asked.

"I don't know," Charlie said. "What do you think, Gaby?"

"Hmm..." Gaby pondered for a moment. "Okay."

So Jacob looked at the pumpkin, proclaiming it the prettiest pumpkin he'd ever seen and vowing he just knew that his pumpkin, a boy, was going to fall for theirs as soon as she had a candle in her mouth.

"Yep, she's definitely going to light his fire," Jacob said.

"Oh, Daddy," Gaby groaned.

Charlie laughed. "Why don't you two go put them out on the porch while I clean up this mess."

So he carried his pumpkin and Gaby carried hers out to the screened porch where they placed them side by side on a wicker table.

"I wish Grandma could see them."

"Well, maybe she can. Charlie would probably let you come over and visit the pumpkin couple." *And I could come with you,* he thought, smiling to himself. Perfectly natural. Why, they might have to come visit the pumpkin couple quite regularly. He was liking the idea more and more.

"Can we, Charlie?" Gaby asked.

She was standing in the doorway, a book of matches in her hand.

"Can you what?"

"Can we come visit the pumpkin couple? Bring Grandma to see?"

"Honey, they're your pumpkins. You can take them home with you."

Hell, Jacob thought. There went that plan.

"No," said Gaby.

"No?" Charlie asked.

"No?" Jacob asked, aware that his *no* sounded a lot more hopeful than Charlie's had.

"I think they belong here," Gaby said, gazing at the pumpkins. "This is their home."

"You think so?" Charlie asked.

Gaby nodded solemnly. "We don't have a place where they can sit outside like this and show their lights."

"That's right," Jacob said. "We don't."

Charlie seemed to be avoiding looking at him. She busied herself lighting the candles inside the pumpkins, keeping her head down. Then she stood back to look at them. Gaby went to her then, leaned in close to her side. Charlie's arm went around her shoulders like it was meant to be there.

Jacob wanted to join them. He wanted to know what it would feel like to stand by Charlie's side with his arm around her waist while she held his daughter tucked at her side. He wanted that badly.

But not as badly as he wanted his daughter to have this moment. If he went to her now, Charlie would spook—and the moment would be over.

"I guess you're right," he heard her say. "They do look like they belong here."

"Can I visit them?" Gaby asked.

"Of course, honey. As often as you like."

"Cool," Gaby said, her voice a mere whisper. She was totally absorbed in looking at the pumpkin couple. In the darkening afternoon, the light from their candles wavered over her face, lit up the childlike wonder in her eyes and highlighted her sweet, happy smile.

"Thanks, Charlie," he whispered.

She looked over at him. "You're welcome," she said simply. But there didn't seem to be anything simple about the look in her eyes. They held almost as much wonder in them as Gaby's did. Her breath was coming deeply, he could see it as her breasts moved under her sweater. It made him ache. Ache for her, ache for this. For simple things like carving pumpkins and sitting on porches.

And a quick kiss shared over a child's head.

Slowly, carefully, he moved over to her, lifting his hand to touch her cheek, letting his fingers trail lower to her mouth. It felt so soft, so warm against his hand. He wanted to taste that mouth. He wanted to feel it tremble again

against his own, wanted to feel her sweet moan when she
came alive to him. And he wanted to feel it now.

He started to lower his head.

"Daddy? I'm hungry!"

Chapter Twelve

"What on earth am I doing?" Charlotte muttered to herself.

Well, she *knew* what she was doing. She was standing at the stove in her kitchen making grilled-cheese sandwiches. Not all that unusual.

Unless you took into consideration who she was making them for.

She could hear Gaby's laughter coming from the bathroom where Jacob was supervising her washing up. The lower rumble of his voice came and then more laughter from Gaby. She smiled to herself. He really did seem to be a good father. The bond she'd noticed earlier between father and daughter was both playful and caring. It was something she'd never had with her own father. She hadn't even had it with Barnabas. Neither side of her family was the playful type.

She flipped the sandwiches over on the griddle, then went to the refrigerator to rummage for fruit. She was cutting up apples and pears when they came back into the kitchen.

Gaby immediately ran over to her to display her hands. "See? All clean!"

"They certainly are," she said, wondering how something as simple as inspecting a child's hands before a meal could bring such a lump to her throat.

She turned her attention to the sandwiches, flipping them over. She must be tired. That was it. Tired from all the upheaval going on in her life. Because surely she couldn't feel like crying just because a child had washed her hands.

She flipped the sandwiches onto a cutting board and cut them crosswise.

"What would you like to drink, Gaby? Juice or milk?"

"Juice!"

"Gaby," Jacob warned.

"Oh, okay," Gaby said with barely a frown. "Milk. I can only have juice in between meals."

"Sounds like a good rule to me," Charlotte said. "Sit down and I'll get you your milk."

"Look, Daddy. Charlie cut the sandwiches the way you do—the way I like them."

Jacob took the glass of milk from her hand after she'd poured it and set it at his daughter's place. "Yes, she did, didn't she? She must know a lot about little girls."

"Do you?" Gaby wanted to know.

Jacob pulled out a chair for her and she sat down. He took the one next to her.

"Well, I was one once. Beyond that—" she ended with a shrug.

Gaby nodded. "That must be why you know about carving pumpkins."

"Actually, that was the first time I've ever carved one."

Jacob looked at her. "You're kidding?"

She shook her head. "Barnabas wasn't the jack-o'-lantern type."

"Didn't you have a mommy, either?" Gaby asked around a mouthful of grilled cheese.

"Oh, I did. Still do. But she wasn't around a lot. I lived with my grandfather most of the time."

"How come?" Gaby asked.

So she told them the story of her father and mother. Of

how they traveled a lot and were no longer together. About how she'd finally come to live with Barnabas for good. About how she seldom saw her parents—then or now.

Gaby was silent for a moment, a solemn look on her little face. "I don't think I'd like that," she finally said.

"Well, I wasn't crazy about it, either. But I love my grandfather very much."

"Oh, I love my grandma, too. But I'd miss my daddy if I didn't see him."

They ate in silence for a few minutes, then Gaby asked, "Can I go visit the pumpkin couple now?"

"Finish your milk first," Charlotte automatically said, then immediately shot a look at Jacob. If he resented her overstepping her bounds, he didn't show it. And neither did Gaby. She happily drained the rest of the milk in her glass, then went skipping off.

"I'm sorry," Charlotte said, once they were alone.

Jacob raised his dark brows. "About what?"

"Well, I shouldn't have been the one to tell her to finish her milk."

"Oh—that. Funny, it seemed perfectly natural to me."

From across the table, he held her gaze, until she felt uncomfortable enough to get up and start clearing the table.

"Charlie..."

The dishes she was holding clattered into the sink.

"It wasn't supposed to be this way," she said.

"What way?" he asked her quietly.

"You were supposed to be my rogue holiday lover, my forty-eight-hour Prince Charming—you weren't supposed to turn into someone's daddy. You were never supposed to be that real to me."

She was at the sink, her back to him, but she heard his chair scrape the floor as he pushed himself away from the table.

Now, he'll leave, she thought. *He'll realize the danger-*

ous ground he was walking on and take his daughter and run.

She waited for the sound of the door shutting behind him. It didn't come.

"But I *am* someone's daddy, Charlie," he said, his voice close to her ear. "And I *am* real."

She closed her eyes. "I think you'd better leave."

"No," he whispered, close enough now for her to feel his breath on her cheek. His arms slid around her from behind, pulling her back into him. "I thought I'd never find you again, Charlie." His voice was quietly fierce. "Don't you know yet what that did to me?"

She bit her lower lip and shook her head. "It wasn't supposed to do anything to you. It was supposed to be just for San Francisco—that was all. No questions, no past, no future. Those were the rules."

"Didn't I tell you?" he asked, and she could hear the smile on his lips. "I'm a master at breaking all the rules."

One of his hands moved lower to rest on her belly. Something inside her tightened—painfully, pleasurably. Her breath quickened as the sensation shot lower, tearing through her on its way to becoming a need.

His other hand moved to her breast and just rested there, cupping the fullness. It was a subtle threat to the rest of her senses. Part of her wanted to shake him off, to tell him not to touch her at all. The other part of her wanted to cover his hand and press it against her, begging for more, for harder, for deeper. For everything.

"I still want you, Charlie," he whispered, and the words darted through her breast, tightening her nipple. "I never stopped. Forty-eight hours wasn't enough. Hell, a lifetime might not be."

"Nobody gets a lifetime," she whispered.

"Of course, they do."

She spun around so she could face him, throwing off his

embrace in the process. "Who? My parents made each other miserable—"

"And you were the little girl who was lost in the chaos." He lifted a hand to touch her cheek. "Are you afraid of getting lost again?"

She jerked her head away from his touch. "Lost? I don't know what you're talking about," she said. But she did. She did know. And it startled and frightened her that he should be able to see her so clearly.

"Every marriage isn't miserable, Charlie. Not everyone gets divorced."

"No, some people die instead. Like Melinda's husband. Like your wife."

His eyes narrowed. "Do you honestly think either Melinda or I would have been better off not pledging our love, not believing in forever?"

"Don't you?"

"No," he said, pulling her back into his arms. "Needing and wanting is part of life," he whispered harshly, his eyes not allowing her to look away. "I want you, Charlie. Whether you like it or not, I want you."

Could he be saying these things to her—the man she thought she would never see again?

He kissed her then and it was everything she'd remembered. Everything. The longing rose inside her swiftly, hotly. She pressed her body to his and he answered her need, his hands skimming down her back to her buttocks, pulling her tight against him. If she'd had any doubt at all that he still wanted her, the hardness in his body would have, at that moment, told her the truth.

Their mouths broke apart, only because they needed to draw breath, and then he was kissing her again, his tongue seeking hers, his body moving against hers—an echo of the way he'd made love to her in San Francisco.

"Charlie," he said, the air rushing out of him. "Damn it, Charlie. I can't let you go again—I can't."

"Daddy!"

He might not have wanted to let go of her again, but he did. He jumped nearly halfway across the floor and threw himself into one of the kitchen chairs just as Gaby came running into the room.

"Daddy, Charlie's got *The Wizard of Oz,*" she said, waving the videocassette into the air. "Can we watch it?"

"Yes!" they both said at the same time.

Charlotte moved first. She took the cassette from Gaby. "I'll set it up for you."

"Will you watch it with me?" Gaby asked, following her into the living room. "You and Daddy?"

"Of course," she said, still trying to catch her breath. "It's one of my favorite movies, too."

THUNK!

"Ouch!" Charlotte gasped.

Jacob laughed softly. "Did I mention," he whispered, "that my little girl can be lethal when she's sleeping?"

Gaby had fallen asleep during the movie, her head against her father, her legs curled up. Or they had been curled up. She had obviously decided to stretch out a little, flinging her sneakered feet sharply into Charlotte's thigh.

"I'll get something to cover her with," she whispered, easing out from under Gaby's feet.

When she came back to the living room with an afghan, Jacob had placed Gaby's head on a pillow. He took the afghan from her hands and covered his daughter's sleeping body. Then he bent and kissed her on the cheek, before saying to Charlotte, "Come on."

"What?" she asked him as he started walking toward the hallway from which she had just come.

At the archway, he turned, put his finger out, and beckoned her.

She shook her head adamantly.

He lowered his chin just enough to make his eyes even more compelling and gave that half smile again.

Irresistible.

This time when he beckoned, she went.

When she reached him, he grabbed her hand and pulled her into her bedroom, leaving the door ajar and the light off.

"We can't!" she hissed.

"We can," he said.

"Gaby is—"

"Asleep. She'll be that way for at least a half hour. Which gives us a good twenty minutes to fool around. Not ideal—but at this point I'll take what I can get. Now, haven't we wasted enough time? Come over here and kiss me."

Again, she went. There didn't seem to be any reason to pretend that she didn't want to.

She wrapped her arms around his waist, he wrapped his around her shoulders and then his mouth was buried in her neck, nibbling, while he walked her backward until her back hit the wall.

"Let's get rid of this sweater," he murmured.

She raised her arms and he pulled it over her head.

And then his hands were all over her at once, cupping her breasts, brushing them to life, skimming up to her face again where he cupped it and looked into her eyes.

"I missed you," he said roughly, before bringing his mouth down to hers.

And she couldn't get enough. How did she ever think that she could live her life without this? She'd waited so long to feel this with a man. She'd found it—thought she'd lost it. And now it was here again.

He was here again.

His mouth still devouring hers, his hands started pulling her turtleneck from her jeans. He slipped his fingers underneath and she gasped into his mouth when he touched her bare flesh.

"Gaby..." she whispered.

"Is sleeping. Just let me touch you, okay? I need to touch you."

And, oh, she needed that, too. Needed to be touched, needed to touch him.

Holding his eyes with hers, she slid her hand down to where she could feel the hardness of him behind the zipper of his jeans.

His lips parted in a grimace of pleasure when she pressed her hand against him.

They held each other's gaze while his hand left her breast and skimmed down until he could cup her between her legs.

"Jacob!" she whispered.

His hand moved to the pull of her zipper. Slowly, he lowered it.

And then his hand was touching her bare flesh.

She jerked and started to cry out. Quickly, he covered her mouth with his own, swallowing the sound.

Suddenly she needed to feel his flesh, too. Needed it badly.

His zipper went down easily. And then he was in her hand. Full. Hot. She touched him the way he touched her, stroking gently at first, then harder. And harder still.

Their mouths clung together, muffling the sounds they made, breathing in each other's ecstasy.

They climbed the spiral together, higher and higher, their silent thrusting in total unison, as if they'd never left that hotel room in San Francisco. As if they'd been making love to each other their entire lives. When they finally exploded, it was together, their bodies shaking with the passion of the sounds they couldn't make.

His body held her there against the wall until her breathing stilled.

"Charlie..." he finally said, easing away from her until she supported her own weight again. He brought his hands up and took her face into their embrace. "To think I might never have found you again."

His voice was harsh, yet the tenderness was there in his touch. She searched his features, looking for some kind of truth to grab on to. Looking to see if the urgency in his voice could possibly be echoed in his eyes.

It was there. Raw. Powerful. It both scared her and thrilled her. But it also filled her with questions.

"Jacob..."

He silenced her with his fingers on her lips.

"No more talk tonight," he said. "Just be with me. For now, just be with me."

CHARLOTTE STOOD AT THE WINDOW in her office Monday morning. The sky was an endless blue, completely free of rain clouds. She wished her head was that clear.

Last night had been hell. When she'd dropped Jacob and Gaby off at his apartment earlier that evening, she'd told herself that what had happened between them in her bedroom was a mistake. At two in the morning she was still trying to convince herself of it. Now, with the sun in her eyes and an ache in her head, she told herself that all she wanted was for him to come through her office door and take her into his arms again.

The door burst open, and she turned. He stood in the open doorway, a question on his face. She smiled at him. In a few long strides he was beside her, pulling her to him. "Good morning, love," he said, and then his mouth covered hers. When he'd kissed her thoroughly, he laid his forehead against hers.

"How did you sleep last night?" he asked.

"Terribly," she answered.

He grinned. "Good. Me, too."

She laughed softly. "I kept wondering what was going on—what it meant."

"And did you come up with anything?"

She raised her eyes to his. "Only that I don't think I like rules, after all."

He laughed and kissed her forehead. "Good, then let's break some more of them."

"Let's," she said, laughing for the sheer joy that was bubbling inside her. "What does your day look like?"

"Hectic." He sighed. "Meetings. Phone calls. And we have to make the final decision on those T-shirts."

"Oh, right."

"Maybe we could do that over lunch."

She grinned. "I like that idea."

"Good." He looked at his watch. "Noon? Nick's?"

She nodded.

He gave her one last kiss, quick and hard.

"I'm getting out of here before I get started again," he said.

She laughed and watched him walk to the door. When he got there, he turned and winked at her. "Noon, baby. Be there."

CHARLOTTE STOLE A LOOK at her watch. It was after eleven-thirty. Was this meeting never going to be over?

She leaned over the desk and tried again.

"Agnes, we don't want to lose your sponsorship, you know that, but—"

"Well, I should think not," Agnes Lembeck said, pulling her back even straighter. She was a big woman, tall, rawboned, and handsome in a cropped-hair, no-nonsense way. "After all," she added, "Lembeck's is special, one of the few remaining independent bookstores. We're a vanishing breed."

"I know that, Agnes. And I mourn it, believe me. But J.J. Tanner was hired to keep this station going and if he feels that your show needs revamping, then we have to listen to him."

"But, romance novels? Lembeck's sponsoring a half hour featuring romance novels?"

"There are several authors in the state," Melinda interjected. "J.J. feels that we should start featuring them in interviews when they have new releases. Perhaps intersperse professional book reviews, such as your own," she was quick to add, "with reviews by listeners. The whole thing could be tied in with promotions for the store."

Agnes looked at Melinda, sniffed, then turned back to Charlotte. "Well, I don't carry many romance novels, Charlotte. You know that."

"Then this could be a chance for you to start." Agnes grimaced, so she quickly added, "Think of it as a chance to get new customers into your shop."

She looked skeptical. "What does Barnabas say about all this?"

Lembeck's had had a long relationship with WEND and Agnes had always respected Barnabas's opinion.

"My grandfather trusts J.J. Tanner and has given him full rein for new ideas."

"And you showed this Mr. Tanner the list of books I wanted to review, along with possible guests?"

"Yes, Miss Lembeck," Melinda said. "We did."

Agnes Lembeck stared at her for a moment. "And what did he say?"

Melinda let out a long breath before she answered. "He said it would kill the afternoon."

"Humph," Agnes scoffed. "He did, did he? We'll just see about that. Agnes Lembeck doesn't take to change easily." She stood. "And you can tell your Mr. Tanner I said so."

Without another word, Agnes left the office, shutting the door soundly behind her.

Charlotte sighed and leaned back in her desk chair. So Agnes didn't like change? Well, Charlotte never had, either. But if turning into an Agnes Lembeck would be the outcome of avoiding change in her life, then she was glad she was meeting Jacob for lunch.

"Well, that wasn't exactly one of my finer moments," Melinda said as she slid down in her chair, stretching her legs out and crossing her ankles. "That woman has always scared the heck out of me. Every time I went into her bookstore as a kid, she followed me around like she thought I was going to hide books in my shoes or something."

"You did fine," Charlotte said as she checked her watch. "No one is going to please Agnes Lembeck by telling her her ideas stink. I thought she took it rather well, considering."

"Has J.J. said anything to you about how I'm doing?"

"No, but then why should he?" Charlotte asked as she fished in her purse for the compact Carrie had provided, along with everything else in the suitcase she'd opened in San Francisco. The compact wasn't the only thing getting use. Today she'd worn one of the skirts—a short straight one in a black knit—along with one of her own sweaters and some black tights and hiking boots. It was surprisingly comfortable, even riding her bike to work that morning.

"I don't know—I sometimes feel really inadequate around here."

Using the mirror in the compact, Charlotte started to touch up her eyes. "That's just that thing you have about Agnes."

"Well, maybe. I'll never forget the time she called me a 'poor relation' and said I should be satisfied with a paperback instead of a hardcover." Melinda shook her head and laughed. "But it's more than that, Charlie. I really don't know enough—but for the first time in my life I think I might want to learn."

Charlotte lowered her lipstick to look at her cousin. She had straightened in her chair and was leaning forward, a sparkle in her eye that spoke of an earnest kind of excitement, not the placid look of resignation she'd often seen on her cousin's face over the past few years.

"I think I might look into taking some courses. Maybe work toward my degree."

"Melinda, I think that's great. If that's what you want, do it. I'll help you any way I can."

Melinda shot to her feet. "Great! I may have to take you up on that when it comes to baby-sitting if I have night courses."

"No problem. Just let me know."

"Thanks."

Melinda left the office and Charlotte picked up her lipstick and started to reapply it.

"Got a hot date, sweetheart?"

Charlotte looked up to find PowerCord leaning in the doorway. "No," she said, popping the lipstick and compact back into her purse.

"Uh-huh," he drawled, sauntering over to her desk. "Who you meeting, sweetheart?"

"Well, I am meeting Jacob over at Nick's Candy Store, but it's business."

PowerCord laughed. "Oh, right. After yesterday you expect me to believe that?"

She narrowed her eyes. "Yesterday?"

"Yeah. I hear you two spent the day together. Nice little home scene with the baby bunting."

Charlotte tried to keep the grin from her mouth, but she was secretly a little pleased that Jacob had been discussing her.

"And from that grin trying to twitch its way onto your face, I'd say the day was successful."

Feeling hot color rising in her cheeks, she ducked her head.

PowerCord laughed again. "I knew it would work. I told him so."

Charlotte's head came up again. "Knew what would work?"

"Dangling Gaby in front of you as bait. Works every time."

Chapter Thirteen

"Hi, Charlie," Nick said. "Your fella's waitin' for you at your usual booth."

"My fella, indeed," Charlotte muttered as she strode straight past Nick without so much as a glance.

She ignored the few called hellos that came her way from the lunch regulars and kept going until she got to the first circular booth on the left.

Her booth.

He was sitting in it, with that damn irresistible smile on his face. Well, it was about to be resisted—big time.

He patted the seat next to him. "Sit down, love. You looked frazzled."

"Angry is the word."

"Uh-oh. Meeting with Lembeck not go well?"

"No, it didn't. But that's not the problem."

"Then why don't you come over here—" he patted the seat again "—slide in next to me, and tell me the problem."

His voice was like honey. Thick, warm and sweet. Less than an hour ago, she would have lapped it up. But that was before her little talk with PowerCord Baker.

"You're the problem, Tanner. And sitting next to you would be like entering the lion's den."

She could see by the look on his face that he thought he

could charm his way out of this one. Like he always had. Like he always would.

But not this time.

"I had a little visit from your friend PowerCord this morning."

"Is he causing you trouble? Because if he is—"

"No, he's causing *you* trouble, Tanner. You really shouldn't go running to him with tales of your latest conquests. He can't seem to keep his mouth shut."

His smile had disappeared completely now. "What are you talking about?"

She glanced around to make sure no one was paying any particular attention to her. Then she placed her hands flat on the table, leaned over it, looked him straight in the eye and lowered her voice. "I'm talking about your little plan to use your daughter as bait—dangle Gaby in front of me, get me hooked, then reel me in. It worked, didn't it, Tanner?" she hissed. "It worked in spades."

He groaned and buried his face in his hands for a quick moment. Then he looked at her again. "That's crazy."

"Oh? You deny you had that conversation with Baker on Saturday?"

"No, but—"

"You deny that he suggested you get me hooked on Gaby so you could get your hooks into me?"

"No, but—"

"It's a despicable way to use a child, Tanner."

"Which is why I rejected it."

She straightened and stared down at him for a moment. "Oh, right. And it was merely coincidence that right after that conversation with PowerCord you went out and bought yourself a ten speed. Merely coincidence that the very next morning you just happened to pull up next to me at a stop sign."

He shook his head. "Look, I'm not going to say I didn't hope to run into you, but—"

Nick came over then. "Here's the chocolate soda you ordered, J.J. Two straws."

"And right on time, too," he said. "The lady seems to need a little cooling off."

"Oh, you think so, do you?" she said, forgetting to keep her voice down. Forgetting that she hated scenes. "Well, I disagree. I think you're the one who needs cooling off. Anyone who would use a child to...to..." She couldn't even say it aloud. "Well, anyone who'll do that definitely needs cooling-off."

She picked up the soda and dumped it in his lap. Then she walked out of the candy store.

She should have known he would come after her—she was barely out the door when he grabbed her from behind and swung her around.

He should have looked ridiculous with chocolate soda dripping down his khakis. He didn't. He still managed to look gorgeous. And angry. He definitely looked angry.

"Why believe him over me?" he demanded.

"Because it all makes sense. You were just looking for another J.J. groupie—and you didn't care how you got her."

He screwed up his face. "Another J.J. groupie? What are you talking about?"

"When I went to WEXL in San Francisco, they thought I was one of your women, begging to find out where you'd gone. They couldn't understand what a man like you was going to do with his nights in a small Midwestern burg like this. Well, I guess they didn't count on your ingenuity when it comes to using a child."

"Charlie, come on. You know radio—any deejay who doesn't look like Quasimodo gets a reputation. It helps the numbers in the book, so maybe the station lets the reputation stand, even fuels the fire a little bit. Before you know it, people who should know better are believing what they hear. Women fall in love with the voice on the radio, Charlie. And I was a voice on the radio for a lot of years.''

''Well, from what I've seen, that voice works pretty well when used directly in the female ear, too.''

His mouth quirked. ''But, you're a special case, love.''

He raised his hand to touch her hair, probably to push a strand behind her ear in that way he had before. She pulled back. ''Don't you dare start working that charm on me now!''

''All right, let's go back to the studio and discuss this,'' he said.

''No!''

''So, you're going to be stubborn, as usual. Okay, we'll finish this right here.''

''It's already finished.''

She started to turn around. He wouldn't let her. He grabbed a hold of her hand.

''What do you think you're doing?''

''I'm getting you to listen to me.''

She was aware that people were starting to look at them. So much for being the Charlotte Riesling who avoided scenes. Dealings with Jacob Tanner seemed to come with scenes built right into them.

''Go ahead, then,'' she said, suddenly eager to get away from the chaos he managed to produce every time she was near him. ''I'm listening. Get it over with so I can get back to work.''

He took a breath. ''I've been with three women since Michelle died. One when I was in New York on business. One when I was in L.A. on business. And you. And you're the only one I ever wanted to be with again. But, as much as I want you, do you really believe I would use Gaby that way? Even to get to you? I bought that bike because everyone in Madison rides a bike. And I thought it'd be a good way for Gaby and me to spend more time together. Sure, I was hoping we'd run into you, but if you think I plotted and planned, then you're wrong."

"But PowerCord said—"

"And why would you believe him instead of me?"

She stared at him, suddenly wondering the same thing herself.

"Want me to tell you why?" he asked reasonably.

She gave a huff of impatience. "I'm sure you're going to."

"Because you're afraid."

She tried for a curled lip, but had no idea if it came off right. "Afraid?" she echoed with disdain. "Afraid of what?"

"Afraid of more abandonment, more rejection. Your life is scattered with it."

His words shook her, but she managed to redirect the feeling and let it fuel her anger. It was that or tears. And she wouldn't cry. Not in front of him. "Don't you dare use your California pop psychology on me!"

He looked down at the sidewalk and back up into her face. "Charlie," he said, far more gently than she deserved, "that's not what I'm doing."

How could he be so reasonable when she felt like her insides were boiling with emotion? It made her resent him even more, made her hurt even more.

How could he have gotten so close, so fast? Close enough to know things about her that she kept hidden, things she held to herself like an invisible shield? And why had she let him? She had been so careful—all her life she had been careful.

"Then what are you doing?" she asked him with a haughty toss of her head.

"I'm only trying to understand why our relationship would—"

She didn't let him finish. "Get one thing straight, Tanner, our relationship is one thing and one thing only. I'm your boss. And that's all I am."

Something flickered in his eyes, something that looked like hurt, but it was gone too quickly for her to know for sure.

At that moment, she didn't want to know for sure. "Charlie..." he began.

She thrust her chin up and dredged her father's haughtiness from some hard place inside her. "Let me go," she said.

And he did. After one long, heartbreaking look, he let go of her hand and she turned and walked away.

But not toward the station. Instead she headed down Main Street the other way. She walked quickly, the crisp wind hitting her face. The lunchtime crowd had thinned, their hustle and bustle replaced by the sound of fallen leaves scattering across the wide sidewalk.

At the end of the block she stopped to wait for the Walk light. The damn thing was taking forever. Impatiently, she looked up and down the street. The nearest car was half a block down. For the first time in her life, Charlotte crossed against the light.

She *walked* when it said Don't Walk.

She'd done a lot of things in the past few weeks that she'd never done before. Her life in Madison had been placid, no-risk. True, crossing against the light when you could see all the way up and down the street for blocks wasn't exactly a huge risk.

But letting J.J. Tanner in was a huge risk. Maybe the biggest of her life.

Halfway down the block, she stopped, and looked through the autumn trees at the Capitol building.

How many times had she stood in this spot, looking up at the solid granite facade? How many times had she counted on it to make her feel like she belonged somewhere, like there was some kind of permanence to life? She didn't know. All she knew was that it didn't seem to be enough anymore.

And maybe it never had been.

She started walking again.

It should never have happened—that brief, frantic episode in her bedroom when reason had fled once more. That madness was supposed to have been left behind in San Francisco. *He* was supposed to have been left behind in San Francisco. It was travesty enough that he should show up in her life again as the program director she wanted to loathe, but then he had to go and get to her again. Use his child—

Her line of thought abruptly tripped, as if she'd caught her toe on a crack in the sidewalk. Okay, she thought. Maybe he hadn't really used Gaby that way. Did that make him right when he'd accused her of grabbing hold of anything to knock them apart again because she was afraid? Afraid of abandonment? Afraid of rejection?

"Boy," she muttered to herself, "does he have your number, or what?"

The only reason she'd been able to finally throw caution to the wind was that she'd been so far from home. The man she'd let into her heart and her body hadn't even had a last name. She'd felt safe—knowing that she would be flying out of his life, knowing that she would never expect anything from him.

And now here he was again, invading her thoughts, her heart. Making her need and want in a way she never had before. That he happened to have a little girl who was plowing her way into that battered heart as well, was the proverbial icing on the cake. Too sweet. Don't touch. But once you got a fingerful you wanted it all.

And everyone knew, you could never have it all.

CHARLOTTE LOOKED AT HER desk calendar. Wednesday. Would this week never end?

She glanced at her watch. It was almost noon. Jacob was down the hall meeting with Macon Merriweather one last time before the transition took place this coming Monday. Once Macon left, Jacob and Melinda would be leaving for a lunch meeting, giving her one hour—maybe two—in which she wouldn't have to worry about running into him in the halls. So far, it had been easy enough to avoid being alone with him. When they did have to meet, it was usually with a third person there—Melinda or one of the deejays. It was better that way, she told herself.

But to traverse the hallways was often perilous. That was the most likely place for her to run into him alone. She'd been practically keeping herself a prisoner in her own office since she'd dumped that soda in his lap on Monday, and she was thoroughly disgusted with herself about that.

She looked at her watch again. Almost home free, she thought. And then the phone rang. She stared at it, wondering if she could just ignore it. On the fifth ring, she snagged up the receiver.

"Charlotte Riesling," she said into the phone.

"It's Melinda again," the voice on the other end of the line said.

"Yes?" she said warily.

"I'm going to try one more time to convince you to join J.J. and me for our lunch meeting."

Charlotte sighed. "Melinda, please—"

"I just don't understand you. WEND means the world to you. If we get this account it will be the biggest WEND has ever had. Both J.J. and I think it's important for you to be there.''

"Look, Melinda, if J.J. could convince Macon Merriweather to sponsor an hour of classic rock, he doesn't need me there to woo a record store that already sells the stuff.''

"It's a statewide chain, Charlotte. And it might go national. We're playing with the big boys now and I'm a beginner. I need you there.''

"No, you don't. Tanner says you're a natural. The two of you can handle it.''

It was Melinda's turn to sigh. "I don't understand you. Just because the man stole a kiss—''

"That's got nothing to do with this—and I'd rather you forgot that that ever happened.''

"All right,'' Melinda said after a moment's hesitation. "It's forgotten. Now come to the meeting.''

"You don't need me. I have total faith in you. Call me tonight and let me know how it went.''

She hung up the phone before Melinda could say anything more.

Not long after that, she heard doors opening and closing, followed by muffled voices passing her office. She waited for ten minutes, then let herself out into the hall. It was time she visited the studio and said a few goodbyes.

She had only intended to stay there a half hour or so, but one thing led to another, and by the time she could pull herself away, the lunch hour was over. She was tempted to poke her head out the studio door and see if the coast was clear but she was afraid of how it would look to anybody watching. Still, she closed the door very slowly behind her, hanging on to that possible escape route for as long as she could.

No one seemed to be in the hall. Quietly, she started down it. Before she left the relative safety of the hallway to cross the more open reception area to reach her end of the hall, she paused and listened. No one seemed to be out there. Just in case—she didn't want to be seen skulking—she walked as normally and as swiftly as possible across the reception area. Not a soul in sight.

When she reached the door to her office, she thrust it open, slipped inside and quickly closed it behind her, listened for a moment, then closed her eyes and turned around to lean her back against it.

"Hiding from someone?"

Her eyes flew open. The damn rogue was lounging back in her desk chair, his feet up on her desk.

"Not anymore," she muttered, pushing away from the door and coming farther into the room. "Aren't you in the wrong office?"

"I'm trying it on for size," he said.

"What's that supposed to mean?"

"You should have been at that meeting today," he said in a far more serious tone.

"You and Melinda could handle it."

"That's not the point."

"Then what is the point?"

"We needed to present a united front."

"That's why I didn't go."

"Skipping the meeting confirmed what everyone has been thinking. Apparently the whole damn town knows you're against me."

"I'm against the change in format," she corrected him.

"Same thing."

She shrugged. "So, what difference does it make? The change is taking place."

"Yes, but your lack of cooperation is making the Temple brothers a little nervous. They're not sure they want to commit to a station that might go down the tubes."

"Why would it go under with the great J.J. Tanner in control?"

"Well, it's like this. We need advertising dollars. And, more specifically, we need Temple Records' advertising dollars."

She stared at him for a moment. "Are you telling me they didn't sign?"

He lowered his chin and fixed her with his dark stare. "That's exactly what I'm telling you."

She squeezed her eyes shut briefly and set her teeth. "All right," she said when she opened her eyes. "I'll take them to dinner—"

He shook his head. "Too late."

"Why too late?"

"The boys are going to New Orleans for Halloween."

"Oh. When do they leave?"

"Not until Friday night."

"Well, then—" She went for the phone.

He placed his hand over hers on the receiver. "They won't talk any more business with us until they get back. Considering the obvious split at the station, they want to think it over."

She slumped against the corner of the desk, suddenly feeling sick. She'd known how important this account was. Behind her, she heard him lower his feet off the desk and push the chair back. The leather creaked as he stood.

He came around in front of her. "You're as stubborn as they come, aren't you? Even when you're bleeding from cutting off that pretty nose to spite your face."

"What are you suggesting?"

"I'm suggesting that you'd better examine your motives because you are about to lose the one thing you've been trying to hold on to."

"I thought that was why you were here, Tanner. To keep that from happening."

"I can't do it alone, Charlie. We can keep going long

enough to launch the new playlists. After that..." He
shrugged and she suddenly felt cold.

"What do you mean, 'After that'?"

"I mean after that we need a big account to guarantee
that other advertisers will come aboard. Otherwise..." He
shrugged again.

"Are you deliberately being obtuse?" she asked him.

He tilted his head and studied her. "You really don't
know, do you? Barnabas has been talking to a network. I
would think you'd be the last one who would want that to
happen to WEND."

She went numb for a moment before she shook off the
feeling. "Barnabas would have told me if things were that
bad."

He shook his head. "You know, for a smart lady, you
can really get screwed up where your heart is concerned.
Of course, things are that bad. Why do you think I'm here
in the first place? This isn't just your loss, you know. The
old man wouldn't be doing this if he didn't have to."

"But he acts like he's accepted it."

"He's resigned to it. He's found a way to make himself
happy over it. But you're so stubborn you won't even help
woo an advertiser that could keep you from losing this
place entirely."

"Oh, and I suppose you're going to tell me that if I'd
been there they would have signed today?"

"It would have helped."

"Even knowing how I feel about what's going on? I'm
not a good liar, Tanner."

He leaned closer to her. "Sure you are. You lie to yourself every time you tell yourself you're not in love with
me."

She stared at him, her heart pounding. He was so close.
If she leaned just slightly forward she would be brushing

his body with her own. Every fiber of her being was screaming for her to move those few inches.

But he was right. She was stubborn.

"You arrogant—"

"Uh-uh," he said as he backed away from her. "Don't lose your temper, love. You might say something you'd regret."

She started advancing on him as he backed toward the door. "You know, I never had a temper until I met you."

"Yeah," he replied. "But you never had a good time, either."

"Out!" she yelled, pointing at the door behind him.

He grinned. "No kiss goodbye?"

"Oh, you just think you're so irresistible, don't you?"

"Yep," he said.

She was frantically looking for something to throw at him when he gave a bark of laughter, blew her a kiss and slipped out the door.

"That man is without a doubt the most egotistical, most infuriating—" she muttered to herself as she stormed around her office. "Who does he think he is?"

She threw herself into her desk chair and threaded her hands into her hair, flinging her head back and staring up at the ceiling. Why, oh, why did he have to be the one to point out to her the damage her stubbornness was causing? Anybody but him! Barnabas. Her mother. Even her father.

But no, it had to be J.J. Tanner who'd finally made her take a look at what she was doing.

She lowered her head. The phone was directly in the path of her gaze. She stared at it. There was only one way she could think of to remedy the situation. And that was to call the Temple brothers and try to smooth things over. Maybe they didn't want to make their decision until after the coming weekend, but trying to push a phone call on them before they went wasn't going to do any more harm than she'd already done.

"YES, AGNES," CHARLOTTE said into the phone. "Yes, I know he can be charming," she agreed out loud, inwardly muttering: *He's a real Prince Charming, all right.* She glanced at her watch. It was Friday afternoon and the Temple brothers' plane was leaving in a few hours. If she couldn't get Agnes Lembeck off the phone soon, she was going to miss her last chance to get in touch with them before they left for New Orleans.

"And, Charlotte," Agnes was saying, "he really does seem to know what he's talking about."

"Of course he does," she said sweetly. "That's why Barnabas hired him."

Charlotte rolled her eyes toward the ceiling and prayed for patience. If she had to go on agreeing with Agnes Lembeck about how wonderful J.J. Tanner was, she was going to scream. Jacob must have pulled his very best plan out of his endless portfolio of charm to win Agnes Lembeck over to this extent. Not only was she sponsoring an hour-long talk show featuring romance novels, she was also considering a live broadcast from Lembeck's Books for sometime in the future.

"Charlotte," Agnes gushed like a schoolgirl, "he's just full of wonderful ideas."

Yeah, thought Charlotte. *He's full of it, that's for sure.*

"And Melinda was so helpful, too. I had no idea she was so bright. Working with a man like J.J. Tanner must be bringing out the best in her."

"Yes, he certainly has a way about him, doesn't he?" Charlotte said, grimacing at Melinda who had just come into her office.

"Oh, got a customer, Charlotte, I'd better go."

Charlotte thankfully said goodbye and hung up the phone.

"If I have to hear one more person gushing about how charming J.J. Tanner is, I'm going to lose it! If he's so charming, why couldn't he get Brian and Richard Temple to sign?"

Melinda sat down in the chair opposite Charlotte's desk. "He really bugs you, doesn't he?"

Charlotte gave her a look. "What do you think?"

Melinda studied her for a moment. "I think he really gets under your skin—and I'm not sure why."

Charlotte gave her a look of incredulity. "Not sure why? The man has turned my life upside down. He's taking WEND away from me."

"Oh, Charlotte, he's not, really. He's merely fixing it so you can still have your beloved WEND."

"Yes, but at what cost? Supermarket openings? Drawings for T-shirts? A retro Donny Osmond hour?"

Melinda laughed. "I've seen the playlist. There is no Donny Osmond."

"Well, thank heavens for that."

"No, thank J.J."

Charlotte made a face. "I'd much rather stick a knife under my thumbnail, thank you."

Melinda laughed and shook her head. "Look, Charlotte, I know this is hard for you. I know you resist change. But it's inevitable. And I would think that you'd be happy to have someone with a reputation in the field like J.J. Tanner has, making the changes."

"Anyone else but him," Charlotte murmured. "Anybody—and the change might not be so hard—or so complicated."

As soon as she'd said the words, she wished she hadn't. She looked up sharply at Melinda to find her cousin watching her with shrewdly speculative eyes.

"Why is it more complicated with him?" Melinda finally asked.

Charlotte got up from behind her desk and paced to the window. The day was gusty. Leaves swirled from the trees and scurried down the street. She wished she could run away with them, right to the Land of Oz with Dorothy.

"Why do you think Carrie filled my suitcase with those clothes?" she asked without turning around.

"It was a whim, I guess," Melinda said. "She thought, and I agree, that you needed a little boost. You were so unhappy about what was happening here."

"Is that all?"

"Well, I guess we both kind of fantasized about you meeting someone. Having a little fling. We thought the clothes might make you feel different enough to take a chance."

Charlotte watched the progress of a young woman wheeling a baby buggy in front of the small church across the street before she spoke. "It worked," she said.

She heard Melinda get up behind her. "What?"

"I had a fling."

"Charlotte! That's wonderful!"

Charlotte shook her head. "No. No, it's not. It was supposed to be a holiday affair. Short. Sweet. No questions asked, no future, no past."

"But that's exactly what we wanted for you!"

"That's how it was *supposed* to be. Unfortunately, it didn't work out that way."

"It didn't?"

"No, it didn't." She took a deep breath. The woman pushing the buggy turned the corner and was soon out of sight. "The man I had the fling with showed up here in Madison."

"He found you? How romantic!"

Charlotte smiled sadly at her own reflection in the window. "And he wasn't even looking," she said almost absently.

"I don't get it. Then how did he—"

Charlotte turned around. "The man was J.J. Tanner."

Melinda stared at her for a moment. "Ho-ly co-ow," she finally said, drawing out the vowels the way one of her children might.

Charlotte thrust her hands into her pockets and started to pace from one end of her office to the other. "Don't you see? He was my rogue holiday lover. My forty-eight-hour Prince Charming. I was never supposed to see him again! He wasn't supposed to turn into someone's father! Let alone of a complete little angel like Gaby. And he certainly wasn't supposed to show up as my new program director!" She glanced at Melinda but kept pacing. "I've got to see him every day! Work with him! And every time I get near him I remember—" She paused, both in words and movement, not knowing how to finish, not knowing how much she wanted to say. "I remember everything," she finally said. *"Everything,"* she repeated, her voice barely above a whisper.

Melinda came to her, placed her hands on Charlotte's upper arms. "Look at me," she said, too softly to be a demand, but Charlotte obeyed it like it was an order. She looked up, straight into her younger cousin's eyes.

"Oh, my God," whispered Melinda. "You're in love with him."

Chapter Fourteen

I am not in love with him, she said to herself once again. Hell, she'd been saying it to herself ever since Melinda left her office an hour ago. But first she had said it to Melinda— several times.

She groaned and looked at the phone. Was Melinda right? Was it all her fault that the Temple brothers hadn't signed yet? Maybe she would try one more time to call them—and then she would leave. It was finally, mercifully, Friday. The transition, WEND's first rock transmission, was taking place on Monday. Anything she still needed to take care of before then, she could do from home.

She glanced at her watch. Maybe she would just turn on the speaker and sit and meditate for a while before the phone call. Maybe it would help.

She stood, walked over to the speaker on the wall and flipped it on.

A Beethoven overture—*Leonore* III. Simple, sensual, relaxing. She went back to her desk and sank into the leather chair that had once belonged to Barnabas. The same chair she'd sat in when she'd first heard the overture so very long ago.

Lord, she was going to miss it.

The music built, then ebbed; drew out, then faded into near nothingness before building and spinning and fading again. She leaned back against the worn, supple leather, closed her eyes, and let the music take her.

By the time the piece came to an end, she felt more peaceful than she had in weeks.

She still had her eyes closed, wondering what would come next, hoping for Debussy. Her eyes flew open on the first note.

It was a piano but it wasn't Debussy.

Charlotte was pretty sure Debussy was never played on a harmonica.

The sounds of simple piano and plaintive harmonica were abruptly joined by a raw voice punishing words into an image.

"'The screen door slams?'" Charlotte repeated to herself. "'Mary's dress waves?'"

By the time the guy was rolling down his window and casing the promised land, guitars and drums nearly drowned out the piano—and Charlotte realized that someone was working from the wrong playlist.

But who? The usual afternoon drive-time deejay had given his last show yesterday. But everyone at WEND knew that the changeover wasn't starting until Monday. Drive time was supposed to be filled in using taped music, promos and reruns of taped earlier shows—a little nostalgia to get everyone into a warm fuzzy mood, Jacob had said. Make them think about loyalty to the station. Give the New WEND a chance.

The promos featuring teasers of songs that were considered classic rock weren't supposed to be used until Sunday. Sunday had always been a big day for WEND, making it the logical day to saturate airtime promoting the New WEND. But Jacob had promised to go easy on the promos, and to use only soft rock lyrics. What she was hearing over the in-house speaker system was anything but soft.

She stormed out of her office and started down the hall.

"What's going on?" she called to Carrie when she passed the reception area.

"I don't know. Barnabas is already on the phone about it," she added, holding up the receiver.

"Tell him I'm on it," she said as she headed toward the studio.

She threw open the door, and there he was, behind the glass, leaning back in the chair in front of the console, headphones on, his head bobbing to the beat of the music.

She didn't bother to knock.

She slammed the door behind her with enough force that he jumped to his feet while at the same time grabbing the headphones and tossing them down. The music abruptly stopped, but she barely noticed.

"What do you think you're doing?" she demanded.

"Just giving our listeners a taste of what they can expect."

"Believe me, Jacob, Sunday will be soon enough for them to find out what their ears are going to be assaulted with unless they change the dial."

"Well, I'm betting a lot of them will have the sense to learn something new and stay."

"Learn something new?" she scoffed. "You mean like that wailing and beating—"

He held up his hands. "Ho—now wait a minute! That was Springsteen. The Boss himself."

"Boss of what? The junkyard band?"

"Oh, that's pretty funny, Charlie. What you just heard was a master of the genre at the very moment of his break out of obscurity."

She crossed her arms. "And we'd all be better off if he had stayed there."

His dark brows shot up. "You don't hear the passion there? The opera? The story?"

"If you're talking about visual images, classical music

doesn't need some guy who can barely carry a tune screaming about what's going on. You feel it—'' she laid her palm against her heart ''—in here.''

''And you didn't feel the power of that night for the people in the song?'' He bent closer to her, tilting his head to the side and lowering his voice nearly imperceptibly. ''The yearning of youth didn't touch you until something just started to ache inside you?''

She stared at his mouth when he said the word *ache*. If there hadn't been an ache there before, there was now.

He saw all of that in the song she'd just heard? Was it possible?

He took another step, bringing him so close she had to look up to see his face. His eyes searched hers.

''You know what I'm talking about, Charlie. I can see it in your eyes. Find me something in your classical music that could make you feel that way.''

She was stunned by the words, stunned by the voice that said them. But she couldn't ignore the challenge. That would be a most dangerous thing to do. Ignore the challenge and she would find herself in his arms in one beat of a snare drum.

''All right,'' she said. ''I will.''

She easily found what she was looking for on the rack behind her and handed it to him. ''Track five.''

He looked at the CD case. ''Debussy?''

''Debussy at his best.'' She thrust up her chin. ''You want yearning? Listen to 'Clair de lune.'''

To her surprise he didn't argue. He flipped open the case and a few seconds later music, *her* music, filled the studio.

He stood across from her and listened. And as he watched her, she could see the change in his face. His mouth softened, his eyes seemed to yearn, just like the notes of the piano. She knew what he was feeling, because she was feeling it, too.

He leaned toward her and the breath caught slightly in her throat. But all he did was turn a dial, lowering the volume of the music in the studio, his gaze on her face all the while, not leaving it even to look at the controls on the console.

"You're right," he said, his voice low, a little lazy. "There is yearning there."

"You feel it?" she asked him softly.

His gaze traveled her face. "Yes—" he swallowed "—I feel it."

She smiled.

He shrugged. "But not quite like I feel it with Springsteen," he said, his voice returning to normal. "See, when—"

Her mouth gaped open. "What?"

"Well, Bruce has got it all over Debussy. When he—"

"You don't know what you're talking about. Debussy was one of the most innovative and influential composers of the late nineteenth and early twentieth centuries."

"Well, that's partly my point. 'Thunder Road' came out in the early seventies. Bruce was yearning the same time we were, love. Why do you think people like classic rock? Because it's singing their song, Charlie."

She looked away from him, at the floor, at the chair— anywhere but at his face. She was wordless for a moment, her own thoughts knocked out of her while she digested what he'd said. While she wondered if Springsteen could possibly have that kind of meaning for anyone.

Then she made the mistake of looking at him. He was still watching her, his mouth starting to quirk into that half grin he always got when he knew he was getting to her.

"Well, I agree," she said, savoring the split-second flash of victory on his face before she added, "but their song is a *lousy* one!"

"Oh, Charlie," he drawled with a little grin, "those are

fighting words. There are lots of Springsteen lovers out there who aren't gonna like your attitude."

The glitter in his dark eyes only made her angrier. "My attitude? What about yours? You are the one who—"

Before she could finish, Carrie burst through the door.

"The mike is on!" she hissed.

They both turned to look at her. "What?"

Carrie pointed a manicured finger at the control console. Jacob groaned, picked up the discarded headphones, flipped a few switches and a taped commercial came on.

Charlotte looked up at the speakers and gritted her teeth before sucking in her breath and asking, "You mean that went out over the air?"

Carrie nodded slowly but emphatically. "Every word you said."

Charlotte buried her face in her hands. "Oh, no—what are we going to do?"

"I don't know what you two are going to do," Carrie said, "but I'm going back to the phones. They're ringing off the hook."

Charlotte groaned. "The listeners must be calling in to complain."

"Why should they?" Jacob shrugged. "We put on a good show."

She stared at him. "A good show?" she repeated. "I am absolutely mortified! What is Barnabas going to say? What are we going to *do?*"

"Baby, it's not that big a deal. Who listens to a classical music station on Friday afternoon, anyway?"

She put her fists on her hips. "Oh, that would be your attitude. The last few days our listeners get to enjoy real music and you desecrate it with that wailing and then with your ridiculous argument."

He gave her a hard look. "There is nothing ridiculous

about anything I said. But since you hired me to save WEND, if you'll excuse me, I'll do just that.''

He sat down at the console and took the mike just as the commercial ended.

''We hope our listeners enjoyed a taste of what's to come on WEND. We expect controversy, we expect passion, we expect opinions—and we also expect you to tune in. The New WEND. Meet us on Monday. Now, back to Debussy.''

He flipped a switch, swung the mike out of the way and grinned. ''Nice save, wouldn't you say?'' he asked her, barely skipping a beat.

''It doesn't matter what I think,'' she told him. ''You've got Barnabas to worry about.''

She swung open the studio door and stormed out.

''Charlotte,'' Carrie called, when she passed the reception desk. ''Barnabas is on the phone.''

''Oh, great.'' She didn't want to deal with Barnabas now. Not yet. ''Tell him I'll call him back,'' she said, walking on to her office and shutting herself inside.

The phone rang before she even had a chance to sit down.

''What?''

''He says don't bother to call him back,'' Carrie said.

Charlotte let out a big breath of relief. ''Thank God.''

''Well, don't thank him yet. It seems Barnabas wants you out at Maple Bluff.''

''Now?'' she croaked.

''Now,'' Carrie answered. ''He insists. And he wants J.J. Tanner to go out there with you.''

''I DON'T KNOW WHY YOU couldn't have taken your own car.''

''It told you,'' Jacob said, ''I don't know where Maple Bluff is.''

"Well, you could have followed me," Charlotte retorted as she adjusted the rearview mirror.

"Oh, right. With you doing your best to lose me? Come on, Charlie, I wasn't born yesterday."

She gave him a sideways glance. "Despite what you might believe, Tanner, I'm not a child and I don't play those kinds of games."

"What kind of games *do* you play, love?" he asked her, reaching out to let his fingertips tangle in her hair.

She flicked his fingers away with a sharp movement of her head. He laughed and turned his attention to the scenery.

The road rose over Lake Mendota, twisting and turning on its way past cushy-looking houses and small estates. Just the sort of place that Jacob figured Barnabas lived. It was very easy to imagine Charlie growing up here, where money was tastefully displayed and taken for granted. He'd heard those tones in her voice more than once—highbrow all the way. No wonder she'd fallen for classical music. It was probably the only thing she'd ever heard growing up.

"Who lives there?" Jacob asked as they rounded a bend in the road to reveal a stately mansion set quite close to the road. A high iron fence surrounded it and Jacob thought he recognized surveillance cameras mounted at the corners.

"That's the governor's mansion," Charlie answered as she flicked on her turn signal. Leave it to Charlie to follow the rules even though hers was the only car on the road.

"Why are you turning in here?" he asked and she pulled into a driveway right across the road.

"This is where Barnabas lives."

She stopped the car and got out. Jacob lagged behind, opening his door slowly, then taking his time getting out as he stared up at the immense stone Tudor.

Charlie was already mounting the front steps so he slammed the car door and hurried to catch up.

She rang the bell.

"Do we have to be announced?" he asked her.

"Of course not."

"Then why—" He'd been about to ask why she didn't just let herself in when the door was opened by a rather stern-looking woman.

"Good afternoon, Sarah," Charlie said as she walked past the woman.

"Humph. He's supposed to be napping."

The tall, spare woman looked Jacob up and down and he had all he could do not to squirm.

"This the one who's been causing all the trouble?" she asked.

"This is J.J. Tanner, Sarah. The new program director."

"Humph. The two of you have him so riled his blood pressure won't come down before midnight. Such goings-on—"

"Where is he?" Charlotte asked and Jacob had to admire her nerve at interrupting Sarah.

"He's in the library. But he's on the phone. Wait in the drawing room."

"We'll wait here if you don't mind, Sarah," Charlotte said.

"Suit yourself."

Sarah gave Jacob one last disapproving look before heading down the hall and disappearing behind a door.

"Man, I hope I wiped my feet properly," Jacob muttered.

"Formidable, isn't she?"

Jacob whistled silently. "How long has she been here?"

Charlotte gave a short, quiet laugh. "No one quite remembers."

"Don't tell me she was here when you were growing up."

"Wish it weren't true, but it is, Tanner. You just met the

woman who made my oatmeal every morning before school.''

Jacob shivered dramatically.

Charlotte laughed for real, then. ''I noticed you didn't try to charm her.''

''Hey, I know when I'm licked.''

''Well, not always,'' he heard her mutter under her breath.

He let it go by. Now wasn't the time for another confrontation about how she felt about him—not that it wouldn't have been entertaining. A lot more entertaining than looking around the dungeon of an entry hall they were standing in.

''I feel a little like I'm being sent to the principal's office—only worse. How do you think he took it?''

''My guess would be not good.''

Jacob strolled over to the enormous staircase to study the portraits lining the way up into the darkness. ''Ancestors of yours? Or did they come with the frames?''

She laughed again and he liked the sound. It had been a long time since he'd heard it quite so freely.

''Ancestors every one,'' she answered. ''The one hanging at the tenth step used to really give me the willies. I'd run as fast as I could past it when I went up to bed at night.''

Jacob counted as he trotted up the stairs. At the tenth he stopped and peered at the portrait hanging there. ''Hmm, I see what you mean,'' he said, studying it. Then he looked down at Charlie. ''Burned at the stake, no doubt?''

She laughed again and he grinned. ''Actually, I believe she refused to die.''

''Ah.'' He came down the stairs again. ''Did you have any fun here at all?'' he asked her.

''Oh, of course. When I first came I hated it. But then I got used to it and Barnabas grew better and better at dealing with me. And it was so much calmer here than on the road with my parents. Despite the gloomy aspect of the place, I felt safer. And, finally, after a few years, Barnabas was able to make me feel loved.''

He studied her for a moment before asking, ''How old were you then?''

She shrugged. ''Maybe eight or nine. I was still only here occasionally then, depending on the whim of my parents, but it was becoming home.''

Jacob looked up at the chandelier overhead, then back at the gloomy ancestors who haunted the staircase. ''I can't even imagine what that would be like. After my father left, my mother and I lived in a studio apartment. It was all she could afford. You could sit in a chair and survey every damn thing we owned.'' He looked into her face. ''But I always knew I was loved.''

She frowned in thought. ''But your father had left. Didn't that—''

He shook his head. ''Naw. I knew that it was him, not me, who had the problem.''

''But how did you know that?''

''Because my mother had told me. The morning I woke up to find him gone, she explained—or at least she explained as much of it as a five-year-old could understand. As I grew older, she would fill in details as she thought I could handle them.''

Charlie stared at him for a moment. Finally she said, ''She told you. That's how you knew. Just like that.''

He walked up to her and raised his hand to her hair. This time she didn't pull away as he tucked a silky strand behind her ear. ''Yes, Charlie,'' he said softly. ''Just like that. Sometimes it really is that simple.''

They were still standing like that, his hand on her hair, her looking up at him in bewilderment, when Sarah came back down the hall.

"He'll see you now," she said. "But don't keep him long, you hear?"

"Yes, Sarah," Charlotte said as she led the way down the hall to the library.

She opened the door.

"Come in, you two. Come in!" boomed Barnabas.

Charlotte glanced back at Jacob. His eyebrows rose and lowered in a shrug and she knew that he was just as surprised at Barnabas's apparent good humor as she was.

"I heard the broadcast this afternoon," Barnabas began.

Charlotte opened her mouth to speak, but Jacob beat her to it.

"Barnabas, I'm sorry for what happened. It's been a while since I've done any hands-on in any studio—let alone in one I'm unfamiliar with. What happened is entirely my fault."

Charlotte was still trying to digest that gallant little speech when Barnabas chuckled.

"So you want complete credit for it, do you J.J.? I think my granddaughter here deserves some of the credit. And since you'll be working together on this—"

Charlotte and Jacob looked at each other, then back at Barnabas.

"What are you talking about, Barnabas?" Charlotte asked.

"I'm talking about our new radio show. Carrie suggested that we call it *Charlie and Jacob Trash the Classics*, but Melinda thought—"

"New radio show?" Charlotte interrupted.

Barnabas chuckled again. "The phone has been ringing off the hook—both at the studio and here at the house. They love it. They want more. And we're going to give them more."

Charlotte looked at Jacob. "What's he talking about?" she mouthed.

Jacob shrugged.

"Grandfather, uh, what are we going to give them more of?"

"You two, my children!"

"Us?" Jacob asked.

"Yes! The public loved the show you two put on this afternoon so much that we're going to make it a daily feature. Just before PowerCord's shift starts. Good lead-in. We'll get lovers of both classic types of music to tune in just to see what you'll play and to listen to you debate the merits of your various selections."

Charlotte felt the panic rise up in her. She was trying to avoid the man, not get into a hot debate with him over which was superior: the sex-driven beat of rock and roll or the sensual enticement of classical music. She didn't need more stimulation around J.J. Tanner. She needed less.

"Grandfather, I don't think—"

"But I do, Charlotte," he said in his best-pulling rank voice. "And so do the Temple brothers."

"What?" they both asked at the same time.

"I just got off the phone with Brian Temple. He and Richard thought it was wonderful how the two of you turned your differences to WEND's advantage. They want to come on board, after all. But only if we give them more of what they heard this afternoon."

Fifteen minutes later, Sarah was showing Charlotte and Jacob to the door.

Charlotte couldn't even look at him. She walked straight to the car, flung open the door and got in.

Jacob followed more slowly. She couldn't help but notice the pleased look on his face when he got in beside her.

"Don't say a word to me," she warned. "Not one word."

And he didn't. She refused to look at him but she was

sure he was sitting there with that same pleased look on his face. Unless, of course, it had turned into one of his maddening grins. He kept his mouth shut nearly all the way back to town. Then he said, "I guess we'll have to spend more time together now."

"One hour a day. That's all," she said emphatically.

"Uh-uh."

She finally did look at him then. "What do you mean?"

"Well, love, we're going to have to have constant meetings to decide which songs to play and to come up with dialogue."

"Nothing doing. Forget it."

"Come on, Charlie. You dropped the ball on Temple Records once before. You can't do it again."

"I have no intention of dropping the ball. I fully intend to give them what they want. And what they want is more of what they heard today. Spontaneous. Unrehearsed. And that's what they're going to get."

Chapter Fifteen

Monday came too soon as far as Charlotte was concerned. Wanting to get to the studio before anyone was there, she'd arrived extra early and was already sequestered in her office by the time anyone else got there. She spent the day doing paperwork and answering the numerous calls that required her attention. And she resolutely, stubbornly kept the speaker in her office turned off. She just didn't want to hear it.

In a matter of hours, she was going to be stuffed into a too-small studio with J.J. Tanner, trying to fight his charm—while thousands of people listened.

That there would be thousands, she was sure. Carrie was keeping her informed of how many times the promo for *Rock the Classics* was played on the air. To make matters even worse, the radio-and-television critic for the local paper had caught their "act," as he called it, and had mentioned the show in his column.

Melinda was ecstatic. "Free publicity, Charlotte! Our first day is going to be a success."

Yeah, thought Charlotte. If she lived through it.

At precisely 2:45 p.m. she headed for the studio.

Jacob was already there. He was sitting at the console, looking particularly virile in a black polo shirt, open at the throat, and a pair of black trousers. When Charlotte had started to dress that morning, she'd taken out her usual Monday outfit. But something strange had happened when she put it on. Instead of feeling comfortable in the bulky dark fabrics, she'd felt encumbered. Stifled. For once, the camouflage of her usual clothing wasn't giving her confidence. It was doing the just opposite. So she'd taken the outfit off, tossed it on a chair, and fetched the red knit minidress from the closet.

Now she was glad she had. Jacob rose from his chair when he saw her. His attitude was wary, but his eyes—his eyes were looking at her in that same heavy, sensual way they had when he'd been coming toward her in her hotel lobby that last night in San Francisco.

Her breathing slowed while she waited for him to take that step closer that he always did. While she waited to feel his fingertips brushing her hair. While she waited for him to try to kiss her.

None of it happened.

Instead, he cleared his throat, pulled out the other chair for her and sat back down.

"What have you decided on?" he asked her.

She swallowed. Well, what she'd decided on was to wonder why she was feeling so disappointed that he hadn't tried to do any of those things.

Out loud, she said, "Rachmaninoff, Symphony no. 2 in E Minor. And you?"

"Foreigner, 'Urgent.'"

He swung the microphone into place. "Sixty seconds," he said.

"What?"

"Till we go on. Sixty seconds. Well, forty-five now."

"But, wait! Who goes first? How are we going to introduce ourselves? How—"

The corners of his softly molded mouth lifted. "I thought you wanted spontaneity, Charlie."

She tightened her jaw. "Making me look bad is only going to make you look bad, Tanner."

"Baby, you can't look bad," he drawled. "You're with me."

She opened her mouth to make some sort of scathing retort, but he put his finger to his lips, then pointed at the On Air sign.

"This is the New WEND," he said into the mike, "and you're about to help us *Rock the Classics* with Charlie and Jacob."

She'd been looking at the microphone, wondering if she was going to be able to talk into it without having her voice shake. But when Jacob spoke, her gaze shot to his face. Oh, Lord, he really did have one of those voices women fell in love with on the radio.

She was still wrapped up in that voice when he swung the mike her way and she became aware that he must have introduced her.

"Sergey Rachmaninoff," she said into the mike, "was the last of the Russian romantic composers. Now, to anyone unfamiliar with classical music, you might think that..."

Jacob watched her as she talked into the mike about Rachmaninoff—the somber romance of his work, the sense of drama, the throb of sensuality. By the time the piece started to play, Jacob was genuinely interested in hearing it.

Yes, he thought, leaning back in his chair and closing his eyes, there was drama. There was also passion. One minute the notes from the piano were floating; the next they were restless; the next, stirring and stentorian. On and on it went, piano, violins, brass. Building to a climax that he felt in his blood—then floating as gently as a snowflake to the ground.

He opened his eyes and languidly turned his head to watch her. Her eyes were closed, too, only instead of relaxing her body into the chair, she was sitting bolt upright, breathing deeply. The thought came to him that she was literally breathing the music in. The red knit dress clung to her full breasts as they rose and fell gently with each breath. The look of her was as intoxicating as the sound of the music.

The piece came to a close. He flipped the mike on.

"So that's Rachmaninoff," he said.

Her eyes opened and he gestured at the mike. She shook her head slightly as if coming out of a trance. Finally her eyes focused, her brain cleared.

"Yes, Jacob. Superb, isn't he? One of his most famous pieces. Even you had to be moved by the melancholy and the passion."

"Oh, I was moved, all right," he said scathingly. "Moved right down the hall to get a box of popcorn before I came back to hear the rest of that soap opera."

Charlie shot him a look. "I see you got the large economy box—sold only to cretins who think better with their mouths full. So keep chewing, Jacob."

Jacob tried not to laugh, but lost it. "Good one, Charlie," he said. "Maybe old Sergey should have tried some. He might have been in a better mood if he'd eaten a little junk food."

"You know, Jacob," she said in the voice of a sweet teacher instructing a not-very-bright pupil, "Sergey Rachmaninoff once said that he composed music because it gave expression to his feelings—just as talking gave voice to his thoughts. However, I'm sure he would agree with me that some people should keep quiet altogether."

Jacob laughed. "Maybe the piece wouldn't have been so gloomy if he'd written some lyrics."

"Once again, the man has to have everything pointed out to him in the overwrought language of rock and roll," she said into the mike. "Let's find out what Jacob has chosen to pollute the airwaves with today."

"Okay, Charlie, move over and prepare to be dazzled. For all you Foreigner fans out there, this song needs no introduction. And for lovers everywhere, it needs no explanation. If the next sounds you hear don't make you think of hot nights, then take your pulse, 'cause you must be half dead."

Charlotte shook her head and laughed, then sat back in her chair, closed her eyes and prepared herself to be bombarded with noise. She wasn't disappointed.

The beat of a drum. Over and over again, finally joined by the wail of an electric guitar. The sound kept coming like a freight train, building momentum, getting louder until a male voice, not very deep but dripping with sex anyway, was added to the mix.

Charlotte tried not to move her foot. But the beat was intoxicating. Although not anywhere near as intoxicating as the words. The simple title of the song said it all: "Urgent." The voice was singing of raw, elemental need. She more than recognized it. She *felt* it. Now, yes—with the help of the music. But last night she'd been all alone in her quiet flat and she'd felt it then, too. That yearning, that need that could push reason aside. She'd been hot with it. Burning. And just like the song, she'd known exactly what she needed to satisfy that need.

Jacob.

On that thought, her eyes flew open.

He was watching her. His chin lowered in that way he had, so that his dark eyes looked even more intense. She looked into those eyes and knew it was more than the music making her need.

He reached over and rubbed his thumb on her bottom lip and she went numb with pleasure. But only for an instant. And then the numbness was replaced by a wave of something so physical rushing through her that her lips parted on a moan.

"Baby," he whispered.

And then she sucked his thumb into her mouth and bit lightly down on it.

It was Jacob's turn to moan. The sound undid her. It was so raw, so real—so true.

She wasn't quite sure who moved first—and maybe it didn't matter. But suddenly she was on her feet and so was he and her mouth was on his, her body crushed to his.

The kiss went on for so long that the song ended. All was quiet. But it was several seconds before they realized that dead air was going out to the listeners.

Jacob grabbed the mike. "Sorry about that folks, but Charlie seems to have come over to the other side. In fact, she was so moved by Foreigner that she moved right on into my arms and kissed me!"

Charlotte gasped. "You rat!"

Jacob laughed. "You heard it here, folks. Our classical dame was so fired up by a rock song that she kissed a rat."

She grabbed the mike. "Ladies and gentlemen. We're going to have to go to a commercial. Jacob's nose is growing so long that, along with his swelled head, the studio is just getting too crowded. Listen to this while we try to let some of the hot air out. We'll be back in a minute to take your calls and requests."

Jacob pushed the button for the commercial and cut the sound and the mike.

"That was a rotten thing to do to me," she said.

"You wanted spontaneity, baby. Your rule. Truth in Broadcasting."

Before she could say another thing, the commercial ended and the calls started coming in, sparking a lively debate on who would be remembered longer, Bob Dylan or Mozart. The rest of the hour was over before she knew it.

"You're going out to Maple Bluff tonight, right?" Melinda asked as she poked her head into Charlotte's office. Barnabas was hosting a party at Maple Bluff that night to celebrate the first broadcasting day at the New WEND. Everyone from the station would be there, along with selected members of the media, a few representatives of state government and a half-dozen Madison big shots.

Oh, and the Temple brothers. Mustn't forget the Temple brothers, Charlotte said to herself. It was all their fault that she was going to have to sit alongside J.J. Tanner every afternoon and try not to want to kiss him.

"I don't know. I'm pretty beat," she said, suddenly not at all sure she wanted to face Jacob again that day.

Melinda came all the way into the office. "Charlotte, you have to," she said earnestly. "Barnabas is counting on it. And what will the Temple brothers think?"

Charlotte sighed. "All right. All right. I'll go."

"Great." Melinda started to leave, then stopped short. "Oh, almost forgot." She turned around and held out a small stack of messages. "Calls that came in about *Rock the Classics.*"

"You're kidding?" Charlotte took them and started to leaf through them.

"Reminiscent of Burns and Allen," she read from one. "Loved it," she read from another. She read the next message over twice, still not sure she'd read it right. "Someone wants an autographed picture of us?" she asked.

"There were several of those. J.J. has the rest. I think we might have a hit on our hands, Charlotte."

Charlotte groaned. All she needed was a nice long run. She might as well start tearing her fingernails out right now, because the torture was going to be just as bad.

Not to mention the ridicule. She knew she was going to be in for it—both on the air and off—from Jacob. He was going to get as much mileage as he could out of the fact that she'd thrown herself at him, she just knew it.

She'd been resisting him for days. Bad enough that she'd had to finally succumb to her feelings for him, but did she have to have done it with an audience? Couldn't she fall in love in private like everyone else?

She lowered her head, threading her hands into her hair. "In love?" she whispered. *You can't be in love with him. It's just sex,* she told herself. *He was your first lover. You've developed an attachment. That's all.*

Only sex.

Well, and maybe that Sunday-afternoon bike ride. And the pumpkin carving—that, too. And Gaby's sweet face when she had fallen asleep during *The Wizard of Oz.* And then there was that romantic night in San Francisco when he'd made her feel so beautiful, so wanted. And listening to the blues on the waterfront. And riding the cable car. And sharing the *tiramisù.*

It was all of that. And more. So much more than she could ever define or explain.

Abruptly, she stood and paced to the window. The sky was that pure, deep blue that only came at this time of year in that magic hour before dark. A young couple came out the front door of the church across the street, hand in hand. Charlotte wondered if they had been meeting with the minister to discuss wedding plans. She wondered if they had already started looking at houses. If they argued over china patterns and then made up in the drive-through of a fast-food restaurant.

"Why on earth am I thinking these thoughts?" she muttered to herself.

But she knew why. It was exactly the reason why she never wanted to see her forty-eight-hour Prince Charming again. Because to fall in love was to start to want things, to start to need things, to ache and laugh and feel. To feel way too much. Way too much.

She suddenly knew she couldn't go out to Maple Bluff and face Jacob. Tomorrow she would have to face him in the studio, and that was soon enough.

When she thought the coast was clear, she gathered up her fleece jacket and started for the door.

The phone rang. The answering system had already been switched on for the night, so she would be able to monitor the call. She couldn't think of anyone that she felt like talking to at the moment.

"Charlotte?" It was Melinda's voice. "I hope you're not gone already. Barnabas has moved the party over to the candy store. We're all here waiting—get a move on."

Nick's Candy Store? Charlotte picked up the receiver to ask how the kind of party Barnabas was giving could possibly be held at Nick's. But Melinda had already hung up.

Damn, now she supposed she had to go. Now that the party was only blocks away, someone would surely come looking if she didn't show up. She would go. But only for as long as it took to shake a few hands.

She let herself out into the hall and headed for the elevator.

IT WAS FULLY DARK WHEN she turned the corner onto Main Street. Rush hour was over but car headlights winked here and there, punctuated by the occasional honk of a horn and the soft whir of ten-speeds zipping past almost as fast as the cars.

There was something nostalgic in the air that night. Something melancholy. An era was ending. But a new one was also beginning. She would try to think of it that way from now on.

Nick's Candy Store looked deserted when she reached

it. She put her hand up to the window and peered in. There seemed to be a glow of light somewhere near the back of the store.

She tried the doorknob. It wasn't locked so she went inside, closing the door quietly behind her. The place was totally dark except for the glow of a candle at her usual booth. As she drew closer she could see that someone was sitting there in the shadows just beyond the flicker of the flame.

It was a man—his head was bent and his face further concealed by a hat that looked like he'd borrowed it from Bogie worn low on his brow.

Now that she was closer she could see that the candle wasn't the only thing on the table. There was a dish of strawberries alongside a plate of chocolate petits fours and a bottle of champagne.

"Who are you?" she asked.

"I'm someone you have unfinished business with," the man answered.

"Jacob?" she gasped.

He raised his head and grinned. "Know anyone else you forgot to eat petits fours with?"

Her hands flew to her mouth as her heart started to thud.

"We did forget our second dessert, didn't we?" she said, when she managed to lower her hands.

He shrugged. "We were a little busy."

"And the strawberries?" she asked him.

"That's what I wanted to feed you the next morning— while I told you that I was in love with you."

"Oh," she said, the exclamation coming out in a little squeak. "Is that some of the unfinished business? You're going to tell me you love me while you feed me strawberries?"

He shook his head slowly. "Nope."

Her heart sank to her stomach, then rose back up into her throat. "Too late?"

"Way too late."

"Oh," she said again.

He slid out of the booth, picked up the bowl of strawberries and started to come toward her.

"Uh, what are you going to do with those?" she asked nervously, images of revenge for soda-throwing dancing in her head.

He selected a strawberry from the crystal bowl. "Oh, I'm still going to feed them to you."

She swallowed hard. "You are?"

"Yep. I'm just going to ask you a question while I feed them to you."

"Oh," she said again. "What question is that?"

He held the strawberry up to her mouth. "Take a bite first."

She was about to refuse until he said, "For once just do it, Charlie. Just trust me."

She opened her mouth and took a bite of the enormous strawberry he held to her lips. The juice exploded on her tongue as she chewed.

"Good, now your mouth is too busy for you to interrupt me."

She gasped and opened her mouth but before she could come up with a retort, he popped the rest of the strawberry between her lips.

"Actually," he said while she chewed, "there are three things I want to ask you."

She swallowed and took a step back so he couldn't fill her mouth with another strawberry when she opened it to speak. "Three things?"

"Right. First, my mother thinks she's found a house for us. Will you come and look at it with me?"

"A house? But I thought when your contract was up..."

"That I'd be moving as soon as I could?" He shook his head. "I want to start planting roots for Gaby—and for myself. Will you come look at the house?"

"Oh. Well, okay. I guess I could do that."

He grinned. "That was amazingly easy."

"And the second thing?"

"I want you to help me find Gaby a superhero cape for Halloween."

She shrugged. "Sure. In fact if we can't find one she likes, I could make her one. And the third?"

"I want you to marry me."

"Oh, well—" Her head shot up. "What?"

"Marry me."

"You, uh, you want to marry me?"

"More than anything," he said.

She stared at him. He had taken the hat off and was holding it in his hand, looking for all the world like a suitor of old who'd brought his girl into Nick's on a Saturday night to pop The Question. Only she was quite sure that no suitor who had ever stood in Nick's Candy Store was as irresistible as Jacob.

She shook off the feeling that all she wanted to do was fall into his arms again and asked, "After what happened to both of our parents' marriages, after losing Michelle, aren't you afraid?"

He took a step toward her and put out a hand. She closed her eyes and concentrated on the touch of his fingers as he smoothed her hair behind her ear. It felt so familiar. So right.

"The only thing I'm afraid of is losing you for a second time."

She opened her eyes. "But why?"

He raised his other hand and laid a finger against her lips, stilling her question. "Didn't I tell you not to ask why?"

"But that was in San Francisco. And this is—"

"Madison. But what difference does it make? You think I want you less, the farther we get from the Pacific Ocean or something?"

She laughed softly, but she was only one step away from crying. The feeling nearly clogged her throat and she had to clear it before she answered. "We know so little about each other."

"That's why I want a lifetime, Charlie. Anything less just wouldn't be enough."

"Oh, Lord," she said, desperately trying to sniff back her tears. "Do you always have to say the most perfect, the most romantic, the most irresistible thing?"

"When I'm talking to you, yes, Charlie. Yes. Because I love you." He glanced at his watch. "So how about it?"

She sniffed. "Do you have to be somewhere?"

"No, it's just that—"

"Because, don't let me keep you. I mean if you have another proposal to make somewhere else tonight, maybe you'd better just—"

He laughed and looked up at the ceiling, slowly shaking his head. "Of all the stubborn... Just say yes, okay?"

She thrust her chin up. "Why should I?"

He grinned. "Well, think of the numbers. The fans will eat it up if we get married."

"Oh, right. For the good of the station. I should marry you so that our show gets a better audience share?"

He put his hands on her upper arms and jerked her closer to him. "No," he said, his dark gaze moving from her eyes to her mouth and back again. "You should marry me because you love me as much as I love you. Do you, Charlie? Do you?"

She felt his hands on her arms, holding her there, and the first thought that came to her was that she wanted to run. Just like she had run that morning in San Francisco, she wanted to run now.

But this wasn't San Francisco. This was Madison.

"Yes," she whispered. "Yes, I love you."

She'd expected a kiss. Instead he looked at his watch again, then he ran to the old-fashioned radio mounted high on the wall at the back of the candy shop. Reaching up, he switched it on.

"This is PowerCord," said a lazy, low voice. "And this is the New WEND *Requests at Seven*. We're going to change our pace a little here with a special song for two lovers at Nick's Candy Store. This one goes out to Charlie and Jacob. Anne Murray and 'Could I Have This Dance for the Rest of My Life?'"

The music—simple and romantic—filled the shop. The candlelight wavered on his face, throwing shadows, but she could still see what was in his eyes when he asked, "Can I, Charlie? Can I have this dance for the rest of my life?"

The tears were starting to spill out of her eyes now. And there wasn't a thing she could do to stop them. "I never used to dance," she said.

"Then it's long past time you started. Say yes, Charlie."

"Yes," she whispered. "Yes."

He held out his arms and she went into them.

He held her close while she cried on his shoulder. When the tears finally ended with a small hiccup, she sniffed again and said, "Now I have a question for you."

He raised his brows. "Oh?"

"What kind of music are we going to have at the wedding?"

She felt the chuckle rumbling through his chest pressed so close to hers.

"Any kind you want, Charlie. Any kind at all."

He's every woman's fantasy, but only one woman's dream come true.

For the first time Harlequin American Romance brings you THE ULTIMATE...in romance, pursuit and seduction—our most sumptuous series ever. Because wealth, looks and a bod are nothing without that one special woman.

THE ULTIMATE...

Pursuit

#711 ~~SHE'S~~ *They're* THE ONE! by Mindy Neff
January 1998

Stud

#715 HOUSE HUSBAND by Linda Cajio
February 1998

Seduction

#723 HER PRINCE CHARMING by Nikki Rivers
April 1998

Catch

#729 MASQUERADE by Mary Anne Wilson
June 1998

Take 4 bestselling love stories FREE

Plus get a FREE surprise gift!

Special Limited-time Offer

Mail to Harlequin Reader Service®

> 3010 Walden Avenue
> P.O. Box 1867
> Buffalo, N.Y. 14240-1867

YES! Please send me 4 free Harlequin American Romance® novels and my free surprise gift. Then send me 4 brand-new novels every month, which I will receive months before they appear in bookstores. Bill me at the low price of $3.34 each plus 25¢ delivery and applicable sales tax, if any.* That's the complete price and a savings of over 10% off the cover prices—quite a bargain! I understand that accepting the books and gift places me under no obligation ever to buy any books. I can always return a shipment and cancel at any time. Even if I never buy another book from Harlequin, the 4 free books and the surprise gift are mine to keep forever.

154 HEN CE7C

Name _____ (PLEASE PRINT)

Address _____ Apt. No. _____

City _____ State _____ Zip _____

This offer is limited to one order per household and not valid to present Harlequin American Romance® subscribers. *Terms and prices are subject to change without notice. Sales tax applicable in N.Y.

UAM-696   ©1990 Harlequin Enterprises Limited

Catch more great

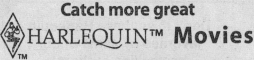

HARLEQUIN™ Movies

featured on the movie channel tmc

Premiering April 11th
Hard to Forget
based on the novel by bestselling
Harlequin Superromance® author
Evelyn A. Crowe

Don't miss next month's movie!
Premiering May 9th
The Awakening
starring Cynthia Geary and David Beecroft
based on the novel by Patricia Coughlin

If you are not currently a subscriber to
The Movie Channel, simply call your
local cable or satellite provider for more
details. Call today, and don't miss out
on the romance!

 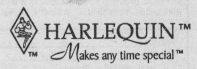

100% pure movies.
100% pure fun.

Makes any time special™

Don't miss these Harlequin favorites by some of our bestselling authors!